BLOOD LUST

"Well met, cousin," the girl said, stepping forward. "I am Isabel."

"My lady." Simon smiled. The cold, ethereal beauty he'd seen on the battlements was real after all. Her astonishing red hair framed a pretty face with hazel eyes and a pert little nose sprinkled with freckles.

"Your cousin," she corrected, smiling back. She took another step forward and embraced him as a kinsman, and for a moment he thought he was lost.

In a single instant, with one innocent touch, the vampire hunger he thought he had learned to control leapt up inside him. As she pressed her warm body to his, he could feel his eyes changing color from brown to greenish gold, feel the fangs grow sharp against his tongue. Not since his first night as a vampire, his first terrible kill, had he felt such hunger and horror. He wanted to destroy this woman, to devour her, innocent or not. He could already taste her. . . .

My Demon's Kiss is also available as an eBook

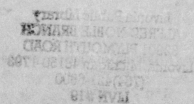

My Demon's Kiss

LUCY BLUE

POCKET BOOKS
New York   London   Toronto   Sydney

This book is a work of fiction. Names, characters, places and incidents are products of the author's imagination or are used fictitiously. Any resemblance to actual events or locales or persons living or dead is entirely coincidental.

An *Original* Publication of POCKET BOOKS

 POCKET BOOKS, a division of Simon & Schuster, Inc.
1230 Avenue of the Americas, New York, NY 10020

Copyright © 2005 by Jayel Wylie

ISBN: 0-7434-6448-6

3 9082 09671 3634

First Pocket Books printing January 2005

10 9 8 7 6 5 4 3 2 1

POCKET and colophon are registered trademarks of Simon & Schuster, Inc.

Cover art by Franco Accornero

Manufactured in the United States of America

For information regarding special discounts for bulk purchases, please contact Simon & Schuster Special Sales at 1-800-456-6798 or business@simonandschuster.com.

Acknowledgments and Thanks

Many thanks to the following for their talent and assistance: Timothy Seldes, nature's most perfect literary agent; Lauren McKenna, senior editor, Pocket Books, whose art and intelligence are only surpassed by her patience; Megan McKeever and Kirsten Ringer, who in addition to their other gifts and graces never fail to put me in touch with Lauren and Timothy; my much-loved family and friends, who are kind enough to still love me back even now; Howard Shore; and Johnny Depp.

My Demon's Kiss

Prologue

Simon stood at the edge of the cliff, shivering in the wind, awestruck by the beauty of the sunset. The burning desert they had crossed just yesterday now lay what seemed a hundred miles below the spot where he now stood, its folds and valleys painted red and purple by the dying sun. Behind him rose the Urals, a range of cruel, cold mountains that seemed to climb forever. Mist curled around his boots, rising from the mossy turf and clinging to the rocks that fell off sharply just in front of him. "Well, Sascha, this is it," he said, smiling at the joke. "We've come to the end of the world."

"No, boy, we have not," his companion grumbled as he fumbled through his pack, obviously unimpressed by the view. "The world goes on forever." He pulled out a bottle and uncorked it with his teeth. "You find the end, the damned thing starts all over," he finished, taking a long swallow.

"Do you think?" Sascha was a Russian, a seasoned mercenary hired by Simon's lord, Francis, the duke of

Lyan, in Damascus to assist his English army in their latest, and hopefully last, Crusader's quest. Sascha's accent was so thick, Simon was the only one of the duke's men who even bothered trying to understand him. But then Simon was a foreigner himself.

"You're very wise, I'm sure," he said now to the Russian as the sun disappeared behind the faraway dunes. Flopping down on the grass beside him, he took the bottle and had a drink. "Still, when I was keeping cows in Ireland, I never thought to see a caliph's garden or a desert either."

Born an Irish slave to a Saxon chieftain, six-year-old Simon had rejoiced to see his master slaughtered by a Norman knight of the great bastard king, William. That knight, Sir Francis, had been made a duke for his success and rewarded with the Irish estate, and in turn he had made Simon's father, Seamus, his castellan. Simon himself had been made a squire of the duke at the age of twelve, and at sixteen he had been knighted for his service in the wars against the Saxon hordes that still raided the Irish coastline. Now, at twenty-six, he was a Crusader in the Holy Land because that was what the duke wished him to be. He was a Norman in his habits but still Irish in his heart. "Black Irish," the girls at home all called him for his dark brown hair and eyes, but his skin was so pale it still glowed white even after three years in the desert.

"None of us should be here," Sascha said. He took

off his ragged boot and shook it, emptying pebbles. "That duke of yours is mad."

"Now why would you say that?" Simon said with a grin. "An entire province to be won to Christ without bloodshed—I call that wisdom indeed." He handed Sascha back his bottle. "And Francis is fifty-five years old, you know. It's time he was taking a wife." He looked back at the caliph's mountain fortress and tried to see it as a cheerful home, but it was quite a stretch. Hunched against the cliffside with its windows glowing yellow in the gloom, it looked more like a mausoleum. "Heathen or not."

"A heathen bride is no great burden," Sascha spat, relacing his boot. "Every woman is a heathen in her heart." He looked back at the palace as well, its jagged towers black against the purple sky. "But there is evil in this place, these mountains—there are stories." He broke off, seeing Simon's face, and laughed. "You think me an old woman, don't you, boy?"

"Aye, I do," Simon answered, smiling back. "I always have." But Sascha's words had awakened a doubt that had been sleeping in his mind ever since they left Damascus. Why should such a powerful caliph as Lucan Kivar have offered the duke his own daughter in marriage, offered to make this foreigner, this heathen in his eyes, heir to his rich estate? "But tell me anyway— what is wrong with these mountains?"

"Simon!" Alan, one of the duke's other knights, was calling to him from the terrace. "Come! It's time."

* * *

The main hall of the caliph's palace was so fine it stole
the breath, a cavernous room bursting with treasures.
A double row of columns down the center were twisted
to look like vines. They were painted gold and studded
floor to ceiling with precious stones arranged to look
like flowers, ruby red and sapphire blue with leaves of
glittering emerald. Rich hangings of velvet hung from
the windows that lined both sides of the hall, their
golden shutters thrown open to let in the cool evening
breeze. Golden sconces held torches between each window, the light they cast dancing and writhing on the
gold and jewels until the eyes were dazzled. Simon saw
Francis at the dais, gazing around at this splendor with
the smile of a man in a dream, and he knew what his
lord must be thinking. By midnight, all of these treasures would be his. But Simon still couldn't shake the
feeling of dread Sascha's mutterings outside had given
him. What sort of marriage rite was celebrated only
after dark?

All the other English knights were smiling—after
Damascus and the desert, this hall must seem like paradise indeed. The caliph's household was present as well,
men in rich robes, some in turbans like men of the East,
some bareheaded and pale as the English, and women
veiled in brightly colored silks drifted among them,
graceful and silent. Tables were laid with a banquet as
yet untouched, and incense burned among the
columns, filling the room with its intoxicating scent.

But as he took his place among the English, Simon could have sworn he smelled something far more foul beneath the smoke, a thick, wet stench of decay. He turned to speak to Alan, to ask him if he smelled it, too, but suddenly a ripple of silver bells rang out from the dais, and the whole crowd turned as one.

The caliph emerged from the curtains, as magnificently dressed as his hall. His people broke into applause, and some of the Englishmen joined in, caught up in the moment. Tall and thin, their host wore cloth of gold that shimmered in the torchlight, its folds embroidered all over in red, queer symbols Simon did not recognize. "Welcome, friends," he said, smiling on the crowd. "I am Lucan Kivar." His head was bare, revealing pale red hair that fell past his shoulders, and he wore a mustache and beard, long and narrow, trailing over his chin. His eyes were brilliant blue.

"He doesn't look much like an Arab, does he?" one of the squires murmured.

"He isn't an Arab, idiot," Alan hissed back. "The heathens in these mountains are as white as you are."

"Well met, my lord," the duke was saying as he stepped up onto the dais. "I am Francis, duke of Lyan."

"Your grace." The caliph nodded, making a deep bow. "You honor us by your presence and your mercy."

A door slammed somewhere behind them, making Simon turn with his hand on the hilt of his sword. "Release me!" a woman was shouting, a black-haired beauty in a blood-red gown who struggled in the grasp of a pair of guards who seemed intent on dragging her down the aisle. "What is this?" she demanded as the crowd parted before them, her eyes meeting Simon's for barely a moment as they passed. "What have you done?" she demanded as they reached the dais.

"Your grace, I present you your bride," the caliph said with a thin, amused smile.

"No," the girl said, shaking her head. "I never agreed to this." She looked around at the English knights, horror dawning in her dark, brown eyes. "I will not. I cannot."

"You will." Kivar cut her off. He looked toward an alcove to one side, and for the first time, Simon noticed a small boy dressed in white satin standing there watching the dais. "You must, Roxanna." Another guard stood behind the boy, and at this, he put a heavy hand on his shoulder.

"Roxanna," the duke repeated in an over-hearty tone, oblivious to the child. He was staring at the girl the same way he had stared at the jewels, as if he couldn't believe his good fortune. "What a beautiful name." He held out his hand, and glancing once at Kivar, she took it, her guards letting her go. "You must not be afraid," the duke said kindly. "Whatever you may think of Christians or Englishmen, I promise you will never be abused."

"You are too good, Christian," she said, looking at her father, who still smiled his thin little smile. "I am not afraid."

I am, Simon thought with bitter humor, his heart beating faster. The girl feared her father, not the duke; the little boy was a hostage. But why did Kivar threaten his own daughter? He moved closer to the dais, pushing past his companions, trying to reach his lord.

"Your letter offered full surrender," Francis, the duke of Lyan, was saying.

"And so you shall have it," the caliph agreed. "You see that my guards are unarmed." He looked down at Simon as he drew closer and smiled. "Unlike your own."

Another figure slipped from behind the draperies—another child, Simon first thought. But while this one stood no taller than the boy in the corner, he was still a man, with a bearded face and thickly muscled arms. From the look of him, he was older than Simon was himself, much older. He hung back in the shadows as if he didn't care to be seen, but when Simon caught his eye, he winked as if they shared a secret.

"Have you brought your Christian priest, as I requested?" Kivar asked the duke.

"Yes, of course," he answered, still watching Roxanna. The wizened friar they'd found in Damascus hurried forward, his black robes fluttering around his skinny ankles. The bride looked horrified, her dark eyes going darker, taking on a reddish cast that made Simon's flesh crawl with a sickening fear. She was crying, he realized, but the tears that spilled down her cheeks were not clear; they were red. Her tears were blood.

"Shall we begin?" the priest said, opening his prayer book.

"No!" Simon took the last step forward and grabbed the duke by the arm. "Your Grace, look at her—look at her face!"

The duke turned to him, obviously angry, but before he could speak, his expression went blank, his eyes wider but empty. Blood trickled from the corner of his mouth as he fell forward into Simon's arms. "Forgive me," Roxanna said softly, the bloody dagger still clutched in her fist.

"Your Grace!" Simon shouted, sinking to his knees beneath the duke's dead weight as chaos erupted in the hall. "Francis!" But the duke was past all hearing.

"Stupid girl," Kivar said, slapping Roxanna as behind them his subjects attacked the English knights. Simon dropped the duke and lunged back to his feet just as a heathen guardsmen lunged at him. The man's lips curled back, and Simon saw his cruel teeth, long and curved like the fangs of a wolf. He clutched at Simon's throat, still coming even as the Irish knight plunged a sword into his side.

"The head!" Roxanna was shouting. "You must take off the head!" The creature laid a hand under Simon's chin to push his head back, exposing his throat as Simon hacked at him with his sword, clumsy but determined. The blade finally made contact with the monster's throat just as it drew back to bite him, cleaving his head from his shoulders.

"Kill him!" the caliph roared as Simon straightened up again, and the knight turned quickly, ready for a new attack. But Kivar had other prey in mind. The guard who held the little boy snatched the child up in a grotesque parody of an embrace, baring his fangs to tear into the tiny throat.

"No!" Roxanna screamed, and Simon saw she had fangs like the others, and her eyes glowed just as red as she turned on Kivar. "Monster! You promised!"

"You betrayed me," the caliph answered, moving toward her, stepping over the fallen duke with barely a ripple of his gold and scarlet robe. "You left me no choice."

For a moment, Simon was paralyzed, a man trapped in a nightmare, powerless. His lord, the man who'd raised him and his father up from slavery to knighthood, lay dead and bleeding at his feet; his sworn companions were being slaughtered all around him, their throats torn out by red-eyed demons from hell. Even the priest was dying, gasping, on his knees, blood gushing through his fingers as he clutched at the wound in his throat. A vampire in a woman's shape crawled toward him, fangs exposed, her torn veil soaked with blood. She caught hold of the cleric's robe and climbed him like a cat, lapping the blood from his skin as she held him, his eyes glazed and desperate with fright.

"No!" Simon barely heard the roar from his own throat, barely realized what he meant to do as he moved toward them, raising his sword. He beheaded the creature with a single stroke, the blade passing through her to cleave the priest as well, but the man of God barely shivered, his broken body sinking to the floor, dead as the duke.

Lucan Kivar was laughing, a high-pitched, lunatic giggle that carried to every corner of the hall over the screams of the dying. "Did I not promise you, my children?" he cried out, arms spread wide. "Behold, I provide you fresh blood!"

Simon felt a snap inside his head, one final shred of reason giving way. He raised his sword like a man in a trance, moving through the pandemonium, and though inside his head he seemed to barely move at all, in truth, he struck like lightning. The guard who fed on the boy looked up, blood smeared across his mouth, and Simon cut him like a blade of grass, his torso falling, split in two, then his head flying upward with another deadly stroke. Barely seeing, Simon whirled around, his blade stabbing up into the belly of another monster, female this time, as she sprang at him, hands outstretched like claws. This one screamed as Simon butchered her, the blood she had just stolen from an English knight bathing them both. Her lips drew back, exposing her fangs, and Simon jerked his broadsword free, pushing her back with his knee. The vampire staggered, clutching her belly, and he brought the blade down like an executioner's axe, slicing off her head.

"That one," Kivar said, laughing with delight as he

pointed at Simon. "Forget the others; that's the one I want."

"Then come and take me!" Simon shouted back, his voice hoarse in his ears. "Or must I come to you?" He advanced on the caliph, cutting through the others as they struck at him, barely slowing. One sank her fangs into his wrist, and pain shot up his arm, a freezing fire.

"Take him, children!" the ruler of these undead monsters ordered, laughing still. "Take all but his heart!" Simon struck the head from the woman feeding from his wrist, and another creature clamped on to his leg, teeth tearing through his leather leggings to reach his flesh. Looking down, he saw the boy the guard had killed, his baby's mouth stretched in a leer.

"Holy Christ," Simon said, breathless with horror, frozen at the sight.

"No!" Roxanna struck the child first with her open hand, and he let Simon go with an offended cry, then she struck his tender throat with her dagger, cleaving off his head. "Don't stop," she ordered Simon, her own eyes glowing scarlet like the others but tears of blood still streaming down her cheeks. "Kill us all—pierce the heart with wood or take the head." One of the other women leapt at her with a scream, and the two of them went rolling, fighting like cats. His paralysis broken, Simon raised his sword again, cutting through the vampires like a reaper cuts through wheat, his own blood flowing from a half a dozen gashes in his flesh.

Their leader was not laughing anymore. His pale

blue eyes glowed red, then green, as his own fangs were exposed. They were longer than the others and more deadly, more like the fangs of a poisonous snake than of any warm-blooded creature. Simon stepped onto the dais, tossing his sword into the air and catching it upside down, his hands wrapped tightly around the hilt, the tip pointed downward. "You wanted me," he said through gritted teeth, driving it with all his strength straight into the vampire's heart. "Here I am."

Kivar smiled, fangs glistening ivory white. "So you are." He seized the knight by the shoulders, his fingers like talons as they dug into his flesh, and as the sword plunged deeper, he yanked Simon closer in a deadly embrace. Simon twisted the blade, and Kivar screamed in pain, but his eyes still glowed with triumph. Smiling as they fell together, he plunged his fangs deep into Simon's throat.

Sudden thunder roared inside Simon's ears, and for a moment he couldn't think what it was. Then he realized it was the pounding of his own heart. Agony like nothing he had ever felt engulfed him, spreading from his throat so quickly that in an instant he could barely sense himself at all. His body, the shape of his limbs, or his consciousness, these things meant nothing; all he knew was pain, both fire and ice. He willed his grip to tighten on the sword, but he could no longer feel its hilt between his hands or see it as he pulled it from the vampire's chest—all the world was blinding, blood-red light and pounding heart and pain. Only when he raised the blade did consciousness return. Kivar released him from the bite and raised his head, Simon's own blood dripping from his mouth. "No," he snarled, a serpent's hiss. "Not yet." Grabbing the cowl of Simon's tunic in his clawlike fist, he crushed him close again and kissed him full on the mouth.

Revulsion struck the knight like a wave, but another feeling followed hard upon it, a joyous warmth that raced along his veins, more potent than the strongest wine. All his sadness, all his fury, all his fear, seemed to evaporate at once. He would not have known the duke if he had seen him, could not have told a stranger his own name. Strong arms enfolded him, lifting him up like a child, and for that moment he allowed it, too weak to resist. He felt the fire leave his lips, and he moaned, bereft, his vision beginning to clear. Then another, purer source was pressed against his mouth, ecstasy poured down his throat, and he fed eagerly, sucking like an infant at his mother's breast. Visions rose before his eyes, a village in flames, and suddenly his fury was returning. Rage without a purpose pounded through him, an overwhelming need to hurt, to kill, to feel the suffering of living souls, consume them as he now consumed this blood.

"Stop, warrior!" The girl, Roxanna, was clutching at his shoulders, tearing at his clothes. "Stop it! You must fight!"

Simon raised his face from Kivar's throat, the rage still coursing through him, stronger still in shame. The creature was a ravaged husk, thin as a skeleton within his robe, his chest and throat ripped open and bleeding, his face dry and wrinkled like some dead thing buried in the sand. But his eyes were bright and knowing, and his ruined lips were twisted in a smile around his fangs. "Mine," he whispered, the rasp of the wind in the trees. "You are mine."

Simon raised his sword again and struck. The skull-like head flew backward, spinning end over end as the body crumpled to the floor. Roxanna rushed forward with a wooden stake, the handle broken from some Englishman's pike, and plunged it into the wasted vampire's breast. A rushing wind swept through the hall, and a wail went up from the monsters still remaining, screams of fear and grief. "Kill us," she was begging as she thrust the stake in again. "Kill us all." Vile-smelling mist rose all around the ruined corpse, and a viscous fluid poured across the dais from the golden robe, the shape of the body and head dissolving.

Another vampire cried out, "Master!" and Simon turned, the sword still trailing from his hand. The hall was thick with corpses, all of his companions dead, but he could not seem to weep for them, could not seem to feel anything at all. A numbing cold was spreading outward from his heart, a stiffness stealing through his limbs as if he were falling asleep. He lifted up his sword, still coated with the creature's blood, and his minions scuttled back in horror, scattering like insects and breaking through the windows to escape.

"You are their master now," Roxanna said behind him, sprawled on the floor. "You are one of us." She looked up at him with pity in her eyes, the dark brown eyes of a woman again. Even smeared with blood, her face was lovely, framed with long, black hair—the duke had found her beautiful. But Simon felt only revulsion, remembering the truth of what she was. "You are a vampire," she said with a sad, fragile smile.

"A vampire," he repeated. "And what is that?"

Her smile turned bitter as she looked around the room at the creatures that were pouring from the hall. "What you have killed," she answered, turning back to him. "What you see before you now."

"No!" He raised the sword to her this time, and the dwarf he had seen before Kivar's attack rushed forward, putting himself between them with another wooden stake held out before him. "You lie," Simon murmured, dropping the sword, suddenly too weak to hold it. The dwarf bent over the girl on the floor, soothing her with words the knight could not understand, stroking her hair. He turned and trudged away from them, past the ruined corpses staring up at him, their faces still frozen in shock.

The gardens were as awful as the hall. Every living creature had been slaughtered, soldiers, horses, even the goats the cook had kept for milk. All lay bloodless on the grass, eyes staring without seeing at the moon. Simon crumpled to his knees, dry sobs wracking through him. He wanted to be sick; his guts were twisting like a nest of vipers, but his body refused to obey. He looked down at the wound in his arm where the female vampire had bitten him, or rather, the spot on his arm where a wound ought to have been. His sleeve was torn, the edges bloodied, but the flesh underneath was unmarked—no tearing in the skin, no bruise from the blow, remained. It wasn't even sore anymore. With dizzy horror, he realized the rest of his wounds were the same, even his throat—he pressed a hand to the spot where Kivar had bitten him and found it whole.

"Boy! Simon!" Sascha came staggering toward him, limping from a deep, bloody gash in his thigh. "Thank Christ, you are alive." Simon climbed back to his feet, and the Russian embraced him like a long-lost brother. "Come." Leaning on Simon for support, he led him toward the garden's high stone gate. "We must leave here now."

"Yes." The roar of thunder filled his ears again as it had when Kivar had bitten him, the deafening drum of a heartbeat. "We have to go home." He tried to think of Ireland, the green fields and the salt wind from the sea. But the heartbeat's thunder filled his consciousness, not from himself this time but from Sascha, and a terrible thirst grew inside him, a hunger that consumed his every thought. "I want to go home."

"I know, boy," Sascha said, patting his cheek, smiling though his face was slick with sweat as if he were in pain. "So you will." He stopped to lean on the gate, panting with exertion, and Simon could smell him, his sweat and his fear as delicious and inviting as the smell of roast venison after a long day's fast. "Just give me one more moment."

"It's all right," Simon answered, his own voice hollow in his ears. "I am all right." The hunger was like a sword piercing his belly—he had never felt such hunger in his life. "I can carry you."

"No," Sascha said, waving him off—or so he thought Sascha must have said; it was becoming hard to hear anything over the pounding rhythm. He felt dizzy and drunk, but a strange, exhilarating strength was rushing through him, too. Indeed, he could have ripped the trees up by the roots, he felt so powerful.

"You are whole?" The Russian was staring at him in wonder. "How can that be?" Dear Sascha, his friend . . . he must save him. He put a hand on Sascha's arm to hold him up, to support him. He was his only friend, the only other man left alive of their company; he must save him.

"I killed them," he told Sascha. He could feel the life in his friend's flesh through his thick leather jacket, the heat of his living blood, and he wanted it, wanted to feed from him as he had seen the others feed from his friends in the hall; he was desperate to taste the blood, to take possession of the pounding heart. But he would not; he would not be this monster, this vampire. He heaved the Russian's arm over his shoulder, headed for the forest. "I killed Lucan Kivar." And Lucan Kivar killed me, he thought as the pain in his belly writhed harder, burning like molten lead. A wolf let out a howl in the distance, an evil, mocking sound that cut through the roar of Sascha's blood, the pounding of the still-beating heart. "These mountains," Simon whispered, looking up, feeling the fangs grow sharp against his tongue. He wanted to resist it, wanted to be what he had always been, but the blood would not be silent, the hunger would not let him go. Vampire . . . he was a vampire. "Sascha . . . you were right."

He flung his friend against the gate with killing force—he heard bones breaking in his back and shoulders, the ripe thud of his skull against the stones. For one clear moment, he saw Sascha's face, saw sadness in his eyes, and his heart cried out in horror. But the demon hunger would not be denied. Snarling like the beast he had become, he sank his teeth into the Russian's throat, his vampire fangs tearing through the vein to reach the hot, sweet blood. His mind reeled, sick with shame, but suddenly his body was in ecstasy again, the same mad joy he'd felt before but better, somehow, warmer and more real. Only when the heartbeat stopped, when Sascha went limp as a rag in his arms, did he stop. Drawing back in horror, he saw Sascha's head lolled on his shoulders, his eyes dead and staring like the rest.

"The first time is always the worst." The dwarf was standing in the shadows, watching. "The need for blood will never be so strong again. Or so I have been told."

Simon stared at him for a moment, the feeling that all of this must surely be a dream taking hold of him again. Then he looked down at Sascha, and the truth made him tremble so violently he thought he must surely collapse. "What am I?" he said, letting the body drop. "Who are you?"

"My lady told you, you are a vampire," the dwarf said, coming closer. He covered Sascha's face with his mantle, a kindly, graceful gesture. "And I am Orlando."

"Orlando," Simon repeated. "And who is that?"

"My lady's servant." He offered Simon a cloth, gesturing toward his own face, and Simon took it, wiping the blood from his mouth as if this were the natural thing to do. "Her father was the caliph here, but Lucan Kivar killed him long ago."

"And the child?"

"Her younger brother." He reached into his pocket and took out a bottle, its glass red as a ruby in the moonlight. "Kivar promised he would let him live to manhood if she did his will," he explained, gazing at it. "But she betrayed him."

Simon remembered the look on her face as Francis fell dead at her feet, the dagger that killed him still clutched in her fist. "She murdered my lord—"

"For a mercy," Orlando said, cutting him off. "Would you rather your lord be like you are?" Simon looked away, unable to answer. "Come, warrior." The dwarf reached up and touched his arm, his head barely reaching Simon's elbow. "We have much to discuss before morning." A crash rang out from the direction of the palace, and Orlando smiled, putting the bottle back into his pocket. "My lady awaits."

The girl was hacking down the shutters in the hall with an axe that should have been much too heavy for her to pick up, much less wield with such vigor. "Orlando, seal the catacombs," she said as they came in. "Most of the others will take shelter in the caves, but some will still be stupid enough to come back."

"The others?" Simon said. She swung the axe again, shattering another window frame.

"The other vampires." She dropped the axe to rip down the draperies. "The sunlight will destroy them—kill all of us." She looked back at Simon. "Unless you kill me first."

"No!" Once again, Orlando hurried to put himself between them. "You can be saved, my lady, you know it—both of you can be absolved of your crimes. The Chalice—"

"The Chalice is a foolish superstition," Roxanna cut him off.

"How can you say so?" he retorted. "How can you speak of superstition, standing here, in this hall, a vampire yourself—"

"A monster," she agreed.

"In body, yes, but not of your own will or your own making," the dwarf insisted. "I swear to you, you can be saved. I have seen it. This warrior—"

"Simon," Simon interrupted, barely listening. The duke still lay where he had fallen. A pair of bluish purple wounds had been torn in his throat, delicate by comparison to the gashes the other corpses wore. "My name is Simon." He knelt beside the body. "Who bit him?"

"I did," Roxanna answered. "We can feed from the dead if we choose."

"And you?" Simon said to Orlando, turning from the girl, unable to so much as look at her. "You are a vampire, too?"

"No, Simon, not me," Orlando said. "Kivar thought me a monster in my own right because of my stature, unworthy of his blood."

"Would that all of us had been the same," Roxanna said, turning away.

"You were not chosen by accident, Simon," Orlando continued, coming to him. "Kivar wanted English knights—he needed English soldiers."

"We don't have time for this," Roxanna said, picking up her axe.

"He knew the Chalice was in England," Orlando continued. "He knew it could destroy him—"

"He is destroyed!" the girl insisted.

"You think so?" Orlando demanded, turning back to her. He snatched up Kivar's empty robe, still dripping with noxious, black-green filth. "You think Lucan Kivar, a creature older than the mountains where we stand, has been reduced to this?" Roxanna didn't answer, but Simon could see from her face that she did not, as dearly as she longed to believe it. "No, my lady, my beloved," the dwarf said, dropping the robe. "He is gone, but he is not destroyed. In my visions, I have dreamed of his return."

"Orlando fancies himself a wizard," Roxanne explained with a brittle, bitter smile. "He came here as a conjurer when I was just a child."

"Wherever he is, whatever he may have become, Kivar will not rest until the Chalice is his, until he has destroyed it," the dwarf said to Simon. "He knows its power; for a thousand years, he has craved it." He looked around at the slaughtered knights. "When he heard of your duke, an English noble, laying siege to a palace already within his control, he knew that his moment had come."

Roxanna had been watching the corpses as well. Suddenly she lunged forward with her axe, and Simon, turning, saw Sir Alan rising from the floor, looking dazed and unhappy. Before he could speak, Roxanna had lopped off his head. "No!" Simon shouted, horrified. "He was alive—"

"He was not, idiot," she shot back, staking the headless stump. "No more alive than you or me or my brother, Alexi—remember what happened to him?" She turned back to Simon, dropping the stake and brushing the hair back from her forehead, her face once more spattered with gore. "He was a vampire." Behind her, Alan's body was dissolving as Kivar's had done, and Simon saw other streaks of the same sort of slime smeared all over the polished floor.

"All of them?" he said weakly, feeling sick again.

"No," she answered, softening her tone. "Most are dead already, their souls released. The victim must consume the monster's blood to become undead himself." She picked up the axe again, then let it fall as if she were suddenly too tired to hold it any longer. "I'm sorry, warrior."

"Simon, you must find the Chalice," Orlando said. "Kivar misjudged you—he could never have expected you to be able to destroy even so much of him as you have. You can destroy him utterly, and in so doing, save yourself and Roxanna. The Chalice is your salvation; drink from it, and you will be restored."

"Orlando, enough," Roxanna said, this stranger who was now his sister in cursed blood. "Leave him alone."

"The Chalice?" Simon repeated, barely hearing her. "You really mean the Holy Grail?" He almost laughed aloud. The son of a bard, he had grown up on tales of Arthur and his knights, of their quest for Christ's last drinking goblet, the vessel of first communion. But Simon was a real knight, not a mythical creature of chivalry; he knew what a real knight was, and he had seen enough so-called holy relics in his day to know what they were, too. "I'm no Galahad, Orlando," he said with a bitter grin.

"Your Holy Grail is a story, a tale told by your priests," Orlando scoffed. "But the Chalice is real." He drew a scroll from his conjurer's cloak and unrolled it. "This belonged to Kivar himself, an ancient text stolen from the tomb of a holy saint. When Kivar found it, he knew the Chalice had indeed gone to England, just as the legends say."

Simon looked down at the rough map of what could have been Britain, he supposed, its shape surrounded on every side by writing, the same queer symbols as on Kivar's ruined robe. In one corner was a drawing of a plain, undecorated wine cup with lines drawn coming out of it as if to represent God's light. Below it was a cross made from a sword and a rough stake of wood. "If this Chalice is real, it is a holy thing," he said, handing the scroll back to Orlando. "Only the purest of knights could ever find it, the most blessed—"

"Another fairy tale," Orlando scoffed. "Are you not a warrior? Are you not on a quest?"

"I was a warrior for him!" He pointed to the duke's dead body, suddenly choking with grief. "I came here only because he wished it—I would gladly have followed him to hell." His vision clouded over red again, this time with tears of blood. "And so I have."

"You are blessed, Simon," Orlando said, smiling. "Think of what just happened in this hall. Look at your companions, all dead—none of them even bothered to fight." He picked up Simon's fallen sword and offered it to him. "You are blessed, sir knight."

"He is right," Roxanna admitted. "A thousand of my father's men could not do what you did." A blood tear of her own slid down her cheek. "Perhaps this chalice does exist; perhaps it still may save you. But not me." She took the sword from Orlando and offered it herself. "If you are a knight, I ask for your help as a woman, a damsel under a curse. Finish me before you go."

Simon took the sword, uncertain what he meant to do, and Orlando flung himself in front of the girl. "You will not," he insisted, his whole manner turning to fury. "You will need my help to find the Chalice, and if she dies, I will never help you."

"I never said I wanted to find your Chalice," Simon protested, but neither of them heard him.

"Wizard, let me go," Roxanna begged, falling to her knees before Orlando. "I only lived so long to save Alexi; you know that." She touched his bearded cheek. "Now he is dead."

"But you can live," the dwarf insisted. "You can be as you were once before, before the monster came—"

"I cannot!" She framed his face in her hands, forcing him to look into her eyes. "Even if my soul were restored to me, even if I could once more walk in the light, I could never be the maid that I was then. I have murdered . . . so many, not just because Kivar forced me to do it but because of my own thirst. You want to call me blameless, but I know in my heart I am not. I have tasted blood." Her tears flowed like an open wound. "Please, don't make me do it anymore."

"No," Orlando promised, taking her hands in his. "I promise I will not." He drew something from his pocket, the ruby-colored bottle Simon had seen him take out in the garden. "Trust me, beloved," he said, taking out the stopper. "I will keep you safe."

She looked first at the bottle, then at Simon. "And if he should fail?"

"I will do as you wish," the dwarf said, holding it out to her.

Simon expected her to take it, to drink some potion it held. But slowly she began to fade, her form turning transparent in the flickering light. As Simon watched in wonder, the vampire melted into mist. A sweet scent filled the air for a moment as the vapor flowed into the bottle. Then suddenly both vapor and perfume were gone, and Orlando put in the stopper.

"She . . . ?"

"She is safe," Orlando said, putting the bottle away in his cloak. "It's a vampire trick; you can do it, too, and more besides." He turned back to Simon. "You have three choices, sir knight." Outside a lark began to sing, a harbinger of the dawn. "You can live as the undead, feeding on the living with no greater purpose. You can wait for the sun to consume you." He held out the scroll again. "Or you can embark on your quest."

Simon took the map with its drawing of this Chalice, this magical prize the wizard spoke of with such faith. In a thousand years, he could never hope to claim it. But he had to try. He wanted to go home.

1

Isabel hurried through the cellar, ignoring the voices of her household calling after her. She was as frightened and worried as anyone in the castle; she had no answers to give.

She lit a torch from her candle and pushed open the ironclad door hidden behind the baskets of new potatoes. Dust danced in the flickering light, rose in little clouds with every step she took down the circular stairway beyond. At its foot stood another door, this one covered so thickly with cobwebs she could barely see the carving that adorned it, the figure of an ancient monk. Only his nose was still clearly visible, sharp and crooked as a falcon's beak.

"Well met, Joseph," she said, giving it a tweak, paying no mind to the dirt. As a child she had studied this carving for hours, holding conversations with the long-dead cleric while her father worked in his study on the other side of the open door. "Have you nothing to say to me?" She took the key from her pocket and fitted it into the lock. "In faith, I need your counsel." Using both hands, she finally forced the key to turn with a grinding squeal. "I fear we may be doomed, the both of us." She shoved at the door with her shoulder, shuddering just a little as a spider raced down her arm and back into the web just over the door. It opened with a screech to reveal her father's study, once her favorite room in the castle, abandoned for the past ten years. It was still as clean and neat as it had always been, as if her father had just that moment left it for the night. Stone coffers were stacked along the walls, sealed shut with covers too heavy for Isabel to lift, but she knew what was inside. She had seen the ancient parchments many times, traced a finger down the pages, studying the writing in a language no one now living could read. Her father's desk was covered with newer scrolls, each neatly tied with a ribbon, and a candle stood waiting to be lit.

Her father had found the castle when he was already long past forty. The ruined keep on an overgrown island, seemingly forgotten, had seemed like paradise on earth to a knight grown weary of battle. He had built a proper motte-and-bailey fortress over the ancient stones and taken a wife from one of the villages nearby, a maid of seventeen with the flame-red hair and green eyes of a Celt. No one had expected their union to produce a child, least of all Sir Gabriel himself. All he wanted was comfort in his waning years, a companion of spirit and good common sense to share his sanctuary.

But late in their first year together, just after his castle was finally completed, his pretty young bride had conceived. Nine months later, Isabel was born, a tiny, red-haired daughter, and his wife was dead.

"There must be something here," the grown-up Isabel muttered, lighting the second candle and settling into her father's chair. She was grasping at straws, she knew, desperately clinging to phantoms in her fear. But she could think of no better choice. Sir Gabriel had explored the texts in all these coffers, and she knew he had learned to read the language of the druids who had first hidden them there. She had always suspected he had even learned some of their magic, though he would never have admitted it. But he had told her many tales of wonder he had read in the ancient scrolls, tales that suggested he had known more than he was willing to say. "I need a conjure, Papa," she said now, untying one of his own scrolls, forbidden to her eyes when he was alive. "Something that can save Charmot." She used the ribbon to tie back her hair and opened the scroll on the desk.

There is no such thing as magic, 'Bella, she could almost hear him answer, the same thing he had always said. No magic but God's grace.

"Where is God's grace now, Papa?" she asked the empty air as her eyes searched the page. "Where was He when you died?" For seventeen years, Sir Gabriel had kept his Charmot fortress at his own expense with no help whatsoever from his king. But before his body had grown cold in its tomb, the king had been ready to claim it. Apprised of Isabel's inheritance, His Majesty had sent a royal herald.

"Make ready, my lady," this stranger had told her, sketching an elegant bow. "Your noble husband will arrive anon." Sixteen years old, still veiled in mourning for her father, sick with grief, she had stared at the herald in wonder, unable to credit her ears. Her husband? What did she need with a husband? As she remembered that moment now, a full ten years later, her jaw still clenched in fury.

"Never mind, poppet," Brautus, the giant captain of her father's guard, had soothed when the herald had gone. "Let him come."

And thus the Black Knight had been born. When the king's chosen favorite had arrived to claim her and Castle Charmot, he had found a demon already in residence, a mountain dressed in chain mail with a coal-black helmet like a devil's head. Brautus had not been a young man even then, but his skills had been more than a match for the puffed-up courtier King Henry had chosen to rule this isolated, mostly profitless manor. Indeed, he had beaten the poor knight so easily, Isabel had been hard pressed not to laugh, watching from the battlements in her best white gown, the perfect damsel in distress. "Save me, sir knight," she had shouted as the poor sot's squires dragged him, broken and addled, back over the natural bridge that almost joined the island to the mainland. "Save me from this monster." But King Henry's man had seen enough of her and her castle already. As soon as he was hoisted on his horse, he had ridden off without a backward glance.

Others had come to challenge the Black Knight, enough to cause a legend to spring up. In the first years, most of the knights who came were as pitiful as the first, the desperate younger sons of minor nobles looking to win a manor of their own, or older men fallen into disgrace hoping to win sanctuary. But as time passed, the true nobles had lost interest in Isabel and her castle, as both proved to be more trouble than they were worth. Mercenaries and villains had begun to come in their place, evil men with little interest in damsels or castles, men who were looking to make a name as a killer even more lethal than the Black Knight of Charmot. And all the while Brautus grew older. Now past sixty, his heart was still as strong, but his limbs were growing weaker by the day. So far he had still managed to vanquish every challenger who came, but victory was less assured with every fight. The month before, his shoulder had been broken in a skirmish with a Flemish mercenary half his age and of nearly the same giant size. Now another challenger was coming, a Frenchman named Michel.

"A cure for fever—useful, Papa, but not what I need." She dropped the first scroll and opened up another. Her father had compiled much of the druids' ancient medicine from his reading in the caverns in a book she kept upstairs. "I need a miracle." Her father would tell her to consult a priest, no doubt, but in faith, she already had. Father Colin from the Chapel of Saint Joseph had been the messenger of her doom. Charmot did not have a village of its own, but it was the only fortress in the region, the only refuge in times of unrest, and the common folk all knew Isabel and pitied her in her plight. They made a kind of spy network on her behalf, watching every road for knights coming to claim her so she and Brautus would always be ready to send them away. That morning, Father Colin had made a rare pilgrimage from his church to tell her he had heard of a blackguard knight newly landed from France, coming with an entourage and boasting of his villainy all the way.

This second scroll was nothing but notes, no coherent narrative—part of her father's research. The corner was decorated with the queer code Sir Gabriel had used to catalog his writings, a mixture of Greek letters and the same Celtic symbols carved into the stone coffers in this study and the walls of the caverns beyond. "Teach me, Papa," she had begged him often, but he had always refused.

"Such matters are not for the innocent, 'Bella," he would say sternly, sending her upstairs to play. But how innocent would she be if this Frenchman should capture her castle?

"Didn't those druids ever require a champion?" she said aloud now. "Who protected their great treasure from the Romans?" She turned another page, an account in Latin of the harvest the year she'd turned ten. She read Latin easily, and French, and some Greek— useless gifts for a woman, perhaps, but it had amused her father to teach her. "Couldn't they call up a demon from hell if they needed one?" The idea had first come to her when Father Colin had told her his news.

"You should flee, my lady," the priest had advised. "Take your womenfolk with you, escape into the forest, take refuge in one of the villages. Leave them the castle; it's all they really want."

"No," she had told him without a second thought. Charmot was her father's castle, his dream; these people were her family. She would not leave them to a villain's rule. And besides, if she should abandon Charmot, what would happen to the druids' scrolls, to dead Saint Joseph and his catacombs? Somehow she felt the need to protect these things as strongly as she needed to protect the castle and its people. They were sacred to her because they had been important to her father, even if he had never really explained to her why. "Brautus will protect us as he always has, or I will conjure a real devil to fight in his stead," she had joked to Father Colin.

"Blasphemy, my lady," the priest had scolded her with a frown. "You must not even jest of such a thing."

But in faith, had she been jesting? The more she had thought about it, the more dark magic had seemed like the perfect solution. If she had been a witch, she would have done it in an instant, blasphemy or not. She

would call up every demon in hell if it meant saving
Charmot. But her father said magic wasn't real. "Send
me a demon," she whispered to the candle's flame, willing the spirits that surely must still haunt these caves to
hear her. "Send me a true Black Knight." The candle
flickered, and for a moment, she thought she heard a
breath of wind, an eerie, groaning sigh.

"My lady." Susannah, one of the castle maids, was
standing in the doorway. "One of the woodsmen from
the river town has come. He says those Frenchmen
have stopped in the tavern and drunk themselves into
a stupor. They will not make it so far as Charmot
tonight."

"May God be praised," Isabel answered, gathering
up her father's scrolls as if that had been her purpose
all along. She had found nothing of use in them, but
perhaps she still might. "At least we shall have one
more night."

The Chapel of Saint Joseph looked like just the sort of
place a magical cup might be found, a Roman temple
half crumbled to ruins in the middle of a misty English
plain. All the clues and signs Simon and Orlando had
found over ten years of searching the world had
brought them to this spot. But the Chalice wasn't there.

"The Saxons raided the church many times," the
priest who kept the chapel explained, holding up his
torch to show them the scorch marks on the cracked
plaster walls. "Anything of value here was stolen long

ago." He gave Simon a piercing look. "What is it you seek, my lord?"

Salvation, Simon almost said, but what would be the point? The priest—Father Colin—had barely blinked an eye to see a knight with armor and a dwarvish squire but no horse standing in his dooryard after dark. Indeed, he had just been returning to the church himself; perhaps he thought they'd been waiting all afternoon.

"Knowledge, Father," Simon told him now. He took a few steps closer to the altar, staring at the cross mounted behind it. Ten years ago, the very sight would have caused his eyes to burn and weep tears of blood. But now he could face it without flinching, at least for a moment, the only pain he felt a cold ache in the hollow that had once held his heart. Crosses could harm him; so could holy water and any relic that had been blessed by a priest. Orlando attributed this to Simon's own faith over any genuine power contained within the objects themselves; either way, he had learned not to risk it. "I am a scholar."

The altarpiece was painted directly on the wall, its colors now faded and flaking away. But he could still make out the empty tomb and the disembodied faces of the angels gathered above it, their robes now crumbled to dust. "A scholar and a knight," he finished, touching the wall.

"My lord has traveled in the Holy Land," Orlando explained. "He has seen many portents of some great power hidden in this place."

"A pilgrim from Our Lord's own lands?" the priest said with awe in his tone.

"From Ireland originally, Father," Simon said, turning back to him with his most winning smile. "But aye." The sky outside the window was almost black now, a deep twilight. "I have seen Jerusalem." He had not fed for fear of frightening the keeper of the church. 'Twas an oddly comic feature of his curse that he should appear most demonic just after he was sated, his eyes aglow with devil's fire. When he was starved and therefore dangerous, he could easily pass for a man. "So will you tell me, Father? Is there holy treasure here?"

"Not here, my lord." Father Colin lit another torch. "But there is a castle." He motioned to a bench beside the window, and Simon sat down. "Another scholar, Sir Gabriel of Charmot, built it on an ancient ruin many years ago. This castle may hold what you seek."

"The castle Charmot?" Simon exchanged a glance with Orlando. They had read the name Charmot in many texts in their travels, but they had thought it was a person, not a place, one of the Chalice's ancient protectors.

"Just so," the priest agreed. "Sir Gabriel was a godly man; I knew him well. He told me there were catacombs beneath the castle, an endless labyrinth of tunnels." He was smiling at Simon with such a look of speculation, the vampire wondered suddenly if the old man might be mad. "If your quest is righteous, perhaps God will lead you to the prize you seek."

Before Simon could form an answer, the bell at the gate rang out. "Another visitor so late?" Father Colin frowned. "I am much blessed tonight." He took up his torch. "Wait here, my lord, may it please you. I would speak with you further on this matter."

"As you wish," Simon answered, rising as the priest went out.

"We should leave this church," Orlando said as soon as he was gone. "We will go to this Castle Charmot, see what they can tell us there."

"Aye, wizard, we will." In their first nights together, Simon had been grateful for Orlando's guidance. But now that he began to understand the demon that he was, he was far less willing to be scolded like a child. "But we still have business here." He had sensed something as soon as the gate bell rang, a scent he had learned to pick out from a thousand others, be they in the multilayered stench of Venice or the clean, cold wind of this plain. He smelled evil. He smelled prey.

"You should give me tithe to stay here, old man." A drunken voice was laughing in the corridor outside. "I am a righteous champion." The door was flung open hard enough to crack against the wall, and a man in armor came in. The knight, if he could rightly hold such title, looked like many of the brigands they had seen in England, more robber than protector. Nearly as tall as Simon but twice as broad, he had the swollen, blotchy face of a longtime drunkard and the swaying gait to match, but his small, pale eyes glittered with wakeful malice. "Tomorrow I fight the Black Knight." He was followed by two other men in leather armor, as dirty and drunk as himself, and a smaller creature swathed head to toe in a stained green mantle—a woman.

The leader saw Simon. "But who are you, sirrah?" His eyes narrowed as he took in his costume, the clothes of a true knight. "What is your business here?"

Simon smiled. "A traveler like yourself."

"Master, I beseech you." Orlando tugged at his sleeve. "We are looked for at another house this night."

"God's helmet, look at that!" the brigand knight exclaimed, his entire manner changing in an instant. "C'est un nain, mes amies—voilà!"

"You are all welcome, my lords," Father Colin interrupted. "Come, sit down—I will go inside and make our supper." He paused beside the woman as if to speak to her, then seemed to think better of it. Glancing once more between Simon and the brigand knight, he hurried away to his lodging.

"Where did you get it?" the brigand knight demanded, still gaping at Orlando like an idiot. "Has it always been so small?"

"Smaller, I would imagine, or hope for the sake of his mother," Simon answered. "But when I met Orlando, he was already full grown."

"Full grown," the knight repeated with a chuckle. His eyes moved to Simon, sizing him up now. "What will you take for him?" Simon felt the dwarf grow tense beside him, and he put his hand on his shoulder. "I am near to acquiring a castle," the Frenchman continued. "I will need a fool. Does it sing?"

"Not that I have heard," Simon answered, trying not to smile. If Orlando had harbored any misgivings about the vampire's intentions, no doubt they were fading away. "My servant is not for sale."

The brigand's smile faded. "Do not be so quick to say it, traveler," he said. "You, come here." He grabbed the woman by the arm and pushed her forward. "I will give you this in trade." He yanked away the mantle, and she let out a shriek of indignation, fighting for it a moment before her arms fell back to her sides. She was barely more than a child with golden hair—a pretty thing when they'd taken her, no doubt. Now her mouth and eye were swollen and bruised, and the thin shift that was her only garment torn and stained with what Simon willfully decided must be mud. She looked at the vampire for barely a moment before looking back down at the floor, but Simon thought he saw the ghost of a smile on her lips, a glimmer of hope in her eyes.

"Your offer is tempting, my lord," Simon said, giving the title an emphasis that was unmistakably ironic. But in truth, he could barely hear his own voice, so loud was the roar of his hunger and the pounding of the brigand's heart in his ears. "But I must decline."

"You must decline?" the man repeated, and his men laughed, coming closer. "I must insist you accept." He

put his hand on his sword hilt, and his henchmen followed suit.

"You would fight me in the church?" Orlando took a
step away, and Simon gave him a wink. *You see?* he
seemed to tell the dwarf. *The idiot leaves me no choice.*
"Before the very cross?"

"Fight you? No, traveler." The brigand smiled, showing rotten teeth. "We will kill you." He unsheathed his
sword.

Simon drew his sword as well, so quickly his oppo-
nents could barely have seen him do it. One moment he
was easy prey, a single fighter standing at rest; the next
he was the demon. The brigand's henchmen lunged at
him first, one armed with mace and dagger, the other
with a sword. Simon killed the swordsman first, parry-
ing his blow like lightning before slicing off his head.
The second stabbed him in the back, plunging in the
dagger to the hilt, but the vampire barely felt it. He
whirled around as the villain raised his mace and
caught him by the wrist, twisting the arm in its socket
like a mortal man might break a winter twig. The
henchman screamed, his eyes rolling wild, and Simon
snarled, sinking his fangs into the henchman's throat.

"Un diable," their master was saying, his face shiny
with sweat. "Tu es Satan." He clutched his broadsword
in both hands, but his body was stinking with fear.

Simon raised his mouth from his first prey's fountain
of blood. "You speak as if you know me." He twisted
the henchman's head to one side with a snap, cutting

off whatever life might still linger inside him. "Are we friends?" He let the corpse fall to the floor.

"Stay away!" The brigand knight dropped his sword and crossed himself. "In the name of Christ, stay back!"

"You dare?" A new rage coursed through Simon, feeding him more surely than the blood now coursing through his veins. "Villain that you are, you call on Christ to save you?" His tongue burned at the mention of the holy name. If he were to wear the cross that hung around this brigand's neck, his cursed flesh would burn with holy fire. "You prey upon the innocent," he said, moving closer. "You would defile His holy church, abuse His priest, and yet you have that right." The injustice was more powerful than any hunger; the rage would no longer be contained. He sprang upon the brigand like a wolf, the two of them rolling together as one as his teeth tore into his heart. The brigand struck him again and again, begging for mercy even as he slashed him with his dagger, but Simon barely heard him, barely felt the pain. All that mattered was the blood, hot and sweet, still laced with the wine this man had drunk and thick with the evil in his heart. This was the food Simon had learned to crave above any other in his ten years as a vampire, the blood of men already damned.

"My holy God . . ." Father Colin had returned. He stood in the doorway, staring in horror at the vampire feeding at the altar of his God. "Merciful Christ . . ." He clutched his rosary for strength, holding his ground as Simon let the dead man fall and rose to his feet. The vampire knew from experience how he appeared, the way his black eyes shone with a devil's flame, the scarlet stain of blood upon his mouth. But the priest did not cower in fear. "Be gone from His church, child of Satan," he ordered. "In God's holy name, I command it."

"You cannot command me, Father," Simon said, though in truth the priest's words did affect him, make him feel a powerful compulsion to obey. This was a truly righteous man, a true priest of the Christ. "You cannot see what you have seen," the vampire said sadly. "You cannot remember this night."

"This night," the priest repeated, his eyes going dim in the trance. Of all the gifts his cursed state had given him, Simon liked this one the least and used it the least often, the power to sway mortal minds. The more innocent his victim, the more easily and deeply he could entrance them, bending their thoughts to his will. "The Black Knight," Father Colin said, understanding dawning in his eyes. "You are Isabel's Black Knight."

"Yes," Simon answered, though in truth he didn't have the slightest notion what the old man meant. Sometimes this happened; a victim's mind would find its own solution, its own way of explaining away the evil it had witnessed. "I am her Black Knight."

"Come," Orlando ordered, bringing Simon his sword. "You must away. The Father and I will take care of this mess." He looked the vampire up and down with a wry smile. "And find you something to wear." Simon looked down at his tunic, slashed and soaked with blood. "Go, warrior," the dwarf repeated, giving him a push.

Outside, it was full dark. Simon stood among the fallen stones of the old Roman temple and closed his eyes, breathing in the cool, misty air as if his body still required it. His flesh was tingling with life, but it was an illusion, vitality stolen from his victim's blood. For a few precious hours after feeding, he would feel almost himself again, a man with a heart and a soul. He would remember Ireland and the dreams he had once held so dear, see the green fields, remember the warmth of the sun on his back. With a dead man's blood still flowing in his veins, he would remember how it had felt to be alive, to yearn for love and home.

But come the morning, he would die again. The blood of the kill would be absorbed by his endless hunger, the only life that was real. He was a beast, a predator that killed for no greater purpose but to rise and kill again. All that was left was the blood and his quest, this endless search for a relic he still could not believe would save him. With every night his cursed body walked, he passed more deeply into the shadow, further from God's grace. Why should this magical Chalice accept him, even if it should exist and somehow he could find it?

Sometimes he envied Roxanna, his sister in cursed blood, sleeping in another world for all these ten years past, a vapor in a bottle. Past all knowledge or control, she no longer felt this yearning he felt now, this illusion of life. If she hungered, Simon did not know and did not care.

The horses of the French knight and his men were tethered just outside the abbey wall. They each looked up at his silent approach, velvet ears laid back as they nickered and chortled in alarm. "You need not fear," he murmured, holding out his hand. "This wolf means you no harm." As a man, he had loved horses as only an Irishman could; there was no mount he could not ride, no stallion he could not tame. "Your master is dead." The largest of the three, a dark brown destrier in armor, planted its hooves and tossed its head, whinnying a warning. "I cannot believe you will mourn him." Almost close enough to touch the velvet nose, he reached for the horse's bridle.

But just as his fingertips made contact, the horse reared up and screamed, flailing the air with its hooves, and its fellows did the same. The first two broke their tethers easily and fled, the destrier shattering the abbey's wooden gates. But the third, a smaller gray mare, was trapped. Eyes rolling white with terror, she twisted and contorted, desperate to escape, but her tether would not break.

"I'm sorry," Simon said, almost pleading, as he drew the knife from his belt. "I swear, love, it's all right." Dodging the flailing hooves, he cut the tether with a snap, and the mare reared away so violently she flung herself onto her back. "No!" he shouted, horrified, certain the horse would be crippled, but she struggled back to her feet. Shrieking once more at the vampire, she galloped away, soaring over the broken gate.

"I'm sorry," Simon repeated, watching as she faded into the night.

"The horses fear you," a voice spoke softly behind him. The girl the French knight had abused was coming toward him, picking her way between the stones of the ruin. "But I do not." In the moonlight, he could barely see her bruises; he saw her for the pretty thing she was or once had been. She stopped before him, letting her mantle fall. "I am not afraid."

"Why are you not?" He touched her cheek with the back of his hand, and she tilted her head, closing her eyes as she leaned into the caress. "You should be frightened, darling." Even his voice sounded like the old Simon, the lilting poet's brogue. "You saw clear enough what I am."

"Yes." She opened her eyes again. "I saw you." She smiled. "But I am yours now."

"No," he said, shaking his head.

"I can do things," she promised. "I can take care of you, and you can keep me safe." She touched his cheek with her fingertips, tracing through the tears of blood. "Why do you weep?"

He smiled. "I weep for you." He took her hand and kissed it before putting it away. "I don't need a cook, little one."

"Good," she answered, moving closer. "I didn't mean cooking."

Her arms came up around his neck as he kissed her, eager for his embrace, and he groaned, despairing and amused. Such sport was but a comfort for the moment, but he ached for the girl even so, the warmth of her body, the parody of love. He pushed her down among the stones, opening her mouth to his to taste her hot little tongue. Her hands slipped up and down his arms, over his shoulders as he lifted her flimsy skirt. The cleft of her sex was as warm as her mouth, as eager to take him inside. He let sensation take him, closing his eyes as he lost himself in her embrace. The bloodlust he felt now was but a little thing after his feeding before, another nagging hunger like the throbbing in his sex, as easily satisfied. When his pretty comforter cried out, he kissed her throat, finding the vein. With both fists clenched tightly in his hair, she arched her hips to meet him, and he bit her, barely piercing her delicate skin, barely feeding as her climax shivered through her, tasting satisfaction in her blood.

He lifted his head and moved faster, looking down into her eyes. "You will forget me." Her lips moved in denial, but she could not speak; she could not look away. "You will forget." He drove into her deeper, holding her pinned to the ground.

"Yes." She gasped as his climax exploded, trembling again. "I will forget."

He kissed her cheek as he withdrew, let her go as her

body went slack. He tugged her shift back down, and she sighed, rolling onto her side. "Sleep, sweet darling," he whispered, and she obeyed, as peaceful as a child. Looking up, he saw Orlando coming toward him, smiling and shaking his head.

"Father Colin is sleeping as well now," the dwarf said when he reached him. "Your spell was very powerful tonight." He looked down at the girl on the ground. "He's too old to be much help anyway."

"I'll do it," Simon answered. In the past ten years, he must have dug hundreds of graves; three more shouldn't take him long. "Give me the purse." He took out a handful of coins and gave them back to Orlando, then tucked the purse under the sleeping girl's arm. "Perhaps she can find her way home."

"The good Father will help her." Simon spread the girl's mantle over her like a blanket, tucking in the corners, and his companion smiled. "Come, warrior. I think I have a plan."

Isabel tied off the bindings on Brautus's shoulder and sat back. "Better?"

"Aye, poppet." The aged giant leaned back against the pillows, the lines of pain on his brow giving the lie away. " 'Tis all but mended." He took her hand and squeezed it. "Let this Frenchman come."

"Tomorrow." She made herself smile. "He will come tomorrow." This great hand had protected her all of her life; this knight was as dear to her as a father.

"Maybe he won't be so bad." If Brautus tried to fight the Frenchman, he would die. "Maybe I should let him marry me without fighting."

"No." His bearded face turned serious, and tears rose in her eyes. "You will not."

"No," she promised, standing up to kiss his cheek. "I will not."

Outside the window, the moon was out, a cold, white sliver. She thought of her father's study, three stories below her now, and the druid's scrolls, full of magic that she could not read, wisdom she could not use. Send me my devil, dear wizards, she thought again, a pagan's silent prayer. Send my true Black Knight.

2

Simon looked up at the castle Charmot, rising stark and gray from its misty island in the purple gloom of twilight. Its outer walls were covered with thorny vines and lichen as if the fortress might have been deserted for some time, but the drawbridge looked almost new, its nail-studded timbers bound in bands of iron. Sir Gabriel might be a recluse, but he was ready to make a defense. Even from the opposite shore of the moat, Simon's vampire hearing could detect movement behind the wall, tense voices speaking quickly, the jingle of the horse's bridle, and the rattle of chain mail armor. He looked down at Orlando, the great sage who had convinced him to come here without so much as a sword. "You're quite certain about this, wizard?" he asked the dwarf, half joking. "This is the only way?"

"Of course not," Orlando answered with a smile. He rang the bell again. "But we can try this way first."

Isabel peered down at the strangers through an arrow slit in the wall. "You see, my lady?" Tom said, standing at her shoulder. The boy had kept watch here all afternoon, waiting for the Frenchman to arrive. "It is a priest, not a knight at all, and a child. They don't even have a horse."

"No." In the failing light, she could barely make out the two figures, could not see their faces at all. But neither of them looked like the sort of brigand they'd been warned was on his way. The larger one was wearing some sort of long robe; he might have been a priest, but he was taller than any man of God she had ever seen before and broader at the shoulders. And while the second figure was certainly small enough to be a child, he didn't move like one. "Tell Brautus to listen and be ready to ride out—he'll know my signal." She touched the boy's shoulder and smiled. "It will be all right."

Simon rang the bell again, losing patience. "Hello?" he called out over the water. "Hello, is anyone there?"

"Hello yourself." The voice was a woman's. Looking up, he saw her standing on the battlements, a beauty with copper-red hair, dressed in a snow-white gown—a creature from a minstrel's swooning lay. "Who are you?" she demanded. "What do you want?"

"I come in search of Sir Gabriel of Charmot." The tall man made her an elegant bow, a most unpriestly gesture, Isabel thought. "I seek his counsel."

"And who is Sir Gabriel to you?" she called out loudly enough for Brautus to hear her in the courtyard. "Who are you to him?"

Simon glanced again at Orlando. "His kinsman," he answered, hating the lie. "If he will but come forth—"

"I speak for him," the woman cut him off. From this distance in the twilight, Simon could barely see her face, vampire or not. But her voice was intoxicating, lilting but not sweet, intelligent but cold. "And I say you are a liar. Sir Gabriel has no kin—or none outside these walls."

"I am his cousin," the man insisted. "Distantly—from Ireland. My name is Simon." He sounded sincere, Isabel thought; more importantly, he sounded Irish, not French. If this was a trick of the brigand she had expected, it was a well-considered one. Her father had never spoken of their having Irish kin, but she supposed it was possible. He had come from a large family in Normandy, and all of his uncles had been knights in service to William Bastard.

"Are you a priest, then?" she called out to this Simon. "A priest and Sir Gabriel's cousin?"

"Not a priest, my lady," Simon answered, meeting Orlando's eyes with a frown. They had quarreled on this point, but Simon would not be moved. Not even for the Chalice would he risk so evil a lie. "A penitent returning home from pilgrimage to the Holy Land. I have had a vision of this castle and my cousin. If I could but speak to him—"

"This castle is cursed, Sir Simon," Isabel cut him off, trying to decide what was to be done. The man said he was her cousin, but how could she be sure? If he really was her kinsman, perhaps she could convince him to help her, assuming he had done more in the Holy Land than pray. But if he wasn't, she might be worse off than she was already. He didn't look dangerous; perhaps Brautus could frighten him away. And if he couldn't, perhaps he really could be of use. She raised her voice, making certain her aged champion could hear her in the courtyard below. "The Black Knight holds it for his own."

"The Black Knight?" Simon repeated. Father Colin had mentioned a Black Knight—he had called Simon by that name when he was in the vampire's trance. Isabel's Black Knight. He looked up at the woman on the battlements. "Isabel?"

"He will judge you, pilgrim," Isabel went on without waiting for a response—but wait, had he said her name? No, it wasn't possible; she hadn't told him what it was. "Perhaps he will let you pass."

The drawbridge began to creak open. "What madness is this?" Orlando muttered, taking a step back.

"I don't know," Simon answered, planting his feet. "But I'd wager you're wishing you had let me keep my sword."

"No," the dwarf said. "It will be all right."

Isabel watched Brautus ride out on Malachi, the jet-black destrier whose sire had been her father's favorite mount. No one could have guessed the Black Knight was really a wounded old man from the way he rode out, bold and terrible as any demon could be. He stopped at the center of the wooden drawbridge, yanking back on the reins to make Malachi paw at the air.

"All who seek to enter these gates must face this demon, pilgrim," she called down to the man who claimed to be her cousin. "Many men have died."

"I don't doubt it," Simon muttered to himself. The creature on the horse was a man, not a demon; Simon's own demonic senses told him as much. But he was impressively frightening; on his feet, he would have towered over Simon. His head and face were covered completely by a black helmet crowned with twisted horns, its visor crafted in a devil's leer.

"I fear no demon born of hell, my lady," Simon called out to the damsel, not sure if he meant this as a comfort or a challenge. Did the Black Knight hold her prisoner? He could smell the man's sweat from where he stood, and blood as well—the Black Knight was already wounded. But Simon smelled no actual malice on him, no tantalizing scent of evil like he had smelled on the French knight, Michel, the night before. He looked up at the girl again. She was leaning on the battlements, watching with obvious interest, but she didn't seem particularly frightened. Could this knight be Sir Gabriel himself? "I have traveled far to seek my cousin's wisdom," Simon said, starting toward the drawbridge. "I will not be turned away."

"As you will, warrior," Orlando muttered. "Just remember, pray, that one of us is mortal."

"So be it, pilgrim," Isabel called back. Malachi reared up again as Brautus wheeled the horse in a circle, but this Simon didn't stop or even slow his pace. Her cousin, if he was that truly, was brave if nothing else. If he really didn't have a sword, Brautus could cut him down easily, even wounded. But she found herself rather hoping he would not. "I shall pray for you," she said, hoping the Black Knight could hear. Whoever this Simon might be, she didn't think he meant them harm. And she found that she wanted to know him, cousin or not. It had been so long since she had met anybody, so long since she had seen any man who wasn't Brautus or some other woman's husband. And if he were brave enough to face down a demon without so much as a slingshot to use in his defense, he might actually have a chance against Michel, assuming she could convince him to fight him.

"Thank you, my lady," Simon said, hoping she was sincere. He had an idea that if the man on the horse thought she wanted Simon to pass, he would allow it. But what about the horse?

"Deliver this penitent, I pray you, Christ," Isabel said aloud. He and his small companion were on the drawbridge now, passing into the shadow of the castle wall where she couldn't see them as clearly. Three more steps, and Simon would be within reach of the Black Knight's sword. "Save him from this demon," she prayed aloud.

The girl's prayer echoed strangely inside Simon's head as he passed into the shadow of the castle. Save him from this demon . . . He felt a tingle on his skin, a burning like he felt in a church, but different, somehow, a comfort instead of a pain. Looking up, he saw a wisp of pure white fabric caught on the evening breeze, the trailing end of her sleeve. *Deliver this penitent,* she prayed on his behalf.

Suddenly the horse reared up, shattering his trance. The Black Knight lurched in the saddle, obviously struggling to keep his seat as the reins snapped in his fist. Simon saw the horse's eyes, dark brown rimmed in red, wild not with terror but with rage. The Black Knight and the damsel might be fooled, but the animal was not; it knew him just for what he was, a monster. The vampire crouched on the drawbridge as the powerful hooves flailed just above him, and Orlando fell on his face beside him, muttering prayers of his own.

But just as Simon thought his skull must be crushed, the stallion fell back. He brought his hooves down harmlessly just in front of Simon and nickered softly, a kind of equine sigh. Simon straightened up again, and the horse lowered its head as if in a nodded salute.

"Go," the Black Knight said, his deep voice gruff inside the helmet, but Simon thought he sounded rather shaken even so. The rider hadn't known his horse meant to attack or that it would suddenly stop. "Go quickly or die!" He raised his sword, and Simon sprinted for the gate, scooping up Orlando as he went. Hoofbeats pounded the drawbridge behind them as they passed beneath the portcullis and into the courtyard beyond.

Isabel watched Brautus gallop into the forest, still

brandishing his sword—Brautus, who by all rights should have been in bed. Waving back, she hurried to the stairs and down into the courtyard.

Simon found himself surrounded by people, more living souls than he had seen together since the terrible night he was cursed. Most were women or children, but a few boys and men were scattered among them—grooms and farmers, from the look of them, no guardsmen, he could see. All of them were staring at him and Orlando, some curious, some obviously frightened. "Look," a boy said, pointing. "The little one's a man."

Isabel watched the stranger and his small companion for a moment from the shelter of the crowd, suddenly shy. He was handsome, this Simon; she hadn't been able to tell before, but now she could see his face. His hair was dark brown, and he wore it long like a Saxon or a Celt—an Irishman, he'd said he was, and he looked it. His beard was dark as well, but barely a beard at all, as if he'd simply missed a day or two of shaving. If he hadn't been so pale, she might never have noticed. His skin was as creamy white as her own and seemed just as fine, too perfect to be a man's. But he was no delicate minstrel. She could see the powerful bulk of his shoulders and arms even under the rough, brown robe he wore, and she thought she saw the pale pink slash of a scar at his throat, his only flaw. Looking around the circle of the household, his eyes finally reached her face, dark brown eyes with thick black lashes.

"Well met, cousin," she managed to say, stepping forward. "I am Isabel."

"My lady." Simon nodded, smiling without thinking about it for the first time in ten years. The cold, ethereal beauty he'd seen on the battlements was a warm, real girl after all. Her astonishing red hair framed a pretty face with hazel eyes and a pert little nose sprinkled with freckles.

"Your cousin," she corrected, smiling back. She took another step forward and embraced him as a kinsman, and for a moment he thought he was lost.

In a single instant, with one innocent touch, the vampire hunger he thought he had learned to control leapt up inside him. As she pressed her warm body to his, he could feel his eyes changing color from brown to greenish gold, feel the fangs grow sharp against his tongue. Not since his first night as a vampire, his first terrible kill, had he felt such hunger and horror. He wanted to destroy this woman, to devour her, innocent or not. He could already taste her. He recoiled from her in horror, fighting for control.

"Forgive me," he said, looking down at the cobblestones, at anything but her face, his voice gone gruff, the demon's voice. "I cannot—"

"No, I am sorry," Isabel cut him off, embarrassed. He sounded so strange, and he had pulled away from her so violently, she didn't know what to think. She had touched him without thinking, a casual, ordinary gesture of greeting, but in that fleeting moment, she had felt something, a kind of coiled, brutal power that might have frightened her if she had felt it for more than a moment. But almost before she realized she was touching him at all, he had pushed her away. "I shouldn't have—"

"No, love, please." The endearment escaped him before he could stop it. Why should touching this girl have struck him so intensely, inspired such a hunger? She was pretty, yes, but what was that to his demonic curse? He had touched many pretty girls in his travels, tavern wenches and whores, most of whom had left his embrace with no more harm than a tumble and the memory of a dream. Why should his pretended cousin be so different? He let his eyes drift to her face again and almost laughed. Her beauty hid none of her feelings; she quite obviously thought he was out of his mind. Perhaps that was it, her innocence, her utter lack of guile. Wenches and whores were one matter, but how long had it been since he touched a truly innocent maid? "Forgive me, cousin," he said with a more calculated smile. "In faith, it isn't you."

"My master is sworn to a quest for salvation, my lady," Orlando interrupted. "He will allow himself no close contact until it is done."

"I see," Isabel nodded, though in truth this made no sense to her at all. She was tired, she suddenly realized; she hadn't slept for two nights running, and now this stranger and his little friend insisted on speaking in riddles. "Actually, I don't see," she corrected. "But I don't suppose it matters." She looked down at the little man standing at her cousin's side. "And what is your name, master?"

"I am Orlando, my lady." He touched his forehead in a strange salute before making her a bow. Tom had taken this man for a child, and indeed he was as small as one. But in fact he was old, as old as Brautus, with a long, gray beard. Underneath his plain, brown cloak, his clothes were brightly colored like a jester's, purple and green all embroidered with gold, and at least a dozen different little pouches and purses hung from his neck and shoulders and belt.

"Welcome, Orlando," she answered him, making a curtsey of her own.

"Orlando is a wizard, Lady Isabel," Simon explained, smiling once again in spite of himself. Sir Gabriel's daughter was kind; she greeted Orlando as gravely as she might any noble squire, as casually as if she welcomed little men into her castle every day. But he must never touch her again, not unless he meant to murder her. "He can tell you such tales, your hair will curl in fright."

"Yes," Orlando agreed with a frown. "I can think of one tale in particular that certain parties would rather not be told." He turned back to the lady. "But where is Sir Gabriel, my lady? Your father, I presume?"

"Yes," Isabel said, looking past him to the others, still watching, curious and afraid, waiting to see what she would do. For the first time in her memory, she felt her father's castle as a burden and wished she could just run away. Even yesterday, when she had been so frightened, she hadn't wanted to leave; she had wanted to protect her home and these people. But suddenly she wanted to be free. She noticed Simon watching her as well and met his brown eyes with her own, and for a strange moment, it seemed he must know exactly what she was thinking. What if this man had been Michel? she thought. What if he had come to claim Charmot and beaten the Black Knight? What if he had wanted her?

"My father is dead," she said brusquely, pushing such fancies away. "Come inside and tell me of your visions, and I will tell you of him."

She led them into the castle's great hall, a large, well-lighted room with a roaring fire on the central hearth. Coming in, Simon was struck again by how long he had kept himself away from the living and how lonely he had been. But he did not dare dwell too long on such fancies. Even now he could hear the beating of these living hearts growing louder in his ears, his vampire hunger ready to rise up and sweep away all reason. I should never have allowed it, he thought, his eyes straying to Isabel's face. I should never have let her touch me.

"Are you hungry?" Isabel asked, and her newfound cousin laughed, a strange, hollow bark of a laugh. "Is that funny?"

"No, my lady," he answered, but his bitter smile said otherwise. "Forgive me."

"My master is fasting," Orlando explained. "It is part of his penitence." The dwarf watched a platter of roast pork pass by in the hands of a serving maid with unmistakably wistful eyes.

"But my servant suffers no such oath," Simon agreed. As difficult as their exile from the living world had been for him, surely it must be worse for Orlando, still a living man himself.

"You don't eat at all?" Isabel asked, beginning to lose patience. Her newfound cousin was a pretty thing, but apparently as useful as a peacock hitched to an oxcart and only half as natural. "How are you not dead?"

"I do eat some things, my lady," Simon said, trying not to smile. "But never meat, and never in company." He had trained himself long ago to not mind the smell of mortal food, though in truth the sight of eating still made him feel rather queasy. "I do not wish to keep you from your supper," he hastened to assure her. "Please, sit down—"

"No," Isabel cut him off, her irritation growing stronger. She had thought she'd missed having a nobleman in the castle, but now that she had one, she wasn't quite so certain. Half a moment through the door, and this Simon was already graciously inviting her to sup at her own table as if it were all up to him. "In truth, I am not hungry."

"You need not fast on my account," Simon protested.

"In faith, I do not." Innocent she might be, Simon

thought, but this was no simpering child. The cold intelligence he had first heard from the battlements had returned full force to her tone, and a spark of temper flashed in her eyes, quite at odds with her delicate appearance. "Hannah," she said, stopping a serving woman. "Set a place for Master Orlando and see he has his fill. My cousin will join me in the solar."

"Wait, my lord," Orlando protested, alarmed. "I must stay with you."

"You need not fear me, master wizard," Isabel said, amused in spite of herself. The dwarf seemed in a proper panic. "I will not feed him honey cakes as soon as your back is turned."

"It isn't that, my lady," Simon said. "Orlando is sworn to assist me in my quest, and he knows much of my visions—"

"More than you know of them yourself?" she interrupted, turning to him with wide, innocent eyes.

Her challenge was unmistakable. "No, cousin," Simon answered, meeting Orlando's eyes over her shoulder. Their best hope for success in this deception was to win this lady's trust, and with it access to the catacombs the priest had spoken of. The wizard nodded slightly. "Of course I will speak with you alone."

"Is he your keeper, then?" Isabel asked as they mounted the stairs and Orlando went to the table.

"No, he is not," Simon answered. "But I think sometimes he forgets."

He followed her to the solar, a surprisingly spartan

room compared to the cozy hall. A servant had come with them to start a fire in the hearth, but the chill would be stubborn with the stone walls bare of any hangings. Two heavy chairs and a weaver's loom were the only furnishings, and these were covered in dust.

"We have little use for this room since my father died," Isabel explained, wiping off a chair. "But we can speak privately here. The hall is full of eager ears, and we have had a rather trying day."

"Most great halls are, I've noticed," Simon agreed. "But why has your day been so trying?"

"You saw the Black Knight, did you not?" she said with a strange little smile. "Would you not call him worrisome?"

"Indeed." He looked at the half-finished tapestry on the loom. "This is nice." It depicted a maiden in a forest, taming a beast—a popular subject for the past hundred years. But this maiden's hair was red, not gold, and the beast that rested its head on her lap was not a unicorn but a wolf. "Did you weave it?"

"Me? No," Isabel said with a laugh. "My mother was the weaver, not me. I have no talent for it."

"Your mother is dead as well?" Simon said, coming to join her.

"She died the same day I was born." She heard pity in his tone, and she would not bear it, not from a stranger, kinsman or not. *Your pride will be your downfall, lady,* Father Colin was fond of telling her. He was probably right. But she was her father's daughter, the lady of Charmot. She would not be pitied. "I did not know her," she said coldly.

"Then I am more sorry yet," Simon answered, sitting down.

"Why?" she asked him with a brittle smile. "What is it to you?" She stared into the flames on the hearth, purposely looking away. In this brighter light, he seemed even more beautiful than he had in the courtyard, his skin more perfect and pale. She had read of saints whose godly habits gave them an angel's appearance. But what did she need with a saint? "Tell me of your vision, cousin," she said aloud, still watching the fire. "What did you want from my father?"

"Better you should tell me, cousin," he answered. "Who is this Black Knight?"

"Why?" she asked again, turning to him. "What will you do to rid me of him? Pray him away?" For a moment, he saw fear behind the temper in her eyes, then her expression softened. "He let you pass; that is enough."

"Is it?" Simon said as she turned away again. For the first time in a decade, he felt something he had thought was gone, a sympathy deeper than a monster's useless pity. This Isabel was brave and pretty; she could pretend to be heartless and cold. But inside she was frightened; he could sense it—frightened nearly to despair. If he had still been the man he was once, he wouldn't have been able to help himself; he would have put his arms around her and promised her the moon and stars to make her smile. But he wasn't that man anymore. He was a vampire. He had no protection to offer her, only a threat more terrible than she could guess, much worse than whatever might be threatening her now.

"Perhaps it was your holiness he feared," she said with the slightest touch of sarcasm, interrupting his thoughts. "As I told you from the battlements, they say he is a demon loosed from hell."

"And well I might believe it, having seen him." She looked back to find him watching her, his deep brown eyes seeming to penetrate her soul.

"But he has never tried to hurt me, or anyone else at Charmot," she went on. "He only comes when a stranger appears—you and your Orlando are the first to pass through our gates since my father died, ten years ago and more."

"Ten years?" Simon repeated, surprised. Father Colin had spoken of Sir Gabriel as if he might have been alive; it had never occurred to Simon to think he might have been dead so long.

"Yes," Isabel nodded, getting out of her chair, the walls too close around her suddenly, as if the tiny room were shrinking. "And he never spoke of you at all, my lord, never mentioned our having any kin, in Ireland or anywhere else." She turned back to him. "I assumed I was alone."

"Perhaps he didn't know," Simon answered, getting up himself. The way she had spoken of being alone touched him far more than he was willing to acknowledge, but whatever this girl's problems might be, he could not help her. "I knew nothing of your father, Lady Isabel, or Charmot either when I left home. I went to the Holy Land in the service of my own lord, Duke Francis of Lyan." Tell as much truth as you can, Orlando had always advised, and he was a much more clever liar than Simon would ever hope to be, vampire or not. "It was in his service that I was cursed, his death that caused me to forsake my ruined honor for the dark."

"Cursed?" she echoed, not certain she had heard.

"Cursed by God," he answered. "You spoke just now of my holiness—a cruel joke, my lady." For a moment, he almost reached for her hand, almost risked touching her again without realizing it. But that could not happen again, ever. "Believe me when I tell you, I have none. God Himself has banished me from the light."

"Has he, in faith?" she said lightly. Why did these knights of chivalry insist on speaking in riddles and poems? she thought. Some of the Black Knight's challengers had gone on for an hour or more before they ever drew a lance. "You must be special then, my lord. Most of us He just torments at random, I think."

"I do not jest, my lady," he answered.

"No, I can see you do not." In truth, no one who saw his eyes as he spoke of this curse could doubt he believed it was real. But it seemed so silly, so extreme— what could any one man possibly have done to offend the Lord Almighty, short of burning down a church?

And Simon hardly seemed the church-burning sort of chap to her. "Forgive me, cousin; I do not mean to mock you," she said. "So tell me—what are the particulars of this holy curse?"

"I cannot tell," he answered. "But to escape it, I have forsworn all comfort—company, food, even the daylight."

"Meaning what?" she asked.

"Meaning I do not see the sun," he answered.

"Ever?" she said, raising her eyebrows. Surely he couldn't be serious.

"Never. During the daylight hours, I hide myself. That was why I came to your gates at twilight." Simon could tell she thought he was mad, but she didn't seem to think he was lying. "But still God's grace has eluded me," he continued. "For many months I wandered in the wilderness, all of my companions lost save for Orlando, an infidel whose life I spared."

"That should count for something, Simon," Isabel pointed out. He was absolutely in earnest; he honestly believed whatever he had done made God hate him so much, he didn't dare to show his face. "You can't truly believe God would want you to murder a man who stands no taller than your belt."

"No," he agreed. "Orlando is a blessing, the only one I have."

"Not quite," she amended. "You live; you have your life—if you were truly cursed, would God not have taken that from you?"

"No," he answered, meeting her eyes. "That I live is the worst of my curse."

"Ridiculous," she scoffed. "Good Lord, man, what did you do?"

He almost smiled. No man could stab to the heart of a question as brutally as any woman. "More sins than I dare tell you, my lady," he answered, the same evasion Adam must have used two days out of the garden, but with far less reason. "But believe me, I do not dare to break my vow."

"But what is the point?" she demanded, confusion giving way to true annoyance. In truth, she wanted to shake him as an impatient mother might shake her unruly child. She had real problems, real fears to be faced, and he was her kinsman, a fine, strapping knight, by all appearances. "Why did you come here?"

"I had a vision," he answered.

"Yes, so you've said," she said, not bothering to even pretend to be polite. As if she cared, as if she could afford to care . . .

"Many months ago, Sir Gabriel came to me in a dream," Simon explained. "He seemed to know everything about me, all the evil I had done and all that I had suffered. He told me that my soul was not yet lost, that I still might find salvation."

Isabel stared at him, barely crediting her ears. "My father came to you?" she said, searching his face for some sign of a lie. "Why should he have come to you?" Why not me? she wanted to scream at him, the fury she felt like a sickness that had come upon her suddenly. Her father had been struck dead in an instant, one moment well, the next lying dead on the ground. She hadn't even seen him die; she had been in the stable waiting for his coming—he had promised to go riding with her. She had heard a shout; someone had screamed, "My lord!" and she had run out to the courtyard. But her father had been dead already, his empty eyes staring up at her but seeing nothing. She needed her father; she needed a knight to protect her, to protect Charmot.

"You are a liar," she said aloud, meeting Simon's eyes. "I don't believe you. I will not—"

"He told me I should come here to Charmot," Simon insisted. He had expected to tell this tale to the man himself, not his grieving daughter. Why should she believe him? Why should she care? He had been lost in his own misery so long, he had forgotten what it was to feel another's pain. If anyone had asked him, he would have denied he could feel real sympathy anymore, would have said it was as foreign to his demon's heart as love. But he felt it now, and it frightened him. He couldn't afford to feel. But somehow he had to reach her, to convince her to believe him and allow him to stay until the Chalice could be found. "He said he was my kinsman; he called my father's name. He said his blood flowed in my cursed heart, and he would help me. He said there was wisdom here that could lead me back to the light."

"No," Isabel insisted. "There is nothing here." The catacombs, she thought, unable to stop herself. Perhaps he meant the catacombs . . . but no. Her father would not have shared his secrets with this stranger, kinsman or not. The wisdom of the druids was too precious; he had always kept it hidden, even from Isabel herself. "There is nothing," she repeated.

"Isabel, please." Simon could see she was lying; he could feel it just as he felt evil in the air when it was near, just as he felt the goodness in her heart. He could force her to tell him the truth, entrance her or even steal her secrets in her blood, drain them from her heart. But he didn't want to hurt her; he wanted her to trust him, more than he had wanted anything in ten long years.

"I said there is nothing here," she repeated. "You should leave here, Simon, now, at once—"

"I cannot," he cut her off. "I will not."

"The Black Knight will make you," she insisted, frustrated tears rising in her eyes, making her angrier still—she never cried, ever; why should she be crying now? "He will kill you—"

"He will not," he interrupted. Against his will, his hands came up to frame her face, forcing her to look into his eyes, and the powerful hunger swept through him, mingled with a burning as if he touched some holy thing. "Listen to me, Isabel," he said, the voice he used to charm his prey stealing into his tone. "You know that he will not. The Black Knight cannot kill me."

"Cannot kill you . . ." She felt dizzy, unable to breathe. Send my true Black Knight, she had prayed to the druids. Send a demon to protect our sanctuary. I am cursed, this man had told her, cursed by God. I must forsake the light. "You are the Black Knight," she said softly, barely as loud as a whisper. "My father sent you to me."

"Yes," Simon answered, barely hearing her, so lost did he feel in her gaze. She trusted him; this innocent believed him. Deliver this penitent, she had prayed as he passed through her gate. Save him from this demon. But he did not break the trance; the spell still lingered in his voice, entrancing this woman, bending her to his will. "Your father sent me to you."

"My lord!" The door to the solar opened, and Orlando came in, breaking the trance. "Have you told Lady Isabel of your vision?" he asked, pretending a servant's respect while his eyes blazed a reproof.

"He has," Isabel answered. She moved away from Simon, her heart beating faster, but she felt calmer, too, now that she knew the truth. "He says there is some wisdom in this castle that can save him from his curse." Did Simon even realize why her father had sent him? He spoke of his curse, of needing some wisdom, some way to break it—what if he knew his curse was to protect her? Would he stay?

"Or so he was told in a vision," Orlando agreed. The dwarf was still staring at Simon, obviously waiting for him to speak, but the vampire could not. He had entranced hundreds of mortals in his nights of darkness, but he had always been in control of the trance. He had never once felt entranced himself. What magic did he feel from this innocent's blood? What new temptation beckoned from her gaze?

"Was his vision true, my lady?" Orlando said at last. "Is there wisdom at Charmot?"

"Perhaps," Isabel answered, her mind racing. If Simon thought there was a way to break his curse at Charmot, he wouldn't dare to leave until he found it. But why should she want him to stay? "What did you do to be cursed, Simon?" she demanded, turning on him. "Did you kill?"

If another woman had asked him that question, testing him before she allowed him to stay in her home, Simon would have known to deny it at once, would have played the harmless penitent to soothe her. But something in Isabel's eyes told him that was not what she wanted at all. "Yes," he answered, meeting her eyes with his own. "More than I can remember, more than I could count."

"And would you do it again?" she pressed him, a shiver racing through her. He might be dressed like a priest; he might be beautiful; he might not even carry a sword. But looking into his eyes as he answered her now, she didn't doubt him for a moment. This man was a killer. "If you had to kill again, could you do it?"

"Yes," he answered, a smile barely curling the corner of his mouth. "If I had to kill, I could."

"Then come," she said, smiling back. If he thought there was a way to break his curse at Charmot, he would want to protect the castle until he found it. And if Michel should show up in the meantime, she would make him see that the catacombs where his cure was hidden would have to be protected. "I will show you."

She led them back out through the hall and down a spiral stairway into an earthen cellar. "There's another door just there," she said, pointing past some barrels into a shadowy corner. "It leads out to the lake at the back of the castle." But she led them in the opposite direction to another, smaller door—Simon had to stoop to follow her. Beyond it was another, much older stairway cut into the natural rock. He looked at Orlando, and the little wizard smiled.

"I will have to lend you the key, I suppose," Isabel said, handing Simon the torch. He looked as shaken as she felt, she suddenly realized. Had he felt the same strange power she had when he touched her? She tried to remember exactly what they had been saying to one another when Orlando came into the solar, but it was difficult, as if it had been a dream. All that seemed certain was that he was meant to be her Black Knight. "If my father's spirit summoned you here, these catacombs would be the reason why."

Simon watched her fit an iron key into a stone carving like the effigy on a tomb, a man in robes holding a sword or a mace; the cobwebs made it impossible to tell which. "Good evening, Joseph," she said, forcing the key to turn. "I have brought you another scholar." The stone door swung open, revealing a circular room.

"These caverns belonged to the druids," Isabel said, lighting her father's candle. "My father made a study of their records." She turned back to Simon and Orlando, both of them staring in wonder. "If he thought there was help for you at Charmot, this is where you will find it."

"Thank you, my lady," Simon said, finally able to speak. Whatever else had passed between him and this woman, these caverns must surely be the reason he had found his way to Charmot. Of all the holy and unholy places he and Orlando had seen in their quest for the Chalice, this was the first time he had thought they might actually find it. The chamber was lined with stone coffins carved with ancient runes like the ones on Kivar's map. Three more tunnels led off from it to make a compass cross with the door through which they had passed.

"Call me Isabel," she answered. "I am your cousin, remember? And don't thank me yet. Each of those coffins is packed full of scrolls, all written in a language unlike any I have ever seen, and there are more in the tunnels besides. You may not live long enough to find this wisdom you seek."

Simon smiled. You just don't know, darling, he thought. I am doomed to live forever. "I do thank you," he answered. "Isabel."

When he smiled that way, she could almost forget to

be afraid, she thought. He would protect her, cursed or not. And perhaps she could help him as well. Perhaps the druids really did hold the key to this silly curse. "I will have some rooms made up for you and Orlando," she said. "Unless you would rather stay together."

"We'll stay here," Orlando answered, going to one of the coffins. "Simon, push this lid off."

"We must begin at once," Simon explained, doing as he was told.

"Very well," she said, amused. This dwarf might be a wizard or not, but he certainly had the manner of one. "Then I will see you at breakfast, I suppose."

"No," Simon cut her off. "I can't—"

"Oh, yes, of course," she said, almost laughing at the absurdity of the thing. "You don't eat."

"Or see the daylight, remember?" he reminded her. "I will stay here, in these caverns, until I have found what I seek." She must have looked horrified, because he smiled. "Orlando will bring me what little I need."

"A bed?" she suggested. "Some blankets so you don't freeze to death—it can get rather chilly down here." She hugged herself, just noticing. "It's rather chilly now."

"We have blankets in my pack," he promised.

"Simon, are you mad?" she demanded, almost losing patience again. "How on earth or in heaven should it please God for you to starve yourself and live in a hole in the ground?"

He looked at Orlando, hoping for help, but the dwarf

just shrugged before going back to the scroll he was perusing. "I don't know, cousin," Simon admitted. "You will just have to trust me that it does."

"Trust you," Isabel repeated. She looked at the little man they said was a wizard, now bent over one of the druids' scrolls as if it might have meant something to him. "No," she decided. She needed Simon's help; she wanted him to stay; but this was too much. Charmot was still hers; these catacombs were hers, whether she could divine their secrets or not. "Come with me."

"Truly, cousin, you needn't trouble yourself," Simon protested.

"Come," she repeated. "Both of you."

She led them back past the web-covered effigy and down the narrow corridor to another, plainer door. "I will have this room made up for you," she said, opening it. "It's dark, hideously damp, no outside light at all— the floor even gets wet when the rains come hard on the lake. It should be perfect." She turned back to Simon with a wry smile. "I cannot possibly make you more uncomfortable unless I have you buried alive in the ground."

Simon smiled back, and even Orlando had to suppress a chuckle. "Very well, my lady. We thank you."

"I assume that since you avoid daylight, you would wish to work through the night," Isabel said briskly.

"Yes," Simon answered.

"Then I will come back in the morning to lock up the catacombs." She took the key Simon was holding. "Pay no mind to any noise you hear—you might wish to sleep on the bare dirt floor, but I will not allow it. My servants will make you and Orlando as proper a chamber as we can manage in this hole—"

"Isabel—"

"And you will allow it." Her tone was firm, and her pretty mouth was set in a line that would broach no further protest.

"Very well." Simon made his most gracious bow, and Orlando followed his lead. "We most humbly thank you, cousin."

"As well you might," she retorted. "Now I will bid you good night."

Simon watched her go with a smile, his arms crossed on his chest. "A very pretty lady," Orlando remarked. "Bossy, but pretty."

"I like her," Simon admitted. "I wish I didn't, but I do."

"It doesn't matter." The dwarf gave his arm a pat as he passed on his way to the door. "If we're to have these catacombs for the night alone, we had best get started."

Later, Isabel stood at the tower window, gazing out at the night. Behind her, Brautus was sleeping, safe in bed at last, his shoulder freshly bound again and only a bit worse for wear. He had returned while she was in the solar with Simon—no doubt they would have much to talk about tomorrow when he woke. Somewhere far below her, Simon and his mysterious servant were rummaging through ancient texts, looking for wisdom that she, as a woman, was apparently too stupid or innocent to ever understand. And somewhere out in the darkness, a villain was moving closer, determined to make her his bride. But that didn't matter any more. Simon would be her Black Knight.

A sudden movement caught her eye, a black shadow moving on the opposite shore of the moat. She watched as it moved closer, into the reflected moonlight from the water, and she saw it was a big, black dog, pacing the water's edge. Suddenly it stopped and sat back on its haunches, facing the castle and her. It stared up at the tower for what could have been a moment or several minutes; she lost track. Why should a stray dog stare at a castle so?

"I'm tired," she said softly, barely aware she had spoken aloud. Blowing out her candle, she left the window to go to her room and sleep.

3

Isabel had suspected Brautus might be shocked to hear she had let Simon stay to explore the catacombs. But she never expected him to be furious.

"Are you mad?" he demanded, risking his shoulder to wrench himself upright in bed as soon as she had told him all that had passed the night before while he was gone from the castle.

"Not that I've noticed." She set his breakfast in front of him. "But how would I know if I were?"

"You are; trust me." He glared at the tray as if he bore it a grudge. "And what would your father say, with me tucked in bed like a suckling babe while his daughter takes some stranger and his imp into his study? This man could be anybody!"

"He is my kinsman," she insisted, spreading a napkin over his chest. "You heard him say as much yourself."

"Aye, I heard him. Who's to say he's not a liar?"

"I say." She handed him a spoon. "I told you. He is my Irish cousin; he used to be a knight; he fell under a curse in the Holy Land." He took it without looking, staring at her instead, incredulous. "Papa came to him in a dream and told him to come to Charmot, that the only way to break this curse of his was here."

"And you believe this bucket of—"

"I do." She sat on the edge of the bed. "I prayed for him, Brautus. I prayed to God and to my father—I even prayed to the pagan gods of the druids. Send me a true Black Knight."

"Oh holy Christ—"

"And so they have," she finished. "Brautus, just think—a knight under a curse, cursed by God Himself, or so Simon believes. Does that not sound like a Black Knight to you? And you saw him. Even under that silly robe, you can see how strong he is. And he must be a good fighter, or else why would he think himself cursed?"

"Because he's so clumsy, he killed his own lord by accident?" Brautus suggested. "Because under that robe, he's a leper? Because he roasts babies on spits and eats them on Ash Wednesday? Faith, girl, where is your head?"

"Brautus, I believe him," she insisted. "Not that God has truly cursed him, no, but I believe that he believes it. And if he thinks the cure is at Charmot, so much the better. He will help us, Brautus; I know it." She paused, still not certain she should tell him the rest. "I asked him."

"Asked him what?" he asked with a frown.

"Asked him why he was cursed," she answered. "I

asked him if he was a killer, and he said yes, that he was. I asked him if he could kill again, if he had to do it, and he said he could."

"Holy Christ," he repeated. "This is my fault." He pushed his porridge away untasted. "I should have let you marry the first little weakling the king sent to claim you and been done—no doubt he'd be dead and buried by now, and you'd be free."

"Don't be ridiculous," she scoffed.

"You were just so young," he went on as if he hadn't heard her. "I couldn't bear the thought of you being some strange man's wife, not yet . . . and now we've come to this." His pale blue eyes looked tired and sad as they finally met her own. "You say this man admitted he was a killer, may God save us. What if he is a liar as well?"

"Then he is a liar. What difference will it make?" She got up from the bed. "He doesn't even have a sword, Brautus; I'm not afraid of him. And if he will help us, if he will defend Charmot, I don't care if he is a leper or any of those other things you said. And if he will not . . ." She didn't even want to think of it. She wanted to believe as she had last night that her problems were solved, that she could finally stop worrying about the future, at least for a little while. Was that so much to ask? "If Simon is a liar and he will not help, how will I be any worse off than I was before? If some brigand comes and takes Charmot away from me, what will it matter if we have a liar in the catacombs?"

"What if this Simon is the brigand?" Brautus asked more gently. "What if all of his tales are no more than a trick to win entrance to the castle without a fight? What if he is the one who has come to claim Charmot and to claim you for his own?"

"No." She shook her head, her back turned on her protector. "If he had wanted to take Charmot, he could have done it last night. If he had meant to make me marry him, or . . ." She broke off with a bitter smile. "Trust me, Brautus. He did not."

"Then he is more the fool."

"And glad am I of it." She turned back to him with a smile. "You needn't act as if his getting through the gate was all my fault, you know." She took the bowl and spoon and sat back down on the bed. "You're the one who let him and Orlando pass."

"No, you don't, my lady," he scolded, taking his breakfast back. "I'm not so feeble yet that I will let you feed me." He took a grudging bite. "I didn't mean to let him pass, if you want to know. That was Malachi."

"Malachi?" she laughed. "Brautus, Malachi is a horse."

"When your friend Simon stepped onto the draw-bridge, I didn't think I would have to lift a hand to turn him away; I thought the horse would do it," he answered. "He broke his reins and reared over him like he meant to stove in his head, wild as an unbroken colt."

"I saw him rear up," Isabel admitted. "But I thought you made him do it."

"Not I—I barely kept my seat." His eyes met hers again. "Then all in a single instant, he changed. He faced that Simon like . . . it was like he bowed to him." His expression clouded, and she heard a tremor in his voice. "You are too young to remember, kitten, but his sire used to bow to your father that way, back in the days of our wars. It made me think perhaps this man was telling the truth, that he was Sir Gabriel's kinsman indeed." His face turned stern again. "But now I hear you tell this tale of a curse and a vision, and I think I must be running mad as well."

"He is my kinsman, Brautus. When the time comes, he will defend Charmot." She gave his hand a squeeze. This tale of Malachi made her even more certain she had made the right choice, even more certain Simon was exactly what she knew him to be, whether he knew it or not. But she knew better than to try to press that point with Brautus. "And if he won't, you can kill him yourself."

Simon yawned again, the strange characters of the ancient code swimming on the scroll before his eyes. After ten years of study, he could decipher much of the writing of the saints and wizards who had hidden the Chalice from the world, almost as much as Orlando could. But not when he was more than half asleep. "It must be nearly dawn," he said, laying the scroll aside.

"Well past it, I would imagine," Orlando agreed. They had decided to read what they could in the scrolls

here in this chamber before moving on to the catacombs themselves. Hopefully they would find some clue
to guide them through the labyrinth. But everything so
far seemed to focus on the history of this lake and island and the rites of the people who had once lived
there—fascinating reading, but not of much use to
their quest. So far neither of them had found any direct
mention of the Chalice at all. But the strong premoni-
tion they shared that it was here remained even so. "No
doubt that silly girl will be down here any moment to
lock us out for the day."

"She isn't a silly girl," Simon said, a faint hint of reproach in his tone. "This castle and these catacombs
are hers, and we are strangers. I cannot blame her for
wanting to keep some kind of control over our study."
He picked up another scroll. "Besides, I like her."

"I know you do," Orlando retorted sharply enough
to make the vampire look up. "And so do I," the dwarf
added. "That will be our greatest difficulty here, I'm
afraid."

"Why should it be?" Simon answered. "I don't intend to bite her, if that is what worries you."

"Just because you don't intend to do it doesn't mean
you won't," Orlando pointed out with a wry smile. "But
no, that is not what worries me, or not all." He put the
scroll he'd been reading back into its stone coffin. "The
Chalice is here at Charmot; we both believe it. Somewhere in these catacombs is the end of our journey, the
prize of our quest. But Lady Isabel knows nothing of

that, or only what little you have told her. Yet she allows you to stay."

"And I, for one, am glad of it," Simon said, rather annoyed. "Are you not?"

"Of course I am," the wizard answered. "But I fear the lady's reasons. She wants something from you, warrior, and I fear I can all too easily guess what."

"She wants me to protect Charmot," Simon answered. For the first time since it had happened, he let himself think back to the moment Isabel had seemed to decide to let him stay, the strange trance they had shared. "She thinks I am some Black Knight, a replacement for the giant we saw at the gates. She thinks her father sent me here to save her from . . . something." He turned away, the drowsiness he always felt during the daylight hours making him feel slow and stupid. "I don't know what she fears exactly, but I could tell she was afraid."

"And you want to protect her, whatever it is—it is in your nature to protect the innocent, vampire or not." He smiled. "And as you said, you like her."

"May the angels pity her for it," Simon retorted. "What protection can I offer anyone, Orlando, whether I like them or not?"

"Who can tell?" the dwarf shot back. "You said yourself, you do not know what threatens this girl, what she fears. Your curse may make you her perfect guardian—the Black Knight, she called you? I call that apt indeed."

"Maybe," Simon allowed, getting up to put away his scroll, but suddenly Orlando grabbed his arm.

"You cannot swear yourself to this woman, warrior," Orlando insisted, sounding urgent, almost fearful. "You cannot do evil to save her, no matter what her need might be."

"Don't be ridiculous," Simon laughed, trying to pull free, but the wizard would not let him go. "What evil could she want? She is barely more than a child, an innocent—"

"An innocent who asked you if you would kill for her, or have you forgotten already?" his mentor cut him off. "And you told her that you could. Something has passed between you already, innocent or not." His grip tightened on Simon's arm. "It may be no more than that, her very innocence, or her pretty face, but already she has laid claim to some part of your loyalty. Did you not hear how quick you were to defend her when I called her a silly girl?"

"That was nothing," Simon protested.

"Was it?" Orlando replied. "Even if she wants no more than to have a noble cousin in her castle, she could still distract you from your quest, make you forget why it is you have come here and what you hope to find."

"Not likely." Simon broke free at last. "Do you think I could forget for one moment what I am, Orlando? Do you not think it preys upon me every moment I am with this woman?"

"I do," Orlando nodded. "But what if what you are is what she needs? And what if that need should oppose your own need for the Chalice?"

"How could it?"

"Who knows?" The dwarf looked tired suddenly, and older than he had ever seemed before. "I have seen too much, warrior; I know how fate can play tricks. We have come here for a reason, but I fear what other forces may be waiting here as well, what other ends we may be brought to."

"You worry too much, old man," Simon said, laying a hand on his shoulder. "Just because Lady Isabel wants my protection doesn't mean I intend to let her have it—I can't. I told her I could kill, but I never promised I would kill for her, nor will I. I cannot swear myself to her; I am already sworn. My choices are already made."

"Are you certain?" Orlando asked. "Can you give your solemn promise? I ask not only for your sake, but for Roxanna—"

"Pardon me, my lord." A serving wench was peering around the door. "My lady is coming downstairs in a moment, and I wondered if you would have us bring you some breakfast." She looked Simon up and down, a kittenish smile barely curling the corners of her pretty mouth. "Your room is already prepared."

"No," Simon answered. "No breakfast." The chit had come upon them so suddenly, he felt a little dizzy, her heartbeat like thunder for a moment in his ears before he grew accustomed to her presence. He had not fed since the brigands at the church; he should not risk being near any living creature until he fed again.

"Tell Lady Isabel I will wait upon my master," Orlando said. "She need not trouble herself." His expression turned stern. "Or send you back ever again."

The girl's smile disappeared. "As you will," she nodded, obviously miffed. "My lady will be here soon." Bobbing a curtsey to Simon, she swept from the room in a huff.

"I don't think I should see Isabel," Simon said when she had gone. The girl's scent still hung in the air, maddening and delicious, and he struggled to shut it out.

"Nor do I," Orlando agreed. "Go and see this room of yours; I shall tell her you're already sleeping."

"Yes." He nodded. But in truth he felt disappointed. He wanted to see his pretended cousin; if he were honest, he would admit he had been looking forward to it all night. But that in itself was dangerous. He shouldn't care to see her, shouldn't be thinking of her at all. Could Orlando be right? Could Isabel truly distract him from his quest? "Orlando, I promise," he said, pausing at the door. "Whatever may happen, I will not abandon the Chalice."

Isabel passed Susannah coming up the stairs as she was going down. "What's the matter?" she asked, laughing at the sour look on the other's girl's usually pleasant face.

"Your kinsman is a beauty, my lady," the serving maid answered. "But that little monster with him can go hang."

"You'd do better to leave both of them in peace," Isabel advised. Susannah was the castle's most notorious flirt; heaven only knew what damage she could do to Simon and his penitence, given free rein. "How did you come here? I didn't see you in the hall."

"I came from outside, through the cellar door," she answered. "I was in the garden, and I suddenly thought perhaps your guests would want me to fetch their breakfast."

"I take it they did not," Isabel said, trying to keep a stern face. "Is Sir Simon's room prepared?"

"Yes, my lady." Properly abashed, the girl bobbed a curtsey and hurried away up the stairs.

The little storeroom was still more a burrow than a proper nobleman's chamber, but it looked much more cozy than it had the night before. Two beds had been carried downstairs in pieces and reassembled, one large and one small, and a pair of chests covered with thick carpets would serve well enough for seating and for storage. The damp earth walls had been hung with plain blue wool on every side, and another, fancier tapestry depicting the golden oak of Charmot on a field of red had been hung over the larger bed. Fresh torches had been mounted in each corner, and a candle stood waiting on a small table beside the larger bed. Someone had even laid out fresh clothes for Simon, a plain black tunic and hose that had once belonged to her father with a clean white shirt for underneath.

She picked up the tunic, remembering the last time her father had worn it as clearly as she remembered coming down the stairs that morning. She pressed her face to its soft folds, breathing deeply as if she might still catch a whiff of his scent. How many times had she pressed her cheek to this tunic and felt his arms close around her, making her feel safe? How had she lasted so long, knowing she would never feel that way again?

Simon stood in the doorway watching. The room was fine, the best he'd had for shelter in quite some time. But it wasn't the room that held him silent and entranced. He had meant to avoid Isabel completely until he had rested and fed, but now that he saw her, he couldn't imagine he could ever look away.

Isabel felt eyes on her and turned around. "Good morrow, cousin," she said with a little laugh, embarrassed. What must he be thinking, seeing her this way? "Did you find what you were looking for?"

"Not yet." He came closer, into the room. "I fear we must impose on you a while longer."

"We don't mind." She laid the tunic on the bed. "Someone must have thought you needed something better to wear," she explained. "It was probably Hannah—she was saying last night it was a disgrace, your being seen in that tatty robe when you're my father's kinsman." He was still watching her, one corner of his mouth turned up in the barest hint of a smile. Stop babbling, she scolded herself; you sound like a fool. "But then, you must prefer the robe, for your penance."

"No," Simon answered. "I don't, as a matter of fact. Thank you." He smiled in truth. "Or thank Hannah." He had been afraid the strange hunger he had felt for her the night before would have grown worse, but strangely, it had not. Being with her now, he could almost forget he hungered for blood at all. "Is she the one you sent down to ask if I wanted breakfast?"

"I didn't send anyone. I just assumed you didn't." She lit the candle on one of the torches. "But that was Susannah who came down on her own," she said. "She and your Orlando will never be friends, I'm afraid. What did he say to her?"

"Nothing, really." How long had it been since he had allowed himself to have this kind of simple conversation with anyone, much less a woman? He found it soothing, fascinating. But what had she been thinking with her face pressed to that tunic? Did he dare to ask? "I think Orlando worries that I might be tempted into sin."

"I'm a bit worried myself," she said with the husky hint of a laugh. "If anyone could tempt you, it would be Susannah."

"I'm not so certain of that." Isabel looked at him, surprised. He almost sounded like he meant to flirt with her. But that was impossible, wasn't it? "So which one is Hannah?" he asked.

"Hannah is older," she answered. "Susannah is her niece. Her husband, Kevin, works in the stables with Tom, their son—Hannah's husband and son, not Susannah's. Susannah isn't married." She sat down on one of the chests. "Then there's Mary and Margaret and Glynnis—they're all in the kitchen. Glynnis is Kevin's mother, and her husband, Wat, used to be the blacksmith in my father's day. But he's too old now to do much more than sharpen plows and such." Simon yawned, sitting on the edge of the bed, and she laughed. "But I'm boring you straight to sleep."

"No, in faith, you're not," he promised. "I want to hear." If he could only tell her just how glad he was to listen, how long it had been since he had heard anyone talk about plain, simple life. As sleepy as he was, he drank in her words like water in a desert. "So are Kevin and his son the only men in their prime in the castle?"

"Nearly," she admitted. For a moment, she thought about Brautus's warning—could Simon be questioning her to learn about Charmot's defenses, planning an attack? But she dismissed the idea as quickly as it came. "But you saw them last night in the courtyard, remember? Raymond and the second Tom help in the fields, such as they are, but they don't live inside the castle proper. Raymond's wife, Mary, used to live here before they were married, but since the baby, she keeps mostly to the cottage in the woods." He was smiling again, obviously amused, and she couldn't help but laugh. "You can't really want to hear all this."

"You'd be surprised." In truth, he didn't care what she said so long as she kept talking. The night before in her fancy white gown, she had seemed like some captured princess in a fairy tale, fluctuating in her manner between chilly restraint and the edge of tears. Today in her plain green jumper, she was relaxed and fun, the sort of girl he would have courted to distraction back when he was able. "You have to remember, I've had no one to talk with but Orlando in quite some time."

"Orlando seems quite entertaining to me," she said with another laugh. "Where is he, by the way?"

"Still reading in your father's study." He didn't want to talk about Orlando or even think of him. Orlando was reality, the world of darkness where he was a monster. He was enjoying this dream. "What of your father's knights-at-arms? Surely he must have had guardsmen when this castle was built."

"He did," she answered, sobering a bit. She must be more cautious, or she'd be telling him everything, Brautus's ruse included. She found it so easy to talk to Simon somehow, even after less than a single day's acquaintance, much easier than any other young man she had ever known. Not that she'd known many—the king's herald, and the occasional peddler. The only strange noblemen she'd seen since her father died had stayed safely on the other side of the wall. But she had often imagined what it might be like to talk with one of them, and it had never seemed possible it could be as simple as this. Unlike the knights who had come to

fight for Charmot, Simon wasn't grand or pompous or
even particularly solemn, cursed as he believed he was;
he was fun. "There used to be a whole regiment here,"
she admitted. "But when Papa died, they all left to find
a new lord." She stood up, suddenly self-conscious. "It's
very quiet at Charmot, you know, and not very prof-
itable. We don't even have a proper village." She took
her father's key out of her pocket. "But I should let you
rest."

"Wait," he said without thinking, getting up and
crossing the room in two long strides to reach her. Stay
here with me, he wanted to say. Talk to me, and laugh,
and let me look at you. Just don't leave me alone.

"What is it?" she asked, gazing up into his eyes. In a
single moment, everything had changed. His smile was
gone, replaced by a look so sad and lost it made her
want to cry. Who are you? she wanted to ask him.
What is this curse that binds you? What has hurt you
so? But of course she could not.

He wanted to touch her, he realized; the hunger he
had thought was gone was not; it had only changed to
something more subtle and dangerous. He could already feel her soft, warm cheek against his palm as he
imagined cradling it there. But he did not dare. "I must
thank you, cousin," he said aloud, forcing back a
tremor from his voice. She was an innocent; that must
be why she affected him so strongly. He had no experience in resisting the lure of noble maidens in his vampire state. Any other beauty of her class would surely

have made him feel the same—he must believe this. Orlando was right; he could not let himself be distracted. "Thank you," he repeated, embracing her as a kinswoman, the same way she had embraced him the night before.

"You are welcome, cousin." His arms closed around her, and for a moment she pressed her cheek against his chest, breathing in the warm, masculine scent that had always meant sanctuary in her father's arms. But something was wrong; something was missing. He didn't . . . but before she could form the thought in her mind, he was letting her go. "You're welcome," she repeated, making herself smile. "Rest well."

"I will," he promised, smiling as she left.

She found Orlando still sitting at her father's desk poring over a scroll, the last of the candles she had left for them burned down to a stub. "Good morning, master," she said, taking the key from her pocket to signal it was time for him to go. "I fear I have come to disturb you."

"Not at all, my lady. The hour is late—or early, I suppose." He rubbed his eyes. "I forget not everyone has changed their days for nights."

"I must admit, I don't see how you manage it, either of you." He had removed his cloak, and many of the little pouches and purses she had noticed him carrying before now hung from the shelves. One lay open on the desk, spilling what looked like a fortune-teller's seeing stones across another scroll. "Or why you'd want to try, for that matter." Orlando must know the details of Simon's curse; why else would he be here to help him? "What purpose can it serve to live forever in the dark?"

He smiled, and his dark brown eyes were warm with what seemed like genuine friendliness for the first time since they'd met. "I cannot tell, my lady." He rolled up his scroll and neatly tied the binding, his small fingers graceful and quick. "There is much about my master that must seem strange to you, I know." He got up from the chair with a thump that should have been comical but was not. His manner was so grave and dignified, even with him dressed in motley colors and barely as tall as her shoulder, she could not think of him as foolish. "But you must trust me when I tell you this. Both of you will be much happier if you do not ask too much of him."

"Ask too many questions, you mean?" she said with a laugh. "I will try, Master Orlando, if you wish, but it will be against my nature, I'm afraid." She helped him put the scrolls away—already he seemed to know exactly which order they should go in, while she didn't have a clue. "My father always said I was far too inquisitive for my own good."

"A healthy curiosity is never a bad thing, even in a woman." He tossed his seer's stones across the desk, gave them a quick study, then scooped them back into their bag. "You were your father's only child?"

"So far as I know," she answered. "But this time yesterday, I didn't know I had a cousin." A rough map had been pinned to the wall, showing Britain and France and a fair percentage of the Mediterranean. "Are these all the places you and Simon have been?"

"Not nearly," he answered. "Was your father born at Charmot?"

"No, in France—Bretagne, actually." She pointed on the map. "He came here to serve King Henry after the wars. But my mother was born in a village very near here, the daughter of a free farmer." She turned to him and smiled. "So I'm half peasant and partly pagan besides."

"That explains your beautiful red hair," he said.

"That explains a lot of things about me." A ruby-colored flask was sitting on a shelf between two stacks of her father's books, but she was certain she had never seen it before. "Is this yours, Orlando?"

"It is."

"It's a pretty thing." She fingered the glass and found it cold to the touch, even colder than she might have expected in this chilly room. "What is inside?"

"A terrible poison." He reached past her to take it, whisking it away to one of his pockets so quickly she could not even see which one. "You must be careful, my lady."

"That is what everyone tells me." She watched him gather the rest of his things. "Will you truly tell me nothing about Simon? How was he cursed?"

"My master has told you far too much already," he answered with a frown.

"But he says you are a wizard, and he was just a knight even before he was cursed," she pointed out. "Can he truly be your master?"

He paused for a moment, then smiled. "What is a master, my lady?" He took the map down from the wall and looked at it. "Simon is my only hope, my warrior and my salvation. My soul is in his hands."

Watching his face, Isabel believed him. "A king should have so beautiful an oath for his retainers," she said. "Though few could swear it with their hearts as you have."

His eyes widened as well as his smile. "Your inquisitive mind has made you wise, Lady Isabel."

"Wise, master wizard?" she said with a laugh. "Nay, not I, I assure you." The candle sputtered, about to go out. "But come, before we are left in the dark. Simon was on his way to bed, I think. Will you come upstairs and have breakfast with me?"

"Aye, my lady," he nodded. "I believe I will."

Simon could hear Isabel talking with Orlando in the study just beyond the thick earthen wall of his room. If he had taxed his demon's senses, he probably could have understood their words. But the sun was climbing higher by the moment, and before he slept, there was something else he wanted to do.

He filled a deep pewter basin from the jug of water Isabel's servants had left for him—the water was still warm. Stripping out of the tattered robe Orlando had stolen for him from Father Colin, he washed quickly, plunging his whole head into the basin and shaking water from his hair like a dog. The good souls who had prepared his room had been kind enough to leave him a razor and a mirror as well. He faced his reflection and grimaced, baring the slight fangs that gave his true nature away even when he was at rest. Some of the texts he had read in his quest had insisted that a vampire's reflection could not be seen, but that was foolishness. He could see himself only too well.

He touched the blue-white scar on his throat. He treasured this scar, gotten in a tavern brawl in Damascus, a wound that had barely been healed on the night he had fallen into darkness. A thief had tried to murder him for his purse and would likely have succeeded if Sascha hadn't been there to save him. Sascha . . . his first vampire kill.

He swiped the razor across his wrist, barely wincing at the pain. Borrowed blood welled for a moment in the wound, the blood of the dead Frenchmen from the chapel still filling his veins. But before the first drop could spill completely from the cut, the flesh began to heal itself, the edges folding back together with a tiny hiss like water on hot coals, a sound so faint no mortal could have heard it. The sound of the devil repairing his own.

He rinsed the razor in the basin and shaved the three day's beard from his face as he heard Orlando's voice coming closer, two pairs of footsteps coming toward the stairs. He expected the dwarf to join him, but they continued on together, their voices fading away as they shut the basement door behind them.

"So I am deserted," he muttered with a wry smile. He caught sight of his face in the mirror again, the mask of a man that hid his true, cursed self. "I wish I could leave me, too." Pushing the thought from his mind with an effort, he finished shaving and stripped out of the rest of his clothes. He held the tunic that had been left for him to his face as Isabel had done, the sweetness of her scent still clinging to the fabric. What had she been thinking? he wondered again.

"What difference does it make?" He laid the tunic aside for later and collapsed onto the bed, letting sleep have him at last.

Isabel watched Orlando devour the breakfast of a man three times his size, not bothering to hide her smile. "I'm glad to see the food at Charmot meets with your approval, master wizard," she said, taking a bite of her own. "Even if the company does not."

"The company is charming," he protested, pausing to look at her, apparently aghast. "Why would you say I do not approve it, my lady?"

"Perhaps I am mistaken." She nodded to Hannah, who went to fetch another platter. "Both my maid and myself got the impression earlier that you found the presence of young ladies rather irritating."

"No, not I," he demurred with a smile. "Distracting,

perhaps, but never irritating." He refilled his cup. "I fear you will be most offended by me while we are here, Lady Isabel, and by my master as well. We have not lived among civilized folk for quite some time."

"So I gathered." She handed him another slab of bread with butter. "I would ask you where you've been, but I know you wouldn't tell me."

"'Tis no great secret. We are scholars, of a sort, in search of ancient writings and wisdom. We have been in many other places like your catacombs." Hannah had returned with the fresh platter of meat, and at the mention of the catacombs, she let it drop to the table with a muffled crash.

"Thank you, Hannah," Isabel said, giving her a smile.

"My lady," she muttered, hurrying away.

"Did I say something wrong?" Orlando asked.

"You mentioned the catacombs," Isabel explained. "Most of the people who live at Charmot think they are bad luck, a place of evil." She refilled his trencher. "The caves were discovered or made by the druids, the ancient folk of this island and the woods around it. The ignorant say they were witches and warlocks who fed on human flesh, and that the scrolls in their catacombs are full of evil magic." She thought the dwarf would laugh at this, but he didn't even smile. "They even say my father cursed himself when he built this castle here," she finished, smiling herself.

"And thus the Black Knight keeps his castle prisoner," he said with a pointed glance over his cup. "Is that what you believe, my lady?"

"No, master wizard, I do not." Tom came into the hall at a trot, giving her an excuse to let the matter drop. "What is it, Tom?"

"Forgive me, my lady," the boy said, glancing at Orlando. "I must speak with you."

"All right." Nodding once more to her guest, she followed Tom back out into the courtyard. "What is it?"

"I rode all the way to the river by the king's road and back to Charmot through the forest," Tom said. "But I never saw a sign of that Frenchman and his men. I even went to the tavern where they were seen. The man there said they left at nightfall, headed for the Chapel of Saint Joseph to take lodging for the night."

"Did you go to the chapel?"

"No, my lady. I was afraid they might still be there, so I turned back before I got close to the village."

And if they are still there? she wanted to ask. Do you not think I need to know it? But Tom was barely sixteen and a stable boy at that; she could hardly expect him to have the courage of a knight errant. She thought again of Simon, sleeping in her cellar even now, and silently cursed his stupid curse.

"Very well," she said aloud. "Keep Master Orlando upstairs for a few minutes—your mother can help you. I need to speak to my cousin alone." The boy looked doubtful. "And if he won't help me, I'll go to the chapel myself."

4

❧ ❧

Simon dreamed of Ireland. He was standing on the beach below his master's castle, the morning sun warm on his back. A nightmare, he thought, tears of relief on his face, real salt tears, not blood. It had all been a dream. A great black horse was galloping through the surf, glad to be free of the ship's hold at last—his horse. He had come home.

He turned back toward the castle, smiling, but the cliffs were gone, and suddenly, it was night. A great, black plain spread out before him, its tall, dead grasses whispering in a freezing wind. Behind him was his village, where everyone was asleep; his mother was sleeping and her kinsmen. All of those who shuddered as he passed them in the daylight and hid from him in the night. Far across the plain, he saw the fires, the lights of the marauding gods. My father, he thought, the killing rage rising inside him. There is my father.

Isabel slipped into her cousin's room, embarrassed but determined. She had tried knocking on the door, but he had not answered, and she had to speak to him.

"Simon?" she called out softly, blinking in the near-darkness. He had put out the torches, leaving only a single candle burning near the door. She picked it up and closed the door behind her before she approached the bed. "Simon?" She hoped her parents in heaven were otherwise distracted at the moment and not watching her invade the bedchamber of a man she'd barely met. "Are you asleep?"

He was. He had thrown the pillows off the bed and most of the covers as well and was lying nearly sideways across it on his back, arms and legs sprawled in every direction and his head hanging upside down over the edge. She smiled, amused in spite of her worries and the oddness of her present situation. She'd thought she was the most unquiet sleeper in England, but apparently with Simon back from the Holy Land, she was not.

"Simon," she said more loudly, but still he didn't stir. His long, dark hair had fallen back from his brow, and his face glowed in the candlelight, the face of an angel. She moved closer, fascinated. His lashes were every bit as long as her own and as dark as his hair, contrasting sharply with the moonlight-colored skin of his finely chiseled cheekbones, his high-arched eyebrows black against his delicate brow. His nose was delicate as well, even at this ridiculous angle, and his mouth was a perfect bow, soft and sweet in repose. He had shaved, apparently; the dark shadow of his beard was gone. In truth, he was almost too pretty; if she had only seen his face, she might have mistaken him for a maid. But his body was definitely masculine; his arms and shoulders and chest were bare above the twisted blankets, thickly curved with lethal-looking muscle. He had said he was a knight errant before his curse, that he had killed more men than he could count, and seeing him now, she believed him. Angel he might be, but only the sword and the lance could have sculpted him to such a shape. But even so, the skin on his body was as milky white and smooth as his face, its creamy perfection unbroken by so much as a freckle.

"What manner of man are you, cousin?" she whispered, feeling a queer little shiver in her stomach as she bent closer to him. He stirred, still restless in his dream, his brow suddenly drawn in a frown, and she found herself holding her breath, entranced by his beauty, close enough to touch.

But that was ridiculous; she didn't want to touch him; she wanted his counsel. He was a man, a noble knight, her kinsman, and her castle was in danger. He should want to help her, and he should know what to do. "Simon," she repeated, giving his shoulder a shake.

Simon came out of his dream in a fury, blind with rage and drunk on the sudden smell of blood so close he could reach out and seize it. "Yes," he snarled, grabbing the woman up by her arms and shoving her back against the wall, the light she held falling to the floor.

"Wait!" Isabel cried out, horrified by his reaction and stunned by how quickly he could move straight out of a sound sleep. "Simon, it's me!" She had dropped the candle when he grabbed her, but not before she had seen he was naked, another frightening shock. "It's Isabel." He was holding her fast against the wall, standing so close to her she could feel her body brush against him with every breath she took. "Don't you remember?"

"Isabel . . ." Her breath was sweet; her mouth was so close he could taste it, and her heartbeat was exquisite. He had never heard such a strong little heart. But she was speaking to him, saying something that ought to have meaning . . . Isabel; she said her name was Isabel. He fought to recover some part of his waking, still-human reason, to remember who she was and why he shouldn't hurt her, but the demon inside him was hungry; it cared only for her blood. He had been sleeping, safe in his lair, and she had come upon him willingly, had touched him uninvited. Surely she must be prey.

"Yes, Isabel. Sir Gabriel's daughter—your cousin, you idiot." She had never been so close to any man before, certainly not a naked one, and suddenly it occurred to her that she didn't really know him from Adam, and they were two full stories under the castle. Even if she screamed, no one would hear her. "I need to talk to you." He leaned even closer, his cheek brushing against hers, and she could hear him breathing, sniffing her hair like a dog. "I . . ." She felt what must have been his mouth brush her ear, and mysteriously, without warning, her knees went weak. "I need your help," she finished, struggling to keep her voice.

The smell of her skin was unbearable, like blossoms of honeysuckle crushed in his fist, and her hair smelled like spring rain. He let one hand slide up her arm and over her shoulder to her throat, her skin like silk and warm with life, the pad of his thumb gently pressing her pulse. But slowly his mind was returning, as much as it could in the full sun of the day. Slowly he remembered who she was and why he was with her. This cavern was her home, a room under her castle. She was Isabel, the maiden with the key to his salvation. But what was she doing down here? Surely he must have warned her somehow; surely she must know to stay away. "No," he answered, his voice like the growl of the wolf. "I cannot help you."

"Are you sleeping?" she said softly, barely louder than a whisper, the sound of his voice dissolving the last of her bravado. "Are you still asleep?" He sounded like a man in a trance, under a deadly spell, and neither the distant, saintly man she had met the night before nor the easy, good-natured knight who had talked with her that morning would have sounded that way or threatened her like this or made her feel so strange, frightened and aching at once. The sensible woman she had always known herself to be wanted him to come back to his senses and let go of her at once. But there was another, new part of her she had never known existed, a stranger who both feared the man who held her and desired him, who trembled to imagine what he might do next and yet still ached to feel it, whatever it was.

"Yes," he answered, touching her mouth, one hand still braced against her shoulder to keep her pinned to the wall, one knee pressed between her own. "I am dreaming." His vampire senses could see her face even in the dark, see her blush as a rose-colored glow. "You should not have come here." He traced the curve of her cheek down to her jaw, the flow of her blood down the fragile flesh of her throat. Her body brushed against him as she gasped, her soft breasts pressed against his chest, deliciously warm through her gown, and every muscle in his body ached to possess her, to crush her in his arms. "You must go away."

"But . . ." No one had ever touched her this way before, as if she were some precious thing to be both possessed and adored. Perhaps she was dreaming as well. "But I can't," she answered, finding her sensible voice. "You must let me go."

His mouth was now so close to hers, he could feel the warmth of her lips on his own, but she couldn't see him in the dark. She could not know what held her. If she had seen him, seen the demon fire in his eyes, seen the fangs that he could feel against his tongue, she would be screaming, burning with terror alone. The desire his demon senses insisted she felt was no more than an illusion. "Yes." He cradled her beautiful face in his hands, closing his eyes for a moment as he leaned his forehead to hers. Then he let her go.

As soon as he stepped back, the spell he had some-how cast over her, stealing her wits, was broken. Now all she felt was embarrassed. "Sleep well, cousin," she mumbled, pushing past him to stumble to the door, tripping over that damned fallen candle as she went.

She plunged out into the tiny corridor and slammed the door behind her, leaning back against it as if to trap some terrible monster inside. Orlando was coming down the stairs, and when he saw her, he looked every bit as horrified as she had felt a moment or so ago.

"Your master is sleeping," she said, straightening up with all the dignity she could muster. "If he should wake before I return, tell him I have gone to church." Nodding once more to the wizard, she walked past him up the stairs.

Simon sat down on the bed, concentrating without thinking on the sound of her heartbeat as it faded, his beautiful prey climbing back to safety. He could feel Orlando just outside the door, and he hoped he would have the presence of mind to stay there—in his present state, he might even attack the wizard, given the chance. But finally she was gone. The deathly trance that was his natural, undisturbed state in the daylight hours stole over him again, sapping the strength from his body, and he sank back down to the bed like a corpse on a slab, falling back down into sleep.

Since her father's death ten years before, Isabel had vis-ited the Chapel of Saint Joseph only rarely. She was supposed to be the captive of a demon, after all. But she had never known the churchyard gate to be closed and barred in the middle of the day. It was a new gate, from the look of it—the timbers were still yellow. Handing Malachi's reins to Tom, who rode on a small brown mare beside her, she climbed down and rang the iron bell. "Do you suppose Father Colin has gone somewhere?" she asked.

"I don't know, my lady," Tom said doubtfully. "Someone was ringing matins this morning when I was on my way home."

The door in the gate opened a crack. "Who is it?" Father Colin's voice demanded, sounding quite unlike him, impatient and fearful at once.

"Father Colin, it's me." She moved to where she could be seen through the crack. "Isabel of Charmot."

"My lady!" He threw the door open wide and rushed out to embrace her like a prodigal returned. "May Christ be praised, you're safe!"

"Yes, quite," she promised, confused. "Father, what has happened? The gate—"

"Some villain let his horse kick down the old one," he explained briskly as he let her go. "Or so the carpenter said must have happened; I never heard a thing." He touched her cheek, a strange, haunted light coming into his eyes. "Not a sound . . ." His expression cleared, and the brisk manner returned. "But hurry, both of you. Come inside."

They followed him through the gardens and entrance chamber into the chapel proper. The shutters were closed in spite of the warmth of the day, and all of the candles were lit as though for a Christmas mass. "Pray pardon the stench, my lady," the priest said, closing and bolting the door behind them. "We are doing what we can to get rid of it."

"What stench, Father?" Two peasant women were on their hands and knees before the altar, she realized, scrubbing the floor. "I don't smell anything."

"You are too kind, child." He lit another rack of candles and moved them closer to where the women were working. "At first I thought a rat must have found its way into the wall and died. But then I saw the stain."

Isabel looked at the floor. "Stain?" she echoed politely, more mystified than ever. The flagstones were irregular in color, but they had always been so, at least so long as she could remember. The bones of Romans were buried beneath them, it was said, they were so old. Perhaps they did seem a bit darker where he pointed, but even with all the candles, she couldn't see much of a difference.

"It was much worse when we started, my lady," one of the women said. "We could see it right well. But now . . ." She let her voice trail off, her eyes moving to the priest.

"But what happened?" Isabel asked. "What was— is—this stain?"

The second woman looked up, her eyes wide with fear. "Blood."

"Hush," Father Colin snapped, making Isabel start with surprise. She had never heard the priest speak so sharply to anyone. "Lady Isabel does not want to hear your foolishness." The woman went back to her work without another word, and he smiled at Isabel. "Never mind, my lady," he said. "Whatever it is, it will soon be gone."

"I have no doubt," she answered, though in truth she was beginning to feel rather frightened. "Father, forgive my intruding when you're so busy, but I came to ask about Michel." Blood before the very altar of chapel? Father Colin acting so strangely? The front gate smashed to pieces? What could have happened here?

"Ask about whom?" the priest said politely.

"Michel," she repeated. "The Frenchman who was coming to fight the Black Knight at Charmot."

"The Black Knight?" he repeated, sounding alarmed. "Do not speak his name, my lady, not here."

"It's all right," she said, taking his arm with a frown. The women on the floor were of this very village; they knew her well, and she knew them; they were privy to the secret of the Black Knight of Charmot. "You came to Charmot to tell me Michel was coming two days ago. Do you not remember?"

"I came to Charmot?" The same strange, haunted look she had noticed at the gate had returned to his eyes. "Yes, of course . . . of course I did. To see your father."

"No, Father Colin." Tom's eyes widened, too. "My father is dead, remember? He has been dead these ten years past."

"Yes," the cleric nodded. "You are a woman now." He patted her hand on his arm and smiled. "Praise God that you are safe."

"But I'm not safe," she said urgently. "Michel has never appeared at Charmot; I haven't seen him. Tom was told that he stopped at the inn by the river with his retinue and that he was coming here to seek lodging." She laid a gentle hand against his cheek, making him meet her eyes. "Can you truly not remember?"

"You must not press him, my lady," the woman who had said the stain was blood warned her, sitting up. "The old and the innocent forget things for a reason, things too evil to be remembered."

"I told you to hush and clean that floor," Father Colin ordered. "I will not have the chapel of Our Lord befouled, not while it is in my charge."

"You see, my lady?" the woman said, doing as she was told.

"Did Michel not come here?" Isabel persisted. A sudden thought occurred to her. "Was it he who shed blood before the altar?"

The priest looked at her helplessly, tears rising in his eyes. "The Black Knight," he said softly, as if fearful that the very walls might hear and seek revenge. "It was the Black Knight."

"What? No . . ." Before she could say more, a terrible

racket broke out from outside, people banging on the bell and pounding on the gate.

"Father Colin!" a rough voice cried out. "For God's pity, let us in!"

"No," the priest murmured, clutching Isabel's arm. "Not again." He looked at her, his face going pale. "Not now, while you are here."

"That is Raymond's voice, Father," Tom said. "Raymond, who works our fields. He and his wife, Mary, were coming to the village today to visit his kin."

"Raymond," the priest repeated. "Yes . . . yes, of course." He gave Isabel's arm a final squeeze before he let her go. "You stay here, my lady. Come with me, boy."

"Wait," Isabel called, chasing after them. Father Colin opened the gate just as she reached them, and there was Raymond with another burly man who looked very like him—his cousin from the village, she realized, recognizing him from the last harvest. They were carrying something between them, something wrapped in a cloth. Something that looked like a person.

"What have you done?" Father Colin demanded. "What foulness have you brought to the house of the Lord?"

"She isn't foul," Raymond said, pale beneath his farmer's tan. "Or she doesn't seem to have been back when she was alive."

They carried the body inside to the priest's private quarters and laid it on the table. Isabel pressed a fist to her mouth as Raymond's cousin pulled back the cloth, stopping herself from screaming. This woman was not just dead.

She looked to be about Isabel's own age; certainly no older. Her throat had been ripped out—the very bone was exposed. Her clothes were torn to shreds all down her front as well as the flesh underneath; from across the room Isabel could make out the shadow of a rough, gaping wound in her breast. But there seemed to be very little blood.

"It must have been a wolf, we think," Raymond said, sounding shaky and near tears. "But none of us have ever heard tell of a wolf devouring a woman's heart straight from her breast."

"And the rest of the flesh has not been eaten," his cousin added. "Only the blood is gone—she hasn't bled a drop since she was found."

"Where?" Father Colin said, his voice sounding hollow and flat. "Where did you find her?"

"On the king's road, Father," Raymond answered. "Right between the ruts just outside the village, in plain sight of anyone who passed."

"Dear God," Tom said, crossing himself. "If I had ridden another mile, I might have found her myself this morning."

"Mary and I found her," Raymond said. "Poor Mary may never get over it—she's with my mother now, and it will be more than I can do to get her to come home with me to the woods." In truth, he looked as though he might not want to go himself. "None in the village seem to know her, Father, though from her clothes she seems a common lass. That's why we've brought her here to you, in hopes that you might recognize her."

"She was here," the old man answered. He moved closer to the body, his hands reaching out as if to touch it, hovering in the air. "I found her yesterday morning sleeping in the garden inside the broken gate. She did not even know how she had come to be there, poor child." He did touch the woman's face, closing her staring eyes. "I tried to convince her to stay here with me, but she would not. She said she had to go home to her parents—some village called Kitley, near the sea, she told me was her home. She had money, a purse full of gold." He looked up from the dead girl to the living men. "Perhaps she was robbed."

"No thief did this, Father," Raymond's cousin said. "Look at the marks on her throat. 'Twas some sort of beast that attacked her."

"A dog?" Isabel said, finding her voice at last. She thought of the dog she had seen the night before, the knowing look in its eyes as it stared at the castle Charmot. "I saw a dog last night beside the lake, a big, black dog I had never seen before."

"A grim," Raymond muttered. He was of old Celtic stock that still spoke of such things, spirits and demons that haunted the druids' old wood.

"My lady, what are you doing here?" the priest demanded, appalled. "I told you to wait in the chapel—boy, take your lady out of here at once."

"No," Isabel protested. "I want to help—"

"There's naught to be done for her now, my lady," Tom said, taking her arm. "Please, come away. Such evil is not for your eyes."

"But . . ." But what could she say? He was right; this woman was past all help.

"We will pray for her," he suggested, steering her to the door.

He led her out of the church to the garden, and Isabel allowed it, barely noticing when he finally let her go. So much was happening so quickly, and none of it made any sense. "That poor woman," she murmured to herself, pacing under the trees that lined the garden wall. She had seen the dead many times before, of course, but never any horror such as that. Just remembering, she felt sick, her hand going back to her mouth. And Father Colin—what could have happened to him? Even before Raymond and his cousin had turned up with the girl, the priest had sounded half out of his wits. He seemed to not remember coming to Charmot at all—he had thought he must have come to see her father. The old and the innocent forget evil, the peasant woman had said. But what evil had the good father forgotten? He spoke of the Black Knight, but that was madness, too. Father Colin knew as well as she did that the Black Knight was no one but Brautus in a devil's armor.

But you prayed for another one, a voice whispered inside her head. Don't you remember?

"No," she insisted aloud, turning around, and she tripped, her foot catching on the gnarled root of an olive tree. She tried to catch herself before she went sprawling, but it was a poor effort. Scraping both palms on the tree as she went, she fell to her hands and knees.

"Damnation!" She tried to sit back on her haunches and bumped her head on a low-hanging branch. "Ouch! Tom!" But the stable boy had gone back inside.

"Lovely." The ground beneath her was soft and wet, the turf disturbed as if someone had been digging there. Her skirt was soaked with loamy black mud. She looked down at her hands and found them coated as well with blood welling up through the mud from her scrapes. "Well done, Isabel," she muttered, sitting back on the root that had tripped her in the first place. "Why don't you make matters worse?"

Her heart was pounding too quickly, she realized, and had been since she'd seen that murdered girl. No wonder she couldn't think. She leaned back against the tree trunk and tried to get her bearings, to make herself be calm. She couldn't afford to get caught up in what might have happened to some peasant from miles away, beyond the prayers Tom had so rightly suggested. She had to be sensible. She had to think of Charmot.

Father Colin couldn't help her, obviously, or no more than he already had. He didn't remember Michel, or at least he said he did not, and why should he lie? Perhaps the Frenchman and his retinue hadn't made it so far as the chapel. She thought again of the dead girl, unable to stop herself, the pitiable sight of her dead body lying on the table in the church. What could have ravaged her so sorely? Could it have attacked Michel and his party as well? Or perhaps . . .

"Of course," she said aloud, her skin prickling with horror. Why hadn't she thought of it before? Michel had told anyone who would listen that he had no fear of the Black Knight of Charmot, that he was far worse than any demon loosed from hell. Why shouldn't she believe him? Why shouldn't she think he had come here, that he was the Black Knight Father Colin had spoken of, whatever the priest might have thought? Heaven only knew what such a monster might have done in the chapel; hell alone could guess the effect it might have had on the priest's memory. Who was to say Michel hadn't murdered that poor girl, or set his dogs on her for sport? Perhaps the dog she had seen had belonged to him as well. But why had he not come yet to Charmot?

"Oh sweet Jesus," she whispered, a terrible thought occurring. What if he were there now? What if he had been watching and waiting; what if he knew she was gone? Brautus was in bed, too ill to rise; Simon knew nothing of Michel and wouldn't come into the daylight if he did. She clambered to her feet, her skinned knees and ruined gown forgotten. She had to get home. She had to talk to Simon, to tell him the truth and convince him to help her, madman saint or not. He was her only hope.

She turned to start back toward the church and stopped, her eye caught by the glint of something shining in the mud. She bent down and lifted it free . . . a cross. A thick silver cross on a tarnished silver chain, the sort of ornament a knight might wear around his neck. Someone must have dropped it here, but how? No one ever came to this corner of the churchyard; the cemetery was on the other side . . . she froze. She looked down again at the ground where she had fallen, the broken turf and soft mud, as if someone had been digging. This was a grave.

"Tom!" she called out, running for the church. "Tom, come quickly! We have to go home!"

At first, Tom had wanted Isabel to stay at the church, where he was certain she would be safe, and Raymond and his cousin had agreed. "Whatever might be out there, it won't dare to come into the church," Raymond had insisted. But she knew this was not so, and so did Father Colin.

"Stay behind your father's walls, my lady, whatever may occur," he had told her, silencing the protests of the other men. "His blessings will protect you there as nowhere else. He was a godly man."

"He was," she had agreed, accepting his kiss on her cheek, though in truth she had barely heard him, so eager was she to leave. "I will stay at Charmot."

Now they had reached the forest, and the sun had already set. Raymond and his cousin had insisted on coming with them, armed with pike and pitchfork for Isabel's protection, but being on foot, they had slowed the party down. But now they were just inside the old druid's grove, no more than two miles from the castle. "Not much longer now," Raymond said with a smile, sounding relieved.

"Not much," she agreed.

Suddenly Tom's mare let out a terrified cry and stopped, refusing to go any farther. "What is it?" Isabel said, bringing her own horse around. Malachi seemed perfectly calm. "What's the matter?"

"I cannot tell, my lady." The little mare spun around again, fighting the reins. "Something has frightened her."

"God save us," Raymond muttered, taking a firmer hold on his pitchfork.

"It's all right," Isabel said. "She probably saw a snake—"

"No, my lady." Raymond's cousin's voice was cold with fear of his own. "Not a snake."

She turned in the direction he was pointing and saw the wolf, the largest of its kind she had ever seen. "Is that it, my lady?" Tom said, still fighting the mare. "Is that the dog you saw?"

"No," she answered softly, surprised she had a voice. The dog she had seen had been smaller, thick through the chest with a broad, triangular head. This was a wolf, long and lean with longer, rougher fur. In the failing light of twilight, she could see it had brought down a stag and was feeding in the center of the druid's grove, not from the belly as an animal would but from the throat, as if it were drinking its blood.

"Blasphemy," Raymond said, moving to stand at Isabel's knee. The stag was still a sacred beast to the common folk of the forest, Christians or not, its flesh and blood a pagan sacrament.

The wolf looked up at the word, and Isabel gasped, her heart racing faster with fear. Its eyes were faintly glowing, with a green, demonic fire. "Sweet holy God," Raymond's cousin whispered. "What manner of devil is that?"

"I don't know." She tightened her grip on Malachi's reins, expecting him to shy, but in truth, her mount seemed far more sanguine than she felt. The wolf was staring straight at her, a single paw laid on the neck of its prey. The stag shivered, still living, and a shiver went through her as well.

"Run for it, my lady," Raymond said urgently, raising his pitchfork, and his cousin raised his pike. "Ride for the castle. We will hold the beast."

"No." Wrapping the reins more tightly around her left hand, she reached for Raymond with her right, her eyes still locked to the wolf's. "Climb on—you, climb on with Tom." Malachi pranced to one side, but Raymond managed to climb on behind her in the saddle, propriety forgotten as he wrapped his arms around her waist.

The wolf watched all of this impassively, no threat in his manner beyond the glow in his eyes. "Go, Tom," she ordered, drawing her father's sword.

"No, my lady," the boy protested. "You should go first—"

"Tom, do what I say." She took a deep breath, willing her heart to slow down before she fainted, and the mare galloped away. The wolf looked away from her for barely a moment, then its eyes swept back to Isabel. "Hold on, Raymond." She lifted the sword as if in warning, and the wolf seemed to smile, its tongue lolling out as it panted at her like a friendly dog, an almost human interest in its eyes as it watched her. Indeed, she could not shake the feeling that it knew her, that in truth this was no wolf at all. She felt the man behind her tighten his grip, heard him whispering something in his people's ancient tongue.

"Go, Malachi!" She wheeled the horse around and nudged him hard with her heels, breaking free of the strange creature's gaze. "Go now!" The horse obeyed, breaking into a gallop as he headed for the castle.

Simon straightened up, melting back into his human form as soon as she was gone. He could take the shape of nearly any animal of roughly his same size, and he often did so to hunt, particularly when people were around. Orlando had told him once that his vampire maker, Kivar, could take and hold the shape of other humans if he chose, at least for a short time. But Simon did not have that gift. He had awakened at sunset nearly starving and had come to the forest to feed, never expecting to see Isabel. What was she doing in the forest?

The stag that had fed him shuddered again at his feet, its strength sapped more by terror than by loss of blood. "Forgive me." He knelt beside the creature, stroking its warm velvet throat, barely touching the wounds his fangs had made. His prey screamed once, raising its head, then collapsed flat on the ground again, and tears rose in the vampire's eyes. He was sated; this beautiful thing need not die.

"Hush now," he soothed, letting his tears fall on the wound. This trick he had discovered quite by accident; Orlando knew nothing about it. The tiny punctures closed with a hiss, healing as his own flesh could heal. "You will be free." Stroking the velvet nose once more, he stood up and stepped back, purposely looking away—as long as he held the gaze of the creature he hunted, it could not run away. "Go!" he shouted, gazing off into the trees. He heard the stag rise to its feet and felt the rush of wind as it thundered into the forest.

5

❧ ❦

Isabel flung her horse's reins to a groom as soon as they stopped in the courtyard and hurried into the hall. "My lady, we were worried, you were gone so long," Hannah said, coming to meet her. "Good heavens, what happened to your gown?"

"Nothing—I'm all right." Everything here seemed peaceful enough; she saw no sign of imminent invasion. Susannah was bringing dinner out of the kitchen, and Orlando was sitting with his feet up by the fire, or had been—he got up as soon as he saw her coming toward him. "Where is Simon?" she asked. "Is he still downstairs?" She started toward the cellar.

"No, my lady," the dwarf said, running to intercept her before she reached the door. "He went to the forest to meditate."

"The forest? Of course." Where else would he have gone, her fortunes being what they were at the moment? He had no armor—not even a sword. She turned back to Hannah. "Go fetch Kevin, please, and any other men inside the gates—Raymond is outside, too. Tell them to bring whatever weapons they can find. They will have to go and find him."

"That is hardly necessary," Orlando protested. "I'm sure he will return within the hour—"

"Not if he is eaten by a wolf," she cut him off. Hannah turned pale, but she ran for the door to the courtyard, calling for her husband as she went.

"A wolf, my lady?" Orlando said as she went. "What wolf?"

"The wolf we saw in the forest." She turned to Susannah, who had set down her tray to come examine Isabel's ruined gown. "Where is Brautus? Is he well?"

"Well enough," Susannah said.

"Go and see if he is able to come down to the hall—help him if you have to." The maid nodded, setting off. "But don't let him know you're helping."

"Have no fear, my lady," the girl said over her shoulder. "I know what to do."

Kevin and the others were already coming in with Hannah, armed with farming implements and axes—Raymond's cousin still carried his ancient-looking battle pike. "Where has he gone?" Kevin asked Orlando.

"I couldn't say," the dwarf answered, giving their weapons a wary glance.

"Did he at least take a horse?" Isabel said.

"No, he did not," Orlando said with an odd little smile. "He did not need one. Truly, you need not fear for him, Lady Isabel. I'm quite certain he is safe."

"You didn't see that wolf, little friend," Raymond's

cousin laughed. "Big as a pony he was, at least, as long as a man is tall, and black as Satan's nightgown."

"Indeed?" Orlando said, arching an eyebrow. "As black as that?"

"More to the point, a woman was killed last night on the king's own road by what may have been this same beast," Isabel interrupted. This seemed to shake the little wizard's composure somewhat—he stared at her, surprised. "Her throat was ripped open and her heart was torn out."

"And her blood," Raymond added. "There was no blood left in her."

"What about the others, my lady?" Kevin said. "Not that I am not heartsick to think your cousin might be devoured, but we have friends in those woods as well."

"I know," Isabel said, touching his arm. "We will bring them all inside, of course."

"But here is your kinsman, my lady," Hannah said as Simon came into the hall. "May the saints be praised."

"Absolutely," Orlando agreed, going to meet his master.

Simon had known Isabel and her retinue were alarmed by his presence in the forest in his wolvish form, and he waited what he'd hoped was a reasonable interval before following them to the castle. But he'd never expected she would have already raised an army before he arrived. "What's wrong?" he asked, going to her but sharing a look with Orlando.

"A wolf, master," the dwarf answered, looking properly solemn in spite of the glimmer of mischief in his eyes. "In the forest. Lady Isabel and her men saw it earlier, and she was quite concerned for your safety."

"That's very kind, cousin," he said, smiling at Isabel, but she didn't seem particularly amused or relieved to see he was safe.

"I have to talk to you," she said.

"Of course." He took her hand by instinct, sensing an agitation in her all out of proportion to a single wolf in the woods. For the first time, he noticed that her gown was soaked with mud, and her warm little hand was trembling in his. And there was something else, some memory that nagged at him . . . somehow he had touched her before. "Are you all right?"

"For the moment." In truth, she was as addled by his touch as she was by everything else. He didn't seem to even remember their last meeting, as if he really had been dreaming when he pinned her to the wall and scared her half to death that morning. Could that really be true? He had changed into her father's clothes as well, the angel now transformed into a noble knight. But she couldn't afford to think about such matters, clothes or dreams either one. There was too much else at stake. "You have to help me, Simon," she said, looking up at him. "You have to help Charmot."

"Of course," he repeated, raising her hand to his lips. Her hair was wild, as disheveled as her gown, and her cheeks were deathly pale, but she was still so beautiful, she took his breath away. Suddenly he remembered; she had come into his room that morning; she had awakened him from sleep. He struggled to remember exactly what had happened, but it was all so fragmented in his mind. He hadn't hurt her, obviously, or she wouldn't be standing here so calmly now, letting him hold her hand. But what had he said to her? What had he done? "Tell me what to do," he said, his guilt at what he might have done to her already making him all the more willing to help her in her trouble now.

"The cottagers," she answered, a shiver racing through her. "Someone has to bring them into the castle."

"Do you have a wagon in the stables?" he asked.

"Of course," Kevin answered for her. "We can be ready in half a moment, my lord."

"Good," Simon nodded. "And these men, can they ride?"

"Some can," the groom said. "We've only the two other horses even so after the team for the wagon. And one of them . . ." His voice trailed off as he looked at Isabel. Brautus was coming in, barely leaning on Susannah's shoulder, and the groom looked at him as well.

"Simon will ride Malachi," Isabel said, looking at Brautus. The ancient knight looked back for a long moment, obviously not pleased. But finally he nodded.

"Yes, my lady," Kevin nodded, hurrying out with the others behind him.

Simon looked at Orlando, Isabel's little hand still

clasped in his own. "You need not fear, cousin," he promised. "We will bring the cottagers to safety."

"Be careful, master," Orlando warned. "They say this wolf has killed before." Simon's eyes widened. "It is said he tore out the throat of a woman last night, devoured her heart, and drained her body of blood."

"A wolf did this?" Simon said. A massive, white-haired knight had just come in and was watching them—the Black Knight unmasked, no doubt. But this tale of a murdered woman was far more disturbing. "That's not possible—why would a wolf—"

"I saw it," Isabel interrupted. She withdrew her hand from his. "I saw the body of the woman who was killed, and I saw the wolf. That one murdered the other is more than I can tell, but it seems quite possible to me."

"You saw the woman's body?" Simon asked.

"At the Chapel of Saint Joseph, the church in the nearest village to Charmot," she answered. "Raymond and his wife found her on the road this morning, and Raymond and his cousin brought her to the church to see if Father Colin knew her."

Simon just stared at her—did he doubt her word? "And did he, my lady?" Orlando asked, but her cousin said nothing. He looked even more pale than usual, and his dark brown eyes were obviously troubled.

"He had seen her, yes," she answered the dwarf. "She had spent the night in the churchyard two nights ago, he said, but she wouldn't tell him how she got there. In truth, she said she couldn't tell, that she didn't know." At this, Simon's expression changed from troubled to horrorstruck, but only for a moment. She looked at Orlando, but the wizard seemed calm. "Did you see this woman?" she asked, turning back to Simon. "Did you know her?"

"No," he answered quickly. "Know her, no . . . we may have seen her—"

"We saw many pilgrims on the road, my lady," Orlando finished for him.

"The horses and wagon are ready, my lord," Kevin said, coming back in, addressing her cousin, not her. But that was what she wanted, wasn't it? She wanted Simon to take up the burden of protecting Charmot; she wanted the people to trust him, for him to care for them. So why did the sight of Kevin deferring to Simon irritate her so? And what did he know about the dead girl at the church? What might he have said if Orlando weren't here to speak for him?

"Very good," Simon answered, nodding, and the groom actually touched his forehead before he went back out, a gesture she had not seen any of her father's retainers make since he had died. They loved her; they called her "my lady." But to many of them, she would never be more than a child. "Isabel," Simon was saying now, turning to her. "We'll talk more when I return." He took her by the shoulders, as gentle as before, and kissed her cheek.

"If you return," she corrected. The same shiver she

always felt when he touched her moved through her again, but now she found it annoying, another sign of her weakness. Was she Susannah now, living to have her head turned by some handsome man and to blazes with everything else? Charmot was in danger; she had no time for such games.

But Simon smiled, amused, not annoyed. "You wound me, my lady," he teased. "Do you doubt me?"

"Why should I not?" she retorted. "It's not as if I know you."

His smile changed just a little, and a darker light came into his eyes. "You're right, little cousin," he said, letting her go. "You do not."

"So you will ride this Malachi, master?" Orlando said.

Simon turned away from her to face his servant with the same challenging smile. "Yes, Orlando, I will." He took Isabel's hand and kissed it again, much more carelessly this time, and Brautus frowned. "We will be back before your dinner is cold, my lady." Making her a bow, he left the hall with Kevin behind him.

"Come, my lady," Susannah urged, hurrying to her before anyone else could speak. "Let us at least change your gown."

Simon followed Kevin out to the courtyard, still pretending a confidence he wished he could feel. He knew Isabel's wolf was no danger, obviously, at least not to him, but that was the least of his worries. The men of

Charmot seemed ridiculously willing for him to lead them—Kevin had adopted him as "my lord" with a speed that made him feel rather dizzy. Then as he emerged from the castle, young Tom came running to him, carrying a sword. "It was Sir Gabriel's," the boy explained, handing it over to him. "Since you've none of your own."

"Thanks," Simon said, belting it on because he couldn't think how to refuse. The others nodded or mumbled their approval—"he's the old lord's kinsman, after all," he heard one of them say.

But he wasn't Sir Gabriel's kinsman, or even a man at all, for that matter—a lie he could live with on its own. But something else was apparently killing the innocent in the woods around Charmot. Something else like him. The girl who had offered herself to him so sweetly at the Chapel of Saint Joseph had found another monster who had treated her even worse. Had she welcomed her death the way she had welcomed him? He shuddered to imagine it—and who or what had killed her? He actually found himself thinking back over the past day and night, trying to think if he could have done it, as if the murder of an innocent might have simply slipped his mind. But of course he had not.

"Careful, my lord," Kevin said as they reached the horses, breaking into his thoughts. The groom took the bridle of the same massive black destrier Simon had thought meant to batter his skull to a pulp when he first arrived at Charmot—Malachi, Isabel had called him. "Malachi doesn't often take to strangers, I'm afraid."

"That's all right," Simon said, making himself smile. "Neither do I." And besides, he was a vampire; no horse would let him come close enough to touch him, much less mount the saddle. He had told Orlando he would ride this beast, but that had been the voice of stupid pride, not reason. Malachi was watching him now, his great head lowered in warning in spite of Kevin's best efforts to make him look up. As soon the vampire drew closer, he pawed the cobblestones with one warning hoof, snorting his displeasure. "Easy, Malachi," Simon said, adopting the low, crooning tone he had learned from his father almost before he could walk. "You should remember me . . ." He drew closer, still expecting the horse to bolt. "You tried to kill me once already." He reached out and touched the horse's velvet nose, marveling as he allowed it. The other horses, a small brown mare and the team hitched to the wagon, had become increasingly restive as he approached, but when the stallion allowed him to touch him, they instinctively relaxed.

"Aren't you a beautiful boy?" Simon said softly, hardly daring to breath as he caressed the horse's neck. Malachi tossed his head and nuzzled his shoulder, and the vampire laughed aloud.

"He is," Kevin agreed with a smile. "You are a horseman, my lord?"

"I was." Still bracing himself to be tossed over the horse's head, he swung onto his back, but the stallion allowed it with barely a snort of protest. "I haven't had a horse of my own in some time." He took the reins, so elated to be in the saddle again, he didn't dare question how it could be so. Malachi pranced to one side as if eager to be off, and he laughed again—what would it be like to give this beast its head, to let him gallop as far and as fast as he would? But now was not the time.

"Come," he said, bringing the stallion about with the lightest tug on the reins. "We promised Lady Isabel we would be quick."

Susannah helped Isabel out of her muddy gown and shift. "You might be a bit more kind to your cousin, my lady," she said, going to the wardrobe. "You could marry worse."

"Don't stand on ceremony, Susannah," Isabel said with a laugh. "By all means, speak your mind." She scrubbed a smudge of mud from her nose as she peered into the mirror. "I think I've been quite kind enough to Simon—too kind, in fact."

"That is Brautus talking, not you." She took out a gown, looked it over, and put it back. "Listen to him, and you'll find yourself in a convent."

"I wish a convent would take me." She gave her reflection a rare long look and almost laughed again. This was not a woman who should be contemplating marriage. Her nose was red now from its scrubbing;

her cheeks were pale and drawn from worry and too little sleep; and her unladylike red hair looked like she'd been nesting swallows in it from her day's adventures.

"You do not." Susannah took out Isabel's best gown and a clean shift. "The last lady I served went into a convent when her husband died, and I thought we would die ourselves." She loosened Isabel's ruined braid with expert fingers and picked up the brush. "You might as well be buried in a grave as that."

"Never mind trying to put it right," Isabel scolded, reaching for the brush. "Just put it back in the braid." She noticed the gown her maid had chosen. "And I am not wearing that."

"Why not?" Susannah held the brush out of Isabel's reach until her mistress gave up and let her continue. "What are you saving it for?"

"My clothes are the least of my worries at the moment." She winced as Susannah attacked a particularly stubborn knot. "I want to talk to Brautus before Simon and the others get back."

"Let him talk to that horrid little wizard—they deserve each other." She pulled part of Isabel's hair back into a braid as before but left most of it loose on her shoulders. "You shouldn't have to worry about wolves and murders—let the men take care of such things."

"Don't you think I'd like to?" Isabel retorted. "Here, stop fussing and give me that silly gown." She stepped into the shift and gown and let Susannah lace up either side. "Why are you suddenly so keen for me to marry

Simon, anyway?" she teased. "I thought you wanted him for yourself."

"I did," the other girl admitted. "But that was before I saw him shaved and dressed like a proper nobleman." She turned Isabel toward herself and examined her mistress's face with an obviously critical eye. "He's much too fine for me. Besides, it's you he wants." She gave each of Isabel's cheeks a pinch.

"Ouch! Have you gone mad?" Isabel demanded, swatting her hands away.

"You need color—"

"What color? Black or blue?" She turned back to the mirror to look over the damage and stopped, surprised. She did look better, softer and more girlish with her hair halfway undone. Even the livid marks Susannah had left on her cheeks had produced their deserved effect, painful or not. "Simon doesn't want me," she insisted. "He is on a quest—"

"Oh aye, he does, quest or not." Susannah laughed, clearing away the other gown. "I've had a bit more experience in such matters than you, my lady. You'll just have to trust me."

"I will have to do no such thing," Isabel retorted, turning her back on the mirror. "I need a protector for Charmot, Susannah, not a husband."

"Isn't one the same as the other?" the maid said, unperturbed, as she went to fetch Isabel's slippers.

"No, it is not." Her father had thought this way, too, and so did the king, she supposed—he had sent her

enough prospects to make her think he did. But it still
seemed wrong to her, this idea that she and Castle
Charmot were in essence the same, part and parcel of a
single prize or burden. "I want my husband to love me,
Susannah, not just my castle."

The other girl smiled. "Then you'd better start
brushing your hair a bit more often and wearing better
clothes."

"Must I, in faith?" So she could either be a castle or a
coiffure and a dress. Was Susannah right? Was this
how Simon saw her? And Brautus, too—his first
thought had been that Simon was trying to charm her
to get at Charmot. "Enough," she decided. "I am going
downstairs."

Simon rode back over the drawbridge at a gallop, following the wagon Kevin had driven ahead. "They're
here!" he heard someone shout from the battlements.
"They're home!"

Kevin's wife, Hannah, rushed out to meet them,
throwing herself into her husband's arms as soon as
his feet touched the ground. "It's all right, girl," he
soothed her with a laugh, hugging her close even so.
"We never saw a thing."

Isabel walked out onto the steps, silently counting
the cottagers as the women and children climbed down
from the wagon into the arms of their men. Everyone
seemed to be accounted for, even ancient Mother Bess,
Kevin's grandmother, who had not left her own

hearthside for as long as Isabel had been alive. "We brought them all, my lady," Raymond said, coming to join her. "Most had already heard and were glad enough to come, once they had an escort to protect them, and Sir Simon convinced the rest."

"Did he, in faith?" Simon was still on horseback; indeed, he looked as if he had been born in the saddle, as if he and Malachi were one. So why had he arrived at Charmot with no horse of his own? "How did he do that?"

"He told them the woods were not safe, and that you had charged him with the duty of bringing them into the castle," Raymond answered. "I cannot tell you how it convinced them, but it did. Blind old Mother Bess had already told her own grandson to sit on an acorn and hatch an oak, that she'd not be run out of her home by any beastie, wolf or not. But when Sir Simon spoke with her, she said, 'As you will, my lord,' as pretty as you please."

Simon saw Isabel watching him and waved. She had changed her gown, he saw, and her hair was different, and when she waved back, she almost smiled. But something was still troubling her, he could tell. Something more than a wolf in the forest. As he watched, Orlando emerged from the castle as well. He touched Isabel's arm and spoke to her, but his eyes were on Simon, their meaning unmistakable. They didn't have time to rescue peasants, not with the Chalice so close and another vampire so close on their trail.

They had seen evidence of others of Simon's cursed kind many times before, often at the very haunts they had chosen to search themselves on their quest for the Chalice. But none had ever killed so near to them or so openly as this. Whoever had killed the girl at the church had found her less than a day after Simon had fed from her himself. Out of this whole countryside, his rival had found the same prey. It was a warning, a threat. For the sake of the people of Charmot as much as for their quest, he and the wizard could not linger here.

One of the women from the wagon had a small child, barely more than an infant, and seeing her, Isabel left Orlando with a happy cry of greeting. She took the little one from his mother and lifted him high in the air, both of them laughing, and what passed for a heart in the vampire's chest clenched more tightly than a fist. What madness was he playing at to even speak to this girl? What could he give her but pain, and what sort of monster would he be if he pretended otherwise?

Isabel kissed little Euan on either cheek and handed him back to his mother. "He's beautiful," she said. "Come, bring him inside." Simon had dismounted, throwing the reins to Kevin, and was coming toward her fast, his face set with a grim, determined scowl. "Raymond said you brought them all," she said as he reached her.

"I suppose," he answered, barely meeting her eyes. "Everyone seems to be safe." He walked past her to Orlando. "Come, wizard; we've lost too much night already."

"Simon, wait." She put a hand on his arm, and he started as if she had struck him. "I need to talk to you," she reminded him, confused. "You said—"

"I can't," he cut her off. "I'm sorry, my lady, but we have no time to lose. My quest is too important." He looked at her at last, and she saw anguish in his eyes, the same pain she had seen there his first night at Charmot when he told her of his curse. "You must forgive me—"

"I won't," she cut him off in turn. "I can't." The others were moving past them into the castle, and she lowered her voice, not wishing to be overheard. "Simon, Charmot must have your help, not as a cursed scholar but as a knight."

"I cannot be a knight," he said. "I told you—"

"Then you're going to have to pretend." Kevin and Hannah passed up the steps and through the arch, among the last to go in. "You've made a good show of it already tonight."

"I know, and I should not have done it." Orlando had joined them, but he said nothing. "But you needed to bring those people inside—"

"Yes, we did," she agreed. "Now we need to protect them, to protect Charmot." She let go of his arm. "I'm sorry, Simon; I know how dearly you want to break this curse of yours, and I want to help you. But you will have to help me first." She took a deep breath, bracing herself to go against a lifetime of conditioning. He was a nobleman, her kinsman; she was supposed to obey him or at the very least keep out of his way. But she could not. "I will not give you the key to the catacombs until you hear what I have to say and promise you will help me."

Simon could hardly believe what he was hearing. This innocent girl, this delicate creature he feared so to harm, was telling him he had no choice but to do her bidding, his own desires be damned. "And if I refuse?"

"You and Orlando can go." Her little jaw was set; her mouth was a thin, determined line even though her lower lip was trembling. "Orlando didn't seem to think the wolf we saw was any threat to you; I shall pray God he was right."

She was serious; that much he could not doubt. How she meant to eject them from her castle was a mystery, though he supposed Kevin and the others would come to her aid if called. "You cannot turn me out," he said, using a touch of his vampire powers of persuasion, a talent that had already served him more than once that night. "I am your kinsman."

"What use is a kinsman who will not help me when I need him?" she answered, looking him square in the eye.

"She has a point, master," Orlando said slowly, and Simon thought he could detect the faintest hint of laughter in his tone. "Besides, what harm can there be in listening to her request?"

Everyone else was finally gone from the courtyard; the three of them were alone. "Where is the key?" Simon asked.

"Why?" she said, taking a step back. "Would you take it from me?"

"Of course not." He shook his head, nonplussed. In truth, he didn't know if he should be angry or amused, the vampire held hostage by a redheaded slip of a girl. "I just thought perhaps Orlando might take it and begin his study while I hear your suit."

Isabel reached into her pocket but didn't take out the key. "And you will do as I ask?"

"If it is within my power, yes." She still didn't look convinced. "You cannot expect more than that."

"No," she grudgingly admitted. The problem was, with this stupid curse, he seemed to think that the simplest things were outside his power when clearly they were not—taking a stroll in the daylight, for example, or eating a decent meal. "I suppose not." She pulled the key out of her pocket. "Come inside and have some food while I explain."

"I'm not hungry," he answered, sitting down on the steps. "Give the key to Orlando, and you can explain right here."

Now he was just being stubborn—just like a man, she thought. "Very well." She held out the key to the wizard. "Here, Orlando."

"Thank you, my lady," he said, taking it. "But perhaps I should listen as well."

"Why?" Simon said. "Can Orlando assist me in my task, my lady?" He wasn't even looking at her now, just sitting on the steps and glaring across the courtyard—pouting, she would have called it if he hadn't been a man full-grown.

"Not really," she admitted, giving Orlando a smile. "Go on, master wizard. I promise he won't be long."

"Yes, go," Simon ordered. He looked back at Orlando and managed a ghost of a smile of his own. "I think I can manage if she tries to throw me out."

"I don't want to throw you out," she said as the dwarf left them alone. She hovered over him for a moment, then sat down on the step beside him, apparently oblivious to her gown. "I want you to stay."

"That's a comfort," he muttered, unable to help himself. He could be managing this problem a great deal better, he knew, with a great deal more diplomacy. But he couldn't seem to reason past her saying she would send him packing if he didn't do as he was told.

"Simon . . . there is no Black Knight." She was turned toward him slightly with one leg tucked beneath her so that when he looked up, their eyes met. "Or rather, he is no demon. He is a man, an old man, one of my father's old retainers. His name is Brautus—you saw him yourself a little while ago before you left." She paused as if waiting for him to speak, but he said nothing—he had already deduced this much on his own. "Ever since my father died, he has been pretending to be the Black Knight to drive off men who want to marry me and claim Charmot, not because he is evil but because I asked him to do it."

"Why?" He turned toward her as well. "Why don't you want to be married?"

"I don't . . . that doesn't matter." She looked away, unable to face him, thinking of what Susannah had said before. "The point is, Brautus is old, and he's been injured. If you had come to challenge him, if you had been the man we thought you were when you and Orlando arrived, you would have beaten him—you probably would have killed him." She shivered, the night air suddenly cold. "And that man is still coming, a brigand named Michel. He said he would defeat the Black Knight and claim Charmot because he was stronger and more wicked than any demon in hell."

"He told you this?" Simon asked with a slight smile. Having met Michel, he could believe it. "I am near to acquiring a castle," the villain had said when he wanted to purchase Orlando. He must have meant Charmot.

"He told everybody," Isabel answered. "I never saw him; none of us here did, but we had word he was coming from Father Colin, the priest at the Chapel of Saint Joseph, the church where I went today. Michel and his men were supposed to be taking lodging there the night before you came here, then coming here to challenge the Black Knight the next day. But he never came. You came instead."

"I call that good fortune," he joked, hating the fear

he could hear in her voice, wanting to drive it away.

"But where did he go?" she persisted. "I went to the church to ask Father Colin, and he said he'd never seen Michel. He acted as if he didn't even remember coming here to tell me about him."

"Perhaps he doesn't remember," Simon said, silently cursing himself. He was the one who had made the old priest forget, not realizing what the end result might be. In truth, this was all his fault. "Perhaps this Michel never went to the church; perhaps he changed his mind about coming to Charmot."

"I don't think so," she answered, shaking her head. "Something happened at the church, something terrible. Father Colin either would not or could not tell me what it was, but I'm positive Michel was there. Someone broke down the gate and spilled blood on the floor of the chapel. And there was something else." She reached into her pocket and took out the cross she had found in the churchyard. "I found this outside the chapel, half buried in a patch of mud." She held it out to Simon, but he didn't take it. "I think it was a grave, Simon, an unblessed grave."

"Why would you think that, sweetheart?" he said, forcing his voice to sound even and calm. He had even managed not to recoil from the cross, though he doubted he could keep up that pretense much longer. He had trained himself to face the cross in all its guises long enough to fool the priests who protected much of the records of the Chalice, but the sight still caused him pain and would grow worse the longer it was before him.

"The grass was all torn away, and the ground was soft," she explained. He was still staring at the cross, but he made no move to touch it. "This looked as if someone had dropped it in haste and stepped on it."

"I think your imagination may have gotten away with you, cousin," he said with laugh. "More likely your Father Colin started planting cabbages and forgot what he was doing halfway through. He probably dropped this himself." He closed her hand around the cross to put it out of his sight, and a sudden flash of heat passed through his flesh into hers. "You said yourself, he forgot he had come to see you," he went on as if he had felt nothing. "How old is Father Colin?"

"Old," she admitted. "But he's always been quite clear in his mind before." She looked at Simon, searching his face. Had he not felt the frisson of fire that had passed between their hands? "This thing feels cursed," she said aloud, holding up the cross again for a moment before stuffing it back into her pocket. "But I know you think I am a silly girl."

"No, I do not." In truth, he was horrified to hear how wise she was, how much of the truth she had guessed. But how was that possible? He had buried Michel himself, and the villain's cross had been around his thick, broken neck. He had hidden all three graves very carefully, replacing the turf down to the last blade of grass. All three had been together, yet Isabel spoke of seeing only one. And somehow the cross had found its way to the surface. "I think you have had a very difficult day," he said, barely thinking of what he was saying, the only possible answer to the puzzle making him feel sick. "First Father Colin acting so strangely, then seeing that dead woman, then encountering the wolf in the woods. Tom and Raymond both said you were very brave."

"Why, because I didn't have hysterics?" she said with a wry smile. "Someone was killed at the chapel, Simon; I'm certain of it, and Father Colin saw it. Someone was murdered and buried, and I'm certain Michel must have done it."

"Michel," he repeated, making himself smile. "The phantom knight who never appeared at Charmot." The villain Simon himself had apparently made immortal.

"Yes," she insisted. "He and his men must have killed someone in front of Father Colin right in front of the altar—that must have driven him mad."

"Isabel," Simon began, trying to calm her.

"And that woman who was killed," she went on, becoming more agitated instead. "What wolf would be so cruel as to rip out the heart of its prey? A man did that, an evil, hateful man." She looked up at him with eyes now wild with fright. "And he wants Charmot. He wants to come here, to defeat the Black Knight and claim my father's castle. I don't care about myself, Simon, I swear."

"Darling, please—"

"If I thought I could save Charmot by not fighting him, that he would be satisfied with just me, I would meet him in the road," she plunged on desperately, all of the thoughts and fears she had hidden for so long pouring out in a single rush. "But he doesn't really want me at all; he's never even seen me. He wants my father's castle, and Brautus can't stop him, not now."

"Darling, this man is not coming," Simon tried to soothe her, silently begging God to let this be the truth.

"He is, Simon!" She was crying now, blind with her tears. "He'll take my father's castle and destroy it, destroy the catacombs and enslave our people, and everything my father ever did will be for nothing. I can't let that happen; I can't." She caught hold of his tunic in both fists, the tunic that had once belonged to her father. "You are a knight. Cursed or not, you could fight him."

"Isabel—"

"You could! You have to." Tears were streaming down her face, but she was demanding, not pleading. "You said yourself, my father came to you, he sent you here. Don't you see? He sent you here to save us as much as yourself—that is your quest." She framed his angel's face in both her hands, refusing to let him turn away. "Swear to me that you will fight Michel, or I swear I will turn you out and let you be damned forever." His eyes were bright with sorrow or with pity; either way, she couldn't bear to see it. She let go of his tunic and tried to turn away, but he wouldn't let her, pulling her close instead. "I will, Simon," she finished, hiding her face in his chest.

"I know you will." He stroked her hair, murmuring meaningless comfort as her fierce little heart beat desperately against his empty breast. "Hush now . . . it's all right." No wonder she was so frightened; inside her mind, Michel had become the monstrous sum of every evil she could possibly imagine. And now, thanks to Simon, he was. "I will fight him." He pressed a kiss to her forehead, holding her more tightly for a moment before he let her go. "If Michel comes to challenge the Black Knight of Charmot, I will make him sorry."

She looked up at him, embarrassed and elated both at once. "Do you promise?"

"I swear." He smiled as he wiped a final tear from her cheek with the pad of his thumb. "What choice do I have?"

"None," she admitted, barely smiling back.

"But you must promise me something as well." He made himself stop touching her—already he could smell her blood, imagine its sweetness; her heartbeat was driving him mad. "Until Michel does come and you need me, you must leave me to my quest." She looked up at him, surprised. "I know you think my vows are foolish, but they are real," he said, still fighting for control. He had no choice but to protect her; it was his fault she was in danger. But he could not endanger her himself, not if he truly hoped to ever win salvation. "You must not tempt me to break them."

What was he saying? she thought. Did he truly mean her presence was temptation to him, that he wanted to be with her? "So I should stop inviting you to breakfast?" she said lightly.

"Yes, that," he said with a smile. "You should stay away from me altogether. Orlando can look after me as little as I need it." He barely touched her cheek again, unable to resist. "Will you promise me?"

"Yes," she answered softly, barely able to speak. "If that is what you wish." No one had ever looked at her the way he was looking at her now. She felt dizzy just meeting his eyes.

"I do not wish it, Isabel." No face had ever seemed so beautiful to him, no life so precious. She was an innocent; she trusted him. She demanded he be her protector. "But it must be so." Even as he said the words, he was bending closer, bringing his lips to hers. Her eyes were open as he kissed her, her mouth soft and warm under his.

Falling, Isabel thought as she realized what he meant to do. I'm falling. His mouth was cool, a pleasant shiver of pressure against her own, and her eyes fell shut as of their own accord, as if she were tasting something so delicious she couldn't bear to see. And so she was. She felt his arms encircle her, her own arms rising around him, and all the time his mouth was pressed to hers, a sensation like nothing she had ever felt before. She lifted her chin, rising into the kiss, and she felt him sigh more than heard it, felt him press her closer.

Stop it! his reason was roaring inside his head; let her go! But he could not, not yet. He brushed her lips with his again, barely a touch, and she pulled him closer, her hands in his hair, kissing him harder with the tender blossom of her mouth still closed. He could open it, he knew, and slip his tongue inside, taste her sweetness . . .

"No." He turned his face away from hers, breaking the kiss.

For a moment, her mind refused to comprehend what he had said; her arms still tried to hold him. Then he took her gently by the wrists. "Isabel, no."

"No," she repeated, withdrawing. "I'm sorry."

"No, don't be sorry." He bent and pressed a kiss to each of her palms, one after the other, his lashes long and dark against his alabaster skin. "But now you understand."

"I think . . ." He looked up at her, and for a moment she saw fire in his eyes, the reflection of the torch's flame, no doubt. "No, Simon," she answered. "I don't."

"Then you must trust me." He made himself let go of her and stand up, out of her reach. "You must stay away." She was such an innocent; even now she was gazing up at him in perfect trust, her brow barely drawn in a frown. "Promise me, Isabel," he said, his voice gone rough with longing as he turned away.

"I promise." He had promised to protect her father's castle in spite of his vows. How could she refuse him? Why should she even want to? But she did . . .

"My lady!" Tom came out of the castle. "Brautus says you must come inside," he said, looking back and forth between them. "Before you catch your death."

Simon smiled. "He is right." He offered Isabel his hand and drew her to her feet. "So we have an accord?"

She let her hand stay soft in his, resisting the mad impulse to hold on. "We do, my lord."

He nodded as he let her go. "Good night."

6

Simon set a guard on the gates before he went to the cellars. If he was right and Michel was a vampire, and Isabel was right and he did mean to attack Charmot, he wanted as much warning as he could get. By the time he made it to Sir Gabriel's study, Orlando had opened every casket and scattered scrolls from one corner of the tiny room to the other.

"Nothing," he said, tossing another aside as the vampire came in and collapsed into a chair. "There's nothing here—or nothing to the purpose." He picked up a random scroll and read, " 'As Ethelred the Wise had recovered the wives of his nephew, he was gifted with forty oxen made as in honor of the Goddess.' I ask you; who could care?"

"Ethelred, I would imagine," Simon said. "Maybe the Goddess. And probably the oxen."

"This is not amusing, Simon," the wizard said with a frown.

"No," Simon admitted. "I know."

"I found another reference to what could be the

Chalice." He riffled through another pile. "Here it is. 'When I had achieved my fullness of age and judgment, I was given knowledge of the truth as it was delivered to my fathers from the distant lands of the East, the weapons and the Vessel of Light.' But he doesn't say what these items are or where they might be found." He dropped the scroll again with a sigh. "Perhaps they never wrote it down." He looked at the scrolls all around him. "Perhaps it was passed from father to son aloud, or priest to acolyte."

"That makes sense," Simon said, not really listening. Hannah had left him a dagger with his borrowed clothes, and he drew it from his belt, a plain, unornamented weapon, but lethally sharp at either edge and beautifully balanced.

"We may have to begin searching the tunnels at random, as much as I hate the thought." Simon didn't answer, and he glared at him, annoyed. "What ails you? Have you heard a word I've said?"

"I heard," Simon answered, putting the dagger away.

"Oh, no." The wizard came and sat with him on the other side of the desk. "What does she want you to do?"

"No more than would be my duty even if she hadn't asked." He met Orlando's eyes with his own. "I think I must have accidentally made Michel a vampire."

"What? Who is Michel?"

"The villain I killed at the church." He explained all that Isabel had told him, from Father Colin's first warning to her finding the unquiet grave. "At least she found it in broad daylight," he finished. "I tremble to imagine what could have happened if she'd found it in the dark."

"Stop trembling," Orlando said. "I don't believe it."

"So Isabel is a liar?" Simon said with a warning frown.

"Of course not," the dwarf answered. "Lady Isabel is a kind, good-hearted young woman who has lived her life among barbarians who still worship the moon. And you, Simon, are a vampire who believes every ill in the world is your fault."

"Orlando, she had the cross Michel was wearing." He got up from his chair. "And what about that girl, the dead girl who was found?"

"She had a cross like five hundred others we've seen," Orlando said, getting up as well. "And even if it were the one this Michel was wearing, what of it? We dropped it dragging his corpse to the grave."

"And the girl?" Simon said, unconvinced.

"The girl was killed by a wolf, just as they believed, or a pack of wild dogs or a brigand on the road." He began gathering up the scrolls and putting them away. "She was a defenseless woman, and you feel guilty for having your way with her and leaving her alone—as well you might, I suppose. But her death was not your doing."

"Her heart and blood were taken," Simon persisted. "Isabel said—"

"No, she did not," the dwarf interrupted. "I listened to them very carefully in the hall, even if you did not. Those peasants said the heart and blood were taken. But Isabel saw only a mutilated corpse."

"But what difference—"

"All the difference." He put a quelling hand on Simon's arm. "This island is crawling with demons, to hear its people tell it; the English live and die by superstition, almost as much as the Irish." The vampire scowled, and he smiled. "It's good that you promised to help her, Simon. She will trust you now, and our work will be accomplished that much more quickly. But she need not fear this man, Michel; she doesn't need for you to slay him. You already have."

"And if I have not?" Orlando always sounded so certain, so reasonable, and Simon knew that he himself was not. His emotions ruled him as they always had; that was why he so often trusted the wizard's judgment over his own. But this time he wasn't so sure.

"Simon, I promise you, you have," the wizard said with a sigh. "Think back to your own making. You drank the blood of Kivar. Did Michel drink your blood?"

"No," Simon admitted. "At least not that I remember."

"You would remember," Orlando promised. "The making of a demon is no idle matter, warrior; you should know that better than I. It does not happen by accident." He smiled. "If it did, you would have a trail of monsters stretching all the way back to the Urals following at your heels."

Simon grimaced at the thought. "You may be right, Orlando," he said, feeling rather foolish but still not quite convinced. "I pray . . . I hope you are. But I will have to make sure."

"You have better business," the dwarf said, losing patience. "The Chalice—"

"I will find the Chalice, if it can be found," Simon cut him off. "But dead or monster, I will find Michel."

Isabel had expected to find Brautus waiting for her in the hall, but he was no longer there. "He went upstairs, my lady," Susannah said. "He told Hannah he was tired."

"So am I," Isabel admitted. "Is everyone settled? Is there room enough for everyone to sleep?" The hall had not been so crowded since before her father died.

"We will manage," she said. "Most people brought their bedding with them." She smiled, an impish gleam in her eye. "I see the gown did its work, by the way."

"What do you mean?" Isabel asked, genuinely confused.

"Sir Simon kissed you," she answered. "I saw it through the window of the solar, and so did Brautus and Tom." Her grin widened. "I told you he wanted you."

"Good night, Susannah." She hurried for the stairs, her face burning scarlet, though she supposed she ought not to have been surprised. The steps leading up to the castle were hardly the most private spot for a tryst.

She made it to her room and slammed the door, heart pounding, and a voice spoke from behind her. "So that's the end of it."

"Brautus!" She whirled around to find him in a chair by the window, propped up on the pillows from her bed. "Are you in pain?" she said more calmly. "Shouldn't you be lying down?"

"I don't need a nursemaid."

"Neither do I." She went to the desk and sat down as if that had been her purpose all along. "Susannah said you saw me kissing Simon."

"Nay, lass, I saw him kissing you." He turned toward her with obvious effort, his face pale and shiny with sweat. "You were just letting him do it."

"I'm sure I'll do better next time." She pulled the bundle of scrolls she'd brought up from her father's study toward her and untied the ribbon. "You needn't worry, Brautus. He made me promise to stay away from him from now on so I don't distract him from his quest."

"Sure he did," the ancient knight said with a scowl. "What is it about a pretty face that turns a sensible woman into a fool?"

"I'm certain I don't know." She fingered the corner of the top scroll, touching the encoded notes her father had scribbled there. If he were here to see her, would he be scolding her as well?

"Isabel, what are you thinking?" he demanded. "Have you no thought for your father's castle, for his people—"

"When have I ever thought of anything else?" The sheer injustice of the charge was enough to drive her mad. "Who was it who secured my father's castle tonight? Who rode out to collect his people to make certain they were safe? Simon—"

"So you were just showing your gratitude?"

"What is it to you?" He blanched as if she had struck him, and hot shame bloomed in her cheeks. Brautus had risked his life time and again to protect her and her virtue; she should have died before she questioned his concern. But he didn't understand; she didn't even understand herself. "Susannah is right," she said, looking away. "You'd put me in a convent if you could."

"I would not!" he protested.

"Then why shouldn't I—"

"Because I do not trust this man. And neither should you. If he were a proper nobleman of name, if anyone had ever heard tell of him, if he courted you openly as a man who deserves you, I would never say him nay."

"He isn't courting me at all," she insisted. "The kiss you saw . . . it just happened. And it won't happen again."

"These things do not just happen, sweeting," he retorted. "And they always happen again."

"Brautus, what would you have me do?" she demanded. "We need him."

"We do not—"

"We do." She knelt on the floor at his feet and took one scarred and aged hand between her own. "I wanted to tell you before, but there was no time." She told him all that she had seen at the Chapel of Saint Joseph and all that had been said, both there and between her and Simon. "He doesn't believe Michel is coming," she finished. "But he promised to defend Charmot if he does."

"And you believe him." He touched her cheek with sadness in his eyes.

"I do." She wished she could make him understand the kinship she felt with Simon, stranger that he was, a connection deeper than the blood they shared. But she knew he would still think she was a fool, that this feeling was no more than another symptom of her foolishness. "And even if I didn't, what better choice do I have? You spoke of my father's castle and his people. How else can I protect them?" She clasped his hand more tightly. "I would do anything to save Charmot. Surely you must know that."

He smiled just as sadly. "Aye, poppet, I do." He caressed her hair with his free hand, then moved as if to stand.

"Here, let me help you." She got up to support him.

He swore a terrible oath that should have made her blush, but she said nothing. He wasn't really swearing at the pain. He leaned on her shoulder, her arm around his waist, and she saw tears in his eyes. "Your father left you in my care, whether he meant to or not."

"I know," she said, fighting back tears of her own. "He left me Charmot the same way." Bracing herself on the chair, she leaned up and kissed his cheek. "And now we will both be safe."

She helped him to his room and into bed, neither of them saying more. What else was left to say? The candles had burned down to almost nothing when she came back to her room, but Susannah or Hannah had come in and put the pillows back and turned down the bed. No doubt they had been listening in the hallway all along.

"Your castle has ears, Papa," she said, going back to the scrolls on the desk. "Ears and eyes and a heart." She looked down at the code again, this mystery that he had always thought would taint her woman's eyes. "And now, I hope, a sword." The letters of the code had always seemed like gibberish to her, a nonsense mixture of symbols, but suddenly she noticed something. On some of the corners, the characters were written upside down.

She shuffled through the pages, turning them as she went. All of the main text was written the same way, but the text in the corners was different. Some notes were written straight up, some upside down, some sideways left or right. But always the note made a perfect triangle, each exactly the same size as the others, thirteen corners in all. She sat down to be closer to the dying light. Even with them all turned straight, the code made no sense, no words she could recognize. But one set of symbols was repeated again and again, at least once on every page. "What is this, Papa?" she whispered. "Did you mean for this to be forgotten?"

She thought of the night Simon had come and the visions he had described of her father. He said there was wisdom here, Simon had told her. Wisdom that could lead the cursed knight back to the light.

"Is this the wisdom, Papa?" she said, speaking to the empty air. "Is this what you sent him to find?" But her father did not speak to her from heaven; he did not come to her in dreams. He had loved her, but she was a woman. She could never understand.

"I will ask Simon," she said, letting his papers fall. "Perhaps I will give them to him."

Simon headed for the stables as soon as the sun had set the following night, determined to see for himself what lay buried at the Chapel of Saint Joseph. Malachi had indulged him the night before; he hoped he would again. "Fair evening, friend," he murmured, ignoring the indignant snorts and whinnies of the other beasts at his approach. "Care to stretch your legs?" Malachi bobbed his head as he reached him, pushing his nose over the railings to be scratched. "There's a lad," he said with a grin as he obliged.

The door slammed behind him, and he was surprised to see Orlando stomping toward him as fast as his small legs would carry him. "I thought you were hungry," the vampire said, turning back to his horse.

"You kissed her?" The little wizard was so furious, the tip of his nose looked blue-white against the flush of his cheeks. "That idiot girl inside said you kissed Lady Isabel. Is that true?"

Simon frowned over his shoulder. "What is it to you if I did?" He went to get the horse's saddle with the dwarf all but scurrying behind him.

"What is it to me? Have you gone mad?" Simon ducked into the horse's stall, where Orlando didn't dare follow. "You must have." Simon shot him a sour look as he saddled the horse but said nothing. "Do you mean to murder our hostess, the innocent creature whose kindness may mean your salvation?" He fastened the bridle, scratching the horse's chin. "Or have you forgotten you are a vampire?"

"Care to shout a little louder, wizard?" Simon said. "They may not have heard you inside."

"I am in earnest, Simon—"

"So am I." He led the horse from its stall, whispering a word of encouragement as he went. "I haven't forgotten anything," he said, petting Malachi's glossy black neck. "And I do not mean to murder anyone."

"Perhaps you should," Orlando retorted. "Your mind is failing from starvation, methinks."

"Too bad you're no more than a mouthful," the vampire shot back. The wizard took a shocked step backward, and he smiled. "Why don't you open that door?"

"What of your quest?" Orlando persisted, following him. "You have a duty—"

"I said I had not forgotten." He swung into the saddle, the feeling of being on horseback soothing him again, making him feel less like a monster, whatever Orlando might say. "I'll be back long before dawn."

"Simon . . ." The dwarf hurried to open the stable doors as the horse broke into a trot.

Isabel had seen Simon crossing the courtyard and had run to her room to fetch her father's scrolls. "Simon!" she called after him as the drawbridge was lowered, running to catch up. But he did not hear.

"I fear he has stolen your horse," a voice spoke beside her—Orlando, coming out of the stable. "But I dare say he will be back."

"I certainly hope so," she said with a smile. "I'm quite attached to that horse."

"I don't wonder," he answered, not smiling back. "It's a fine animal." He was watching her with an expression that was not entirely friendly, she realized "Besides, he promised to defend your castle."

"Simon? Yes, he did." She started back toward the hall, and he followed. "He told you, of course."

"And you promised to leave him alone." She stopped in the archway and turned to him, surprised. "And yet here you are."

He was smiling now, but this was still no offhand remark. "I wanted to show him—to tell him something," she said. Just how much had Simon told his strange little servant about the night before? "I think I can help him."

"You can't," he answered in a tone as cold as stone, all pretense of pleasantry fading.

"How can you be so certain?" she retorted. Her own servants did not speak to her this way; why should she bear it from him, wizard or not? "And what business is it of yours?"

"You cannot help Simon, my lady, only hurt him." People in the hall were giving them curious looks, and she let him lead her into the solar more to avoid questions than because she cared to hear what he would say. "He is not the man you think he is, Lady Isabel, as much as he would like to be." She saw him fumble in his pocket as if to touch something inside. "His quest is more important than you could ever guess, his vows more deadly to break."

"Orlando, what is this curse?" she demanded. "What is this great sin he has committed?"

The corner of his mouth curled up in a wry, bitter grin. "Would that I could tell you, my lady," he answered. "Would that I could make you understand."

"When have I shown you anything but kindness, Orlando?" she asked. "Why should you dislike me so?"

"Dislike you? Nay, lady, I swear it is not so," he protested. "In truth, I like you very much, more than I care to admit. It is for your protection as much as for my master's that I would warn you." He took her hand between his own in a warm but powerful grip. "He cares for you, I know, and I fear it. He could destroy you, my lady, destroy you body and soul." She opened her mouth to protest, but the look in his eyes stopped the words before they were spoken. "And that would destroy him."

"Orlando, I don't understand." She tightened her hand around his, holding on when he would let go.

"Stay away from my master, my lady," he answered. "I can tell you no more plainly. If you want to help him, stay away."

Simon found the gates of the churchyard closed and barred for the night. Leaning down from Malachi's saddle, he rang the iron bell. With any luck, the priest would not know him at all. He could entrance him again, open the grave he had made behind the chapel, and make certain Michel was where he belonged, make certain Orlando was right. And if he was not . . .

"Begone!" The priest had thrown open the door in the gate and was coming out holding a cross-shaped staff before him, a pottery vessel in his other hand. "Fiend from hell, begone from here, I say!"

Malachi reared up and screamed as if the cross repelled him as much as it did the vampire. "Easy," Simon ordered, fighting to control the horse as he turned his face away, his eyes burning from the sight. "Father, please—I mean you no harm—"

"I said begone!" The old man flung the vessel with surprising strength, dousing the vampire in holy water. This time, Simon was the one who screamed, his face melting as if in flame. Malachi turned of his own accord, recoiling as the reins went slack, and through his own cries of pain, Simon heard the door slam shut again and the bolt smash home.

"Well done, Father Colin," he muttered when he could speak. His flesh was already beginning to heal, but he still would not have dared to look into a mirror for fear of what he would see for at least a little longer. Malachi pranced and snorted, pawing the road as if angry on his rider's behalf. "No, he did right, friend," Simon said as he took up the reins, giving the horse a pat. "He did right." There would be no visit to the churchyard, at least not tonight. And with the priest so vigilant, it was hard to imagine another vampire coming and going under his very nose. Perhaps Orlando was right after all.

He heard a rustle behind him and another sound that might have been a laugh, and he turned the horse in a tight circle, his right hand on his borrowed sword. "Who is there?" Malachi nickered low in his throat in alarm, a shiver running through him. "What is it?"

The glimmer of a pair of eyes stared out at him from the brush, and as he wrapped the reins more tightly around his fist to control his mount, he heard a low, throaty growl. "Steady," he murmured, drawing his sword as the shape of the creature drew closer, black as the shadows, too black to see clearly, even with vampire eyes. Malachi snorted, more angry than fearful, and Simon smiled. "Yes, we shall have him. Whatever he is."

Suddenly the animal sprang toward them, clearing the destrier's shoulder in a single leap and the vampire's head in another, its claws slashing deep into Simon's chest and Malachi's flank as it went. The horse whirled around with a cry of pure fury almost before the vampire tugged at the reins, plunging into the forest in pursuit.

The chase went on for miles through trees and brush so thick Simon could barely glimpse his quarry. But he could smell him, sense his malice, and apparently so could Malachi—the horse never faltered or slowed, even without a trail. Suddenly the woods opened up into a clearing—the same circle of trees where Simon had brought down the stag, he realized, slowing the horse to a walk. And standing at its center was the wolf.

Malachi reared once and stopped, facing the beast unafraid, but Simon wouldn't risk losing the only horse in Christendom who could bear his presence. He climbed down slowly, gripping his sword, and the wolf's yellow eyes never wavered, watching his every move. Simon had never seen himself in wolvish form, but he imagined this beast could have been his twin. Its coat was black as pitch, and its shoulders, hackles raised in warning, were as broad as Simon's own. It bared its fangs in a snarl as the vampire drew closer, and Simon had the strange and rather horrifying thought that this was how he must appear to his prey, ravenous and cruel.

He raised the sword in his right hand and drew his dagger with his left, he and the wolf circling one another, drawing nearer with every step. For a moment, Simon wondered if this creature might be Michel, a vampire in a different predator's shape, but he quickly dismissed the thought. A vampire would have wanted his hands as well as his teeth for a battle, would have wanted to fight as a man. His eyes locked to the wolf's in challenge, his lips drawing back over fangs of his own. The creature froze, and he saw a moment's flash of fear inside his golden eyes. Then in an instant, he attacked.

He felt the animal's full weight coming down on him as he fell backward, but he knew the wolf could not do him serious harm—even if it ripped out his throat, his vampire flesh would heal. Fangs tore at his shoulder as he raised the sword, slashing the throat of the wolf as his dagger plunged into its belly. Hot blood poured over his face, irresistible, and he drank as a man in a desert, drank until he was drunk on it, cruel life flowing into his heart.

An hour after Orlando had left her, Isabel was still in the solar, studying her mother's half-made tapestry for the first time since she was a child. In the background was a castle that could have been Charmot, its towers rising above the fanciful wood, and the maiden looked like Isabel herself, her crimson hair falling to her knees. Crouching before her was a wolf, its head laid in her lap. Yellow eyes gazed up at her in love as she stared off into space, seemingly oblivious. But one white hand was laid upon the deadly monster's throat.

"My lady!" Hannah was calling, running through the door. "Lady Isabel, come quickly! Sir Simon has slaughtered the wolf!"

She followed Hannah and the other women out into the courtyard where the men were already gathered, their voices raised in merry celebration. A great black shape lay on the ground before Simon—the carcass of the wolf.

"Killed him on his own, he did, in pitch-black darkness, yet!" Kevin was laughing as she drew closer.

"Is he all right?" Simon was just standing there, neither smiling nor speaking, Malachi still waiting at his back. "Simon, are you hurt?" His tunic was torn at the shoulder and chest, and he seemed to be covered in blood.

Simon looked at her, this innocent he could not have. The wolf's blood was still coursing through his veins, creating the illusion of life, of desire, of need. Turning, he pushed Raymond and his cousin out of the way, stripping out of the ruined tunic as he went. He plunged his head into the rain barrel, washing away the blood, filling his mouth with water and spitting it out on the ground.

"Simon?" Isabel repeated, following him, confused. Orlando had come out of the castle as well, and he was watching her with warning in his eyes, but she chose to ignore him. "Simon, I said are you hurt?"

He turned to her, still streaming icy water, and gathered her into his arms. She opened her mouth to protest, and he kissed her, his mouth crushing hers, his tongue parting her lips to push inside. She felt as if the ground were dissolving beneath her, but he held her close, so tightly she couldn't breathe, his arms a threat and sanctuary at once. Her hands slid over his shoulders, bare and sleek, and he should have been warm, but he wasn't; his skin was cool but flawless, an angel's flesh under her touch. Somewhere in the world people were laughing and applauding, calling her name and his, but that was far away. Here was only her angel, her Simon, his arms around her, his body pressed to hers, his tongue inside her mouth, and she was frightened and brave at the same time; she felt starved for something she had never tasted. She slipped her tongue between his teeth, exploring, and he let her, his movement urging her own.

Then suddenly, it was over. Simon was letting her go. He set her back on her feet again, his mouth barely curled in a smile. "I am well, my lady." As the men laughed and clapped him on the back and the women howled and scolded in protest, he picked up his tunic and walked away, stepping over the wolf he had killed on his way to the castle. Orlando looked at Isabel for a moment with a face she could not read before he followed.

"Are you all right, my lady?" Hannah said, giving her husband a swat. "Brautus will have that puppy's head for this."

"No, it's all right. I'm all right." She looked down at the wolf lying dead at her feet, its yellow eyes still staring. "He made the castle safe again. That is all that matters."

7

Isabel sat by the hearth in the great hall, pretending to mend a torn stocking and watching Hannah fasten a wreath of spring flowers on Susannah's head. "I like the other one better, the one with the rosebuds."

"Do you think?" the maid asked, admiring her reflection in Isabel's best silver mirror. "I'm afraid all that yellow will make my face look green."

"Orange, more likely, from pure vanity," Hannah scolded with a smile.

The May Night dance in the druid's circle was a tradition far older than Castle Charmot. People came for miles around to dance in the grove of the ancients, or so Isabel had been told. "You mustn't tease the Queen of the May, Hannah," she warned. "She might put a spell on you."

"You should come with us, my lady," Susannah suggested. "You could even bring your cousin."

"Do you think so?" Isabel said sarcastically, pulling a wry face.

"Hush," Hannah scolded, giving Susannah a swat

for good measure. "Lady Isabel has no interest in such goings-on, nor does Sir Simon."

"But it's nice of you to think of us, Susannah," Isabel said.

In truth she couldn't have invited Simon anywhere, even if she'd had the nerve or the inclination to do it. She hadn't laid eyes on him in weeks. The last time she had seen him had been the night he killed the wolf and kissed her for his reward—for so the whole household had chosen to style it. Everyone thought the nobles, Isabel and Simon, must have quarreled about it afterward out of everyone's hearing. They all guessed that she must have banished him to the catacombs for good for his impertinence. "That Irish devil's intentions were plain enough," she had heard old Wat laughing in the stables when he didn't realize she was passing by. "A right shame it is Sir Gabriel brought our lady up to be so damned particular."

But in truth it was Simon who had stayed away from her. Orlando had emerged from the cellars every day or so to fetch food from the kitchen, and many nights she heard Malachi galloping over the drawbridge long after she had gone to bed. But she had honored her promise to leave him in peace, and he apparently preferred to do the same to her.

"Don't mind her; come with us," Susannah persisted. She took the sewing from Isabel's lap and replaced it with the rosebud wreath. "The woods are safe; Sir Simon has made certain of that."

"I know," Isabel said, trying to hand back the wreath. "It isn't that." No one else had been attacked since Simon had killed the wolf; not so much as a single lamb had been lost, and there had been no sign of the brigand knight, Michel. The men of the household were all convinced that Simon was patrolling the forests on his midnight rides. "He'll scare off any beastie that dares to cross him, I'll wager," Kevin had told his wife, and Hannah had repeated his words to her mistress.

"Susannah, enough," Hannah said now in a tone to put down any argument. "Go and see if Kevin has the wagon ready, why don't you?"

"All right, all right." Susannah took the wreath but laid it back in Isabel's lap. "Just in case you change your mind."

"You mustn't mind her, my lady," Hannah said when the other girl was gone. "She's just a peasant and a child; she doesn't understand your position."

"It's all right," Isabel said, setting the wreath aside. "She meant well." She picked up her sewing, trying not to remember that she and Susannah were nearly the same age or that her own mother had been a peasant lass herself. She must have danced in the druid's grove before her Norman husband came to claim her, Isabel thought. But her daughter was born a noblewoman, the lady of Charmot.

She worked her way through a whole basket of mending as the rest of the household made ready for the celebration and left, all of them bidding her fair evening as they went. "Be careful tonight, young Thomas," she called out to Tom as he walked through the hall with a cask of mead on his shoulder. "They say on May Night, the fairies come out in the wood."

He grinned, blushing scarlet. "A man can only hope."

Finally she heard the wagon roll away over the drawbridge, leaving her alone but for Simon and Orlando in the catacombs below and Brautus in his room above, or so she assumed. But just as she was about to go into the kitchen and find herself and Brautus some supper, someone came back in through the archway— Raymond's wife, Mary, looking lovely in a pale green gown with her own wreath of flowers in her hair. "Forgive me, my lady," she said, coming into the shadowy hall. "I need to speak to you." She held out a fat little pouch. "I need to give you this. Raymond says I am a fool, but I'm afraid . . . I can't go to the circle until you take it from me."

Isabel took the ragged purse, a soft leather bag trimmed in brightly colored silk, wine and peacock blue. "Where did you get this?" Most of the people of Charmot and the villages around it never saw two coins together in their lives, but the purse was full near to bursting with copper, silver, even gold.

"That dead woman we found had it hidden in her skirt," Mary explained. "The one the wolf killed." Isabel looked up at her in shock. "We knew it was wrong to take it, but Raymond said . . ." She looked away. "We thought there might be a new lord at Charmot, that we might have to move away, and with that money, we could start over, maybe even go to London. I have a cousin there."

Isabel could hardly blame them; she'd been thinking of running away herself that day. "That girl had this?" she said, more shocked at that. The dead woman had been a peasant; where could she have gotten such a treasure? Some of the coins she recognized as English in origin, the same as ones she had herself, but many of them were strange and obviously old. She tipped a pile into her hand, and a large gold piece embossed with the image of a Roman Caesar rolled out.

"Yes," Mary nodded. The longer she talked, the calmer she sounded, as if the very act of putting the purse into Isabel's hands had driven her fears away. "Raymond said she wouldn't need it any more, and we did, or so we thought. But now that your lord . . . your cousin has come . . ." Isabel looked up at her again, and she blushed, but she didn't look away this time. "You could give it to Father Colin."

"I could give it to him?" She poured the coins back into the bag. "Why me?"

"You're the lady of the castle," Mary said as if this were a perfectly obvious reason. "You might have such a purse yourself, left to you by your father the lord."

"I don't," Isabel said with a laugh.

"But Father Colin doesn't know that," she pointed out. "You could give it to the church, and he would never question it. You wouldn't even have to say where you got it." She wanted absolution, Isabel could see, someone in authority to tell her she could dance now in the druid's circle without fear of retribution for her and her husband's great sin of looking out for themselves. So she had come to the lady of Charmot, a spinster virgin who had never danced there and never would. Thanks, Papa, Isabel thought with an inward bitterness that was becoming something of a habit with her. You left me a fine legacy indeed.

"I'll take care of it," she said aloud, managing a smile. "Go enjoy the dance."

Mary's face broke into a smile. "Thank you, my lady." She bobbed a peasant's curtsey. "Thank you so much." Before her lady could answer, she had gone.

Isabel studied the purse again. Strange characters she could not read were embroidered in the leather in a tarnished golden thread. She fished out the gold coin she had seen before and held it between her fingers. Perhaps the next time a suitor appeared, she could pay him a ransom to leave her in peace. Or perhaps she would give it to Father Colin as Mary had wanted, buy them all a bit of indulgence for their sins. But just now, she didn't much care.

She dropped the coin back into the purse and the purse into her pocket. Brautus would need his supper.

Simon felt his way along the cavern wall, loath to trust even his demon's sight in this dark, dank hole. "The floor is wet again," he told Orlando, who was creeping a few paces behind him. "Bring the light."

The two of them had been fumbling in the dark like fools in a fable for weeks now, searching Sir Gabriel's catacombs and coming no closer to finding the Chalice than they'd been the night they started. The tunnels seemed to twist for miles, deeper and deeper, water occasionally pouring through the ceiling in icy silver drapes or seeping through the floor. Orlando had produced a phosphorescent powder from one of his many purses that left a glimmering, reflective trail as they went; otherwise they would have lost themselves forever.

"Here," Orlando said, handing over the torch. "Oh, dear."

As Simon had suspected, the puddle at his feet already glowed—they had crossed this path before. "Lovely," the vampire grumbled, stalking ahead to the next turning in search of a fresh tunnel. But in truth, he thought, what was the point? They had no idea how long the glow in this powder might last once Orlando dropped it—for all they could tell, they'd been retracing their own steps for days. "It's hopeless," he grumbled aloud, stopping to lean against the wall. "We will never find anything like this."

"And what would you suggest we do instead, warrior?" Orlando said, stumbling as he hurried to catch up. "I would love to hear."

"I don't know." The wall opposite him was painted

with rough figures, men and women in a circle, most
with bright red hair. They seemed to be dancing, arms
upraised, and a spiky blue and yellow shape at the center of the circle could have been a fire. The catacombs
were covered in such paintings, and they always made
Simon feel strange, as if he had forgotten something
important, something just out of his memory's reach.
At first, Orlando had been convinced this was a good
omen, that the crude figures and Simon's reaction to
them would somehow point them to the Chalice. But
after weeks, they had found no more pattern and order
to the paintings than they had to the tunnels themselves.

He raised the torch closer to the painting, studying a
single female dancer with long, red locks entwined
around her slender form. "Isabel," he murmured. Her
mother was a native of this island and the forests
around it; she had woven a figure very like this one in
her tapestry, a maiden taming a wolf.

"What are you thinking, warrior?" the wizard said.
Simon started back the way they had come, leaving his
companion to chase after him. "What is in your head?"

"Isabel," he answered without slowing down. He
reached Sir Gabriel's study and fastened the torch into a
holder on the wall. "She may know something," he explained as Orlando caught up at last, looking vexed and
out of breath. "We should have asked her long since."

"No, Simon," the dwarf said, alarmed. "You must
stay away from her—"

"Why must I?" But he knew the answer. For weeks he had avoided his pretended cousin, venturing from the catacombs only in the dead of night when he was sure she would be sleeping. He had kissed her, not carelessly, not for the pleasure of a moment, but because he had needed her kiss. And he knew that was dangerous, not only to him but to his quest.

But if she could help them, if she knew some piece of local legend or myth that could lead them to the Chalice, wasn't that worth the risk? The sooner his quest was accomplished, the sooner he could leave Charmot, and the sooner Isabel would be safe.

"Stay here and keep looking if you wish," he told Orlando. "I won't be long."

"Wait," the wizard ordered, pushing past the vampire to reach the dead knight's desk. He tossed his fortune-teller's bones across it and studied them for a moment, his expression first grave, then alarmed. "No," he decided. "I forbid you to go to her."

"You forbid me?" Simon echoed, incredulous.

"I will speak to Lady Isabel myself, if you think she may have something of value to tell us," Orlando said briskly. "You must not go near her, this night or any other. You have a duty, warrior, a better promise to keep."

"Orlando, I will not abandon the Chalice," Simon said, trying to be patient. "I've already told you."

"I speak not just of the Chalice, warrior." He reached into the pocket closest to his heart and took out the ruby-colored bottle that held the essence of Roxanna, the little sultana he loved. "She trusts you to save her," he said, his eyes alight with feeling. "She will need you, a warrior who understands her kind and her past, who can protect her when her curse is broken."

"No, Orlando." In his mind, he could see his vampire sister holding the dagger that had killed Duke Francis, his beloved patron's blood staining the blade in her hand, a monster's tears of scarlet on her face. "That will never be." He started to walk past the dwarf, unwilling to say more, but Orlando blocked his way.

"No," he insisted, putting up his wizened little hands as if to hold the vampire back by force. "You will not— you will destroy her—"

"I will not." For the first time in all their years together, Simon lifted the tiny wizard off his feet, an indignity past all forgiving.

"I will tell her!" Orlando raged, struggling in his grasp. "I will tell Lady Isabel the truth!"

"No, you won't." He put him down on the far side of the room, then crossed to the door again in three long strides. "I'm sorry," he said, going out and closing the door before the dwarf could catch him. He turned the key and left it in the lock. "I will be back here as quickly as I can."

Isabel came back down the circular stair with the tray Brautus had barely touched, feeling very put upon and cross. Her ancient friend had been in an extremely foul temper. His shoulder was still not healing as it should have done long ago, and it pained him very much. "One more thing to fret about," she grumbled to herself as she rounded the corner into the great hall.

"What did you say?" Simon asked from the shadows by the hearth, making her scream and drop the tray in fright.

"Holy Christ!" she swore, scowling at him, her hand pressed to her heart, Brautus's dinner smashed and splattered on the rushes at her feet.

"I'm sorry," he said, trying not to laugh. The usually reserved young lady of Charmot had shrieked as if she'd been bitten on the bottom by a goose. Muttering a response he was glad he couldn't quite make out, she bent down to start picking up the dropped tray. "Where is everyone?" he asked. He had already searched the courtyard and the stables without finding another soul.

"What do you care?" she countered, scraping up a puddle of stew in a half-moon of broken crockery. "What are you doing up here?"

"Let me help you." He bent down to pick up the flagon that was spilling wine into the rushes. She slapped his hand away, cutting her own hand on another shard of broken bowl in the process.

"Shit!" she swore, flinging the shard she still held halfway across the room. His eyes went wide, and she was glad; she hoped he fainted from the shock. She was sick unto death of being polite to him; suddenly every grievance that oppressed her felt like his fault, unjust as that surely must be. But she was in no mood to be reasonable.

"Forgive me." He stood up slowly, tearing his gaze away from the wound in her palm with an effort. He closed his eyes, the sudden perfume of her blood making him feel drunk.

"They went to the druid's grove, to the May Night dance." She yanked the kerchief from her head and knotted it around her hand as best she could, since her knight errant seemed to have no interest in attending her. In faith, the great wolf-killer of Charmot looked as if he might be about to be sick. "Up here amongst the living, today was the first of May."

Simon looked at her, shocked, but she had gone back to gathering up the mess she'd made, oblivious to how keenly her barb had found its mark. "Why didn't you go?"

"Because I can't." She picked up the tray and headed for the kitchen, and Simon followed. "The May Night dance is a peasant festival." She dumped the tray in the refuse barrel, then stripped out of her ruined apron and threw it in as well. "I am the lady of Charmot." She caught sight of her reflection in the mirror Susannah had left on the table. "All appearances to the contrary," she muttered, setting it aside with its glass turned down.

"And that makes such a difference?" Simon said. "Back in Ireland, we had May dances, too, and the duke and his knights found it no shame to attend."

"The duke and his knights were men, I suspect. I am a woman." She filled a bowl with water and unknotted the makeshift bandage from her wounded hand. "Forgive me; I thought you had noticed."

"I did indeed," he answered, smiling at her sarcasm.

"You noticed, but you don't understand." The shallow gash had already stopped bleeding, but it stung when she washed it even so, adding still more fuel to her already raging temper. "My father's legacy depends on my character. If my behavior is not above reproach at every moment, Charmot and all he built here could be lost."

"Did your father tell you this?" Simon said, watching her face as she spoke, her expressions more telling than her words. She was angry, but she was hurt as well.

"No one had to tell me, Simon," she retorted. "I am not a fool. This castle has no lord, no master, and has had none for ten years past, and for whatever reason, the king has decided he wants it. The only reason he has sent single knights to claim it in single combat instead of troops to lay siege to the walls is that I am here, a titled virgin of good repute with a claim to the manor of blood. I am the lady of Charmot." She had never spoken of this with anyone, even Brautus, but in truth, it was the great truth of her life, and she knew it only too well. "If I'm just some peasant girl, dancing in a pagan grove, I'm nothing for the king to fret about, and Charmot is nothing but an empty fortress, ripe for the picking. And my father—" She broke off, turning away. "No one has to tell me how to behave, Simon," she finished, emptying the bowl. "I am not a child."

"No," he said tenderly, touched more than he cared to confess by what she'd said. He reached to take her wounded hand. "You are not."

"Stop it," she said, snatching her hand away. "I am not that, either."

He froze, shocked by her rebuff. "Not what?"

"Not some doe-eyed simpleton like Susannah who lives and quivers for the moment you might touch me," she retorted, the words coming more quickly than her thoughts, she realized, as if she'd been waiting to say them for weeks. "Or some Eve in the garden, waiting to tempt you, some worldly vice you must give up like sunshine or fruitcake or whatever else it is you think God would forbid you." He didn't answer, just stared back at her with those dark angel's eyes, a painted saint she could worship but never really touch. "But why do I even tell you this?" she said, turning away from his cold beauty. "Why do I always end up telling you everything that comes into my head, things that I've never spoken to another soul? You never tell me anything."

"Do I not?" he countered, moving around her to see her face, his own temper starting to rise. How dare this child attack him this way, this innocent little snip who thought the world began and ended at the gates of her father's castle? She had told him she was not a child—

no, in faith, she was an infant. "The first night I came here, I told you more than any soul living has ever known of my quest—"

"Your curse, you mean?" she demanded, incredulous. "Aye, Simon, that you told me, and shall I tell you what I think of it? I think it's bollocks. A curse that damns a man to live in darkness on bread crusts and go poking around in old crypts full of dead papers—what mad sort of idiot could believe in such a thing?"

"You think I am a liar, then?" he answered, furious now in truth. He was a liar, but that did not mean he cared to be called one, least of all by her.

"No, cousin," she said, her face very near to his. "I think you are a fool." His expression darkened, and she took a half-conscious step backward, quelled a bit by the look in his eyes in spite of her own fury. "Someone—Orlando, I suspect—has told you that you are a monster, that you deserve to be punished for some great evil, and you, poor fool, believe him."

"I should show you," he said with a smile that was more like a snarl. "I should let you see just what sort of monster I am."

"In faith, Simon, I wish you would," she retorted. "At least then I might have some chance of understanding you. What sort of monster are you?" He looked away, his jaw set in a sullen scowl quite different from any other expression she had ever seen him make. All the saintliness was gone, the angelic reserve that made him seem so distant even when he kissed her that she wanted to scream. "What is this terrible thing that you have done to make God despise you?"

"I cannot tell you—"

"Why not?" She moved around him, trying to make him face her. "Do you think I will despise you, too, that I will try to turn you out? We both know I couldn't do that now even if I wanted you gone, which, by the by, I do not. You're a good man, Simon, I swear it, and I am as fond of you as I have ever been of any friend I have ever had. I can't believe you could have done anything so terrible—"

"Isabel, stop it," he ordered, trying to walk away, to shut out her words before it was too late. He didn't want to be her friend, and he could not be anything else. "You don't know what you ask of me—"

"But I do." She caught his arm. "I'm asking you to trust me as I have been forced to trust you. You say that your salvation is here at Charmot, but you will not tell me why." The sorrow in his face as he turned away again was enough to make her almost regret her harsh words, and she softened her tone. "You want me to help you—"

"I want you to leave me alone!" he said, turning on her in fury.

"You do not!" she retorted, her own full rage returning in a flash. "If you did, you wouldn't—what are you doing here now, Simon? Why are you not in the catacombs with Orlando? Why did you kiss me, not once, mind, but twice?"

He opened his mouth to answer, but he couldn't say the words, couldn't tell her the truth. "Isabel, I'm sorry," he began instead.

"No!" she shouted, her temper exploding completely. "You will not dare to be sorry, you bastard; I'm sick of it!" Never in her life had she dreamed of such a thing, screaming like a banshee at a man, much less a noble knight, but she couldn't help herself. "If you want to kiss me, kiss me and suffer the consequences. If I don't like it, I'll be glad enough in future to tell you so. I may be a virgin, but I'm not a coward or a child."

"So you said," he answered with a sardonic, disbelieving smile.

"And if you don't really wish to kiss me, if you've done so in the past out of some misguided sense of obligation, please, feel free to leave off," she went on, undeterred. "I've lived this long without your kisses; I think I can manage to live a little longer. If you want to be left alone, then stay away from me. I swear I will not trouble you. Have I broken our agreement even once since it was made?"

"No," he muttered, still scowling.

"No, nor will I." The sheer conceit of the man suddenly struck her as comic, it was so ridiculous. "You keep coming to me, yet I'm the one who must be warned to stay away, who must promise to leave you in peace to suffer your great sorrow undisturbed. Well, worry no more, sir knight." She suddenly felt as if a great weight had been lifted from her, blown away in righteous fury. "From this moment, you are safe from me." Flinging the bowl she had used into the washing basin, she stormed out, slamming the kitchen door behind her.

She heard his footsteps behind her and turned just as he caught her halfway across the great hall, sweeping her into his arms. "I didn't promise." His voice was almost a growl, and his dark brown eyes met hers with a hunger that made her feel faint. "I never promised I would stay away." She opened her mouth to snap out her reply and regain her fury, and he kissed her, crushing her so close she could barely breathe, much less protest.

Oh, no, she thought, still fighting inside, struggling in his embrace. She balled up her fists against his chest, trying to push him away. He wouldn't steal her reason with a kiss this time. He wouldn't make her long for him then skulk back into hiding. This time she would be the one to pull away.

His tongue pushed into her mouth, the same kind of delicious invasion that had haunted her dreams for weeks, but this time she bit him, not hard enough to draw blood, but hard enough to hurt him. But still he didn't let her go. If anything, he pressed her closer, kissed her harder, drawing her lower lip between his teeth to gently bite her back. Her mind cried out in fury, but her knees went weak. Furious or not, her body refused to resist him, but still she was raging inside. She slumped against his chest, giving herself over to his kiss, but when he moved to pull away, she caught a double handful of his shirt. "No, you don't," she warned him. "Not this time." She saw the same old anguish in his eyes, and it made her want to scream. "Don't do it, Simon." She loosened her grip on his shirt, but her eyes still held him. "Leave me now, and you leave me forever."

For one horrifying moment, she thought he meant to do just that. He let her go and turned his face away. But just as tears were rising in her eyes, just as she was about to turn away herself, he caught her and kissed her again.

Simon kissed her hard, resolve and reason falling into flame. She possessed him; he couldn't let her go. He pushed her back against the heavy table, still wanting to hurt her, to punish her for capturing him so completely, her innocence be damned. He kissed the corners of her mouth, her jawline, her throat, and her tiny sigh of pleasure just goaded him on. She wanted him; she turned her face up to his kiss, her arms hanging slack at her sides, and when he lifted her onto the table, she reached for him, raking her fingers through his hair. She knew him not as a vampire, the demon in the dark he had been for so many others for so long, but as Simon, the man he had been, and she wanted him, reached for him, melted at his kiss. His anger dissolved into longing, a desire more sweet than any hunger for blood. When he drew back, her green eyes gazed up into his, fearless and warm, and he smiled, caressing her cheek. "How could I leave you?"

He kissed her again, their faces now level, and she wrapped her arms around his neck, one leg twining around him, driving him mad. How could she be real, this wild young spirit in his arms, so sensible and cold one moment, so fevered and wanton the next? His hands moved up and down her sides as his kiss moved to her throat, the heat of her soft flesh like the taste of her skin, maddening and sweet. No one else had ever touched her, he thought as he caressed her. No other man had ever tasted her kisses or pressed her close and felt her surrender. Her passion was for him alone with no trace of calculation, no pretense of maidenly scorn. If she scorned him, he would know it; when she kissed him, it was real.

"Isabel," he murmured, kissing her jaw, and she shivered, loving the sound of her name in his mouth and the longing she heard in his voice. He pushed her skirt up to her thighs, and she trembled, feeling deliciously wicked. They were alone in the castle but for Brautus, who was sleeping, and Orlando, who would not leave the catacombs. No one would come to disturb them or see what they did; no one would charge in to save her. For once in her life, she was free.

His hands moved over her legs, pushing them up in an ungainly position with her knees bent to caress the backs of her thighs, and she breathed in sharply, appalled and elated at once. She felt dizzy, drunk with a desire so intense she could hardly believe it was real. She had imagined kisses before he had come to Charmot; she had tried to imagine her marriage bed, to piece together some notion of what it would be like from the horrors and romances she had been told. But she could not have dreamed of such a fire as she felt in Simon's arms. Nothing was as she had expected it to be; everything was better, strange and new. He arched over her, moving to stand between her upraised knees, and she reached for him again, drew his face down to hers to kiss his mouth.

Simon felt her pulse in her lips and heard the pounding of her heart. Sweet blood rushed through her, warming her skin; he could taste it on her tongue, enticing him to murder. But her blood could never be enough. He broke the kiss; her lips parted with living breath as he bent down and kissed her again. He eased her back farther on the table, caressing the curve of her thigh, soft flesh over powerful muscle. She rose up to kiss him, draping her arms around his shoulders, pressing her body to his. Her hand went to the lacing at the bodice of her gown, baring her skin to his touch. She gasped again, catching his wrist, and a maiden's modest blush painted her cheeks at last, captivating him. "Yes," he murmured, bending closer, kissing her sweet lips. Her grip loosened and turned into a caress, her fingertips stroking the back of his hand as he lifted each breast from its binding.

He kissed each one in turn, his mouth closing

around each delicate pink nipple, feeling it harden to a burning peak against his tongue. Another sudden flush swept over her, warming his mouth as she sighed. His hand closed gently over one cream mound, a miracle of softness, as his mouth moved lower, but her gown still held him back. Rising up again, he tore it from her, ripping the bodice open to the waist.

"Simon!" She should have been frightened or at least ashamed, but she wasn't; she laughed aloud. He smiled at her, his angel's smile, and a thrill of elation swept through her, burning deeper as he leaned down to suckle her breast. "Good," she heard herself murmur without ever meaning to speak. "Your mouth feels so good." Her hand stole half-consciously to her other breast as he tore her gown still further, still suckling her as he pushed it completely away. His hands were shaking as he stroked her hips, and she smiled, moaning softly as he moved to kiss her other breast, nudging her own hand away.

He kissed her stomach, his hands around her waist, and her body arched upward, beyond her control. Her hands found his shoulders, hard muscle curved beneath the soft, thin linen that he wore, and she tore at his shirt as he'd torn at her gown, wishing she was strong enough to rip it completely away.

"Wait," he murmured, laughing. "Wait, sweetheart." He licked a trail across her stomach to her sex, kissing her there as he would kiss her mouth, and she cried out as his tongue slid inside her, making her burn with sweet shock. Then he was standing, bending over her again to kiss her lightly as he pulled his shirt over his head. Weak and shaking, she reached up to touch his cheek.

"My angel," she whispered. His eyelids fell, his lashes dark against his cheek as she touched him. She traced the curve of his lower lip with her fingertips, and a strange thought passed through her mind, a detail forgotten before it was defined. Why do I not feel his breath? She let her touch trail down his chest, and he groaned, leaning closer, brushing his cheek against hers. Her palm slipped lower, and he kissed her, holding her close. She felt the swell of his erection brush her hip, and for a single moment she was afraid, not of pain but of sin. She belonged to Charmot; she belonged to her father; she had no right to give herself away. But Charmot could never comfort her, could never hold her close. She twined her arms around Simon's neck, pressing a flurry of kisses all over his beautiful face.

He cradled her cheek in his hand as he kissed her, then his mouth moved to her throat. His palm caressed her hip, his other arm cradling her waist, holding her to him, caught fast. He kissed her mouth again, capturing her sigh, and for a moment, her tongue touched something too sharp in his mouth. Then his touch moved tenderly between her legs, his hand touching her sex the same way that his tongue had done it, making her cry out in pleasure and shock. A burning thrill raced through her faster and faster as his hand opened her up, so tender but insistent, his mouth still brushing gently over hers to steal her breath. He moved closer between her thighs, and she felt his sex again, still enclosed in his hose.

She wrapped her hand around his wrist again, not to stop him this time but to hold him, and she shivered to feel her fingers would not meet around it. Half-consciously guiding his hand ever deeper against the swollen, tender folds of her most sensitive flesh, she slowly sat up on the table, gasping again at the sudden change of pressure in his touch. Pressing a kiss to the scar on his throat, she slid her own hands down his stomach, pushing down his hose. His sex sprang up between them, pale and perfect as the rest of him, the first one she had ever seen. Entranced, she traced its shape with her fingers, raising her eyes to meet his.

He caught her wrist and pushed her back prone on the table, pinning her beneath him as his mouth dipped down to hers. With one hand braced against the table, he pushed her legs farther apart with the other, guiding himself inside her. She laughed aloud again in shock, the pain so sweet she could hardly think of it as pain at all. This ecstasy was what she was supposed to fear? She brought her hips up eagerly to meet him, urging him to go faster, and a deeper wave of pleasure rippled through her, making her feel weak.

Simon tried to make himself go slowly, but it was a losing fight, his desire for her so intense it hurt him. He loved her, he realized, rocking deeper, the knowledge like a knife twisted inside his lifeless heart even as his flesh shuddered with pleasure. He couldn't stay away from her because he loved her as he had never loved another as a vampire or a man. The torches had never been lit, and the shadows from the firelight made a veil across her precious face as he kissed her. She closed her eyes, her hips rising in rhythm with his own, and he bent closer, bracing his weight on his arms to kiss her eyelids, her forehead, her cheek. He kissed her mouth as her body arched beneath him, quickening her pace, and he matched his strokes to her rhythm as she clung to him, her nails scratching his flesh. His lips strayed to her tender throat, trailing kisses down the vein . . . but no. He drove into her harder, his climax beginning to rise.

"Simon!" she cried out, hands braced against the table as ripples of pleasure erupted in a single, overwhelming wave. She tried to say his name again, to hold him close, but every muscle in her body felt like liquid flame, powerless and burning. She felt him spill inside her, cold as water from a spring . . . why was he so cold? He was kissing her, raising her up in his arms, and she clung to him, wrapping her arms around him as if to warm his flesh, bereft as he slipped from inside her.

"Sweetheart," he murmured, kissing her cheek as he held her upright. "I will be back." He cradled her jaw in his hand as he kissed her. "I swear, I will be back."

"What . . . ?" He was letting her go; he was leaving

her. "No," she said, gathering her gown around her as he donned his hose. "You can't—"

"I have to, angel." He kissed her mouth again, so quickly she barely felt it. "Go upstairs and wait for me." He pressed a kiss to her hand, first the palm, then the pulse at her wrist. "I will be right back."

8

Simon saddled Malachi more by feel than vision, his mind so full he could barely see at all. The hunger for blood possessed him now like a demon indeed, more powerful than it had been since his first night as a vampire. No deathless feeding on a stag or sheep would satisfy him now; he needed human blood.

Malachi shied as he tried to mount, sensing the change in his nature, no doubt. "It's all right, friend," he promised, climbing into the saddle, keeping his seat with an effort as the animal pranced and pawed. "You know now I mean you no harm." The stallion was still restless, but he made no effort to throw him off, even when Simon let the reins go slack. With barely a nudge to his sides, the horse broke into a gallop, thundering over the drawbridge as if the demon was behind him rather than on his back. Once clear of the castle, they turned and plunged into the forest, the trees whipping past them in a blur, and Simon relaxed somewhat. But where could he go?

He thought of the peasant festival Isabel had spoken

of, the May Night dance. Not so long ago, such a gathering would have been like a banquet for him. In a hundred different cities, from the carnivals of Italy to the harvest rites of France, the vampire had moved among the revelers, the noble stranger with an angel's face, feeding lightly here and there from any likely-looking wench and leaving her weakened but elated. Sometimes he even committed a murder outright; such festivals nearly always attracted at least one or two hearts black enough to satisfy his craving for evil as well as for blood. But here at Charmot, he was no stranger; he was Sir Simon, protector of the castle, the lady's sometime suitor. Even if he should find some peasant blackguard who knew nothing of him, he would almost certainly be spotted by someone else who did. He didn't dare risk it, even now. But somehow he had to feed.

Malachi broke from the trees onto the king's road, and Simon let him make the turn onto the easier ground, the sudden burst of speed exhilarating even in his distress. But when his demon's hearing detected voices some half a mile ahead, he slowed the horse to a walk, long before whoever was speaking could have detected him.

"Turn off the road," a man with a thick Scottish burr was saying, and the vampire smiled. Even from this distance, he could smell the malice on this one. He would do nicely. "We have brought him far enough."

Simon left his own horse hidden in the trees and crept closer on foot, moving silently through the woods on the other side of the road. There were three horses stopped in a clearing, but only two of them were properly mounted, one by the brigand who had spoken, the other by another man a little smaller but dressed much the same in dark leather armor. A third man was slung over his horse's saddle like a sack of grain, to all appearances dead. As Simon moved closer, he could hear a third heartbeat, weakening but still alive.

"We should see if there is a house nearby," the second brigand was saying. "We do not want him found."

"Why not?" the first one said with a laugh. "Who will know him here?" He cut a strap binding the third man to his horse and gave him a vicious kick, making him slump to the ground. "Farewell, Lord Tristan DuMaine," he said, spitting on him for good measure.

"Aye, my lord, farewell," the second one said, standing in the stirrups to make a mocking bow. "We will enjoy your castle."

Simon sprang out of the shadows, transforming himself as he went into the great, black wolf. "Damn me, Christ!" the first brigand swore as the vampire lay hold of him, a manly oath that rose into a scream as the fangs tore into his flesh. Simon felt his body come alive as the blood rushed down his throat, warming him at last as love could not. He fell to the ground with his prey, curving over him in ecstasy, roaring in rage as he transformed back into the shape of a man. The brigand shuddered, too weak now to scream, all but an empty husk. His horse reared away from them in terror, and Simon snarled, baring his fangs. The animal cried out and fled, dragging his dying master behind him, one foot still tangled in his stirrup.

The second brigand had drawn his crossbow and managed to aim it at Simon, but as the vampire looked up, he froze, apparently too terrified to fire. Simon smiled, wiping his bloody mouth on his bare arm. "What the devil are you?" the brigand stammered, the crossbow twitching in his grip.

"You guess it already." He grabbed the brigand by the tunic, and he fired, the bolt passing through Simon's shoulder with a sickening thud. "I am the devil." The vampire yanked the pointed rod of metal from his undead flesh almost without thinking as he dragged his prey down from his horse, using it to stab a fountain in the thickly muscled throat. Still holding the man dangling before him by the tunic, he bent his head and drank, an evil parody of a lover's embrace. Mine, a voice murmured deep inside Simon's mind, the voice of the demon Kivar. You are mine.

"No!" the vampire roared, flinging the dying man from him. The brigand's head struck a tree with an ominous crack, lolling on his shoulders as he slumped, lifeless, to the ground. "No," Simon repeated, sinking to his knees. "I am not . . . I am done." But it was always the same when the hunger took hold of him; he always heard the voice of Kivar, reminding him of what he was. And even now, the demon was not satisfied.

Before him lay the dying knight the brigands had meant to abandon. His armor had been stripped from him, his clothes underneath soaked and stained with blood from wounds in his chest, stomach, and arms. His face was a bruised and bloody pulp. But his eyes were open.

Simon bent closer, listening to the fading music of the fallen warrior's heart. What had he done to make those others so despise him? The vampire could sense no evil in him, only rage, a desperate desire for revenge more powerful than his own impending death. If he saw the monster bending over him, he did not show it; Simon smelled no fear. But he was dying; nothing could save him now. Acting as much for mercy as for his own waning hunger, he struck, sinking his fangs into the young man's throat.

The knight, Tristan, they had called him, lurched upward with surprising strength, fighting death with a will Simon could taste in his blood, the power of the righteous and the wronged. One of his shoulders had obviously been shattered, but with his other arm he struck at the monster who would finish him with a true warrior's fury. Simon sank his fangs in deeper, unable to stop himself, drawing the blood from the man's very heart, his goodness like the sweetest wine after ten years feeding on the bitter bile of evil.

Then suddenly he howled in pain as the knight bit him back. Unschooled human teeth tore into the bare flesh of his shoulder, and a power like nothing he had ever felt before swept through him, making him feel faint. Furious, he devoured the last drop of life from his prey in a single gulp, making the living heart stop dead in an instant. But this knight, this Tristan, still clung to him, still fed from him, his teeth growing longer and sharp. "No!" Simon roared, flinging him away, and the knight flopped like a rag doll on the ground, his green eyes staring as in death, his mouth smeared with blood. But his bruises were already fading.

"No," Simon repeated, pressing a hand to the wound in his shoulder, but it was already healed. In his mind, he saw the face of Kivar as he made Simon what he was, thin, cracked lips drawn back from his ivory fangs. Now Simon had done the same.

"No," he said again, climbing to his feet. He had not made another vampire; surely he could not. He had never done such a thing before in ten long years and a thousand murders. He had briefly thought when Isabel had told him about that dead girl and shown him that cross that he might have, but Orlando had been convinced that had been a wolf, and Simon had soon known he was right. He had killed the wolf himself, just as he had killed this man before him. The man was dead; the healing Simon thought he saw was only a trick of the moonlight. He tried to walk away, backing into the trees.

Then the knight sat up.

He sprang to his feet with feline grace, falling to a crouch when he saw Simon was still there. "Stay back," he ordered, reaching for the fallen brigand's sword.

"Stop," Simon answered, cursing himself for a fool. He had no sword; he hadn't bothered to bring one. Indeed, he was barely dressed. "You don't understand what has happened—"

"I live," the new-made demon cut him off. "That is enough." Standing, he was nearly Simon's height, but his complexion was slightly darker even as a vampire, and his hair was blond.

"But you do not," Simon said, taking a step closer.

"You killed them," Tristan said, looking at the dead brigand slumped against the tree. "You killed them both with no weapons; I saw you." He lifted the sword and stared at his own arm as if amazed to find it whole. "Will I now kill in this fashion?" He spoke English with a careful accent, as if it were not his native tongue—a Frenchman, perhaps, though his name, Tristan, was Irish or Scots.

"You can," Simon admitted. Somehow he must get the sword away from this new brother and destroy him, now, for his own good. This man was no demon murderer.

Tristan smiled. "That is all I need to know." The horse he had been carried on was still waiting behind him, apparently unalarmed by this change in his master. Before Simon could stop him, Tristan had leapt onto the horse's bare back and galloped away. Simon gave chase for a mile or so, even transmuting into the wolf to run faster, but it was no use. His new-made brother was gone.

"Lovely," he muttered, turning back. "Orlando is going to kill me."

Isabel sat in the window of her tower room, wearing only Simon's shirt and watching for his return. In the distance, she could see the smoky, orange glow of a fire rising from the trees. She tried to imagine what it must be like to be Susannah, the Queen of the May, dancing at the center of the throng instead of watching the lights from above, or to have been her mother so many years ago, the peasant beauty who had won a foreign noble's heart. But she couldn't even imagine it; she had no frame of reference. Her whole world was this castle, her legacy and prison. But tonight, if only for a moment, she had broken free. "I will be back," Simon had promised, leaving her again. "Go upstairs and wait for me." And so she had. But had he meant his promise? Even if he did come back, would he be coming for her?

She went to the table and opened her father's scrolls. She had meant to show them to Simon weeks ago, show him the strange patterns she had discovered in the corner notes, thinking it might help him find whatever it was he was seeking in the catacombs. But he had made her promise to leave him alone, and Orlando had warned her of some great danger if she did not, some mysterious evil that would destroy her and Simon both. So she had stayed away.

But now . . . were things really so different? Simon had made love to her, but he still hadn't told her why he believed he was cursed or what it was he hoped to find at Charmot. Whatever it was, it obviously had nothing to do with her. So why should she want him to find it? If he did, he would almost certainly leave; who would protect the castle then? Angry tears rose in her eyes, the tears she had refused to shed before when she had raged at him. As if she cared for nothing but Charmot . . . what would she do if he left her?

She tore off the corner of a scroll, a blasphemy—these had belonged to her father. But her father was dead. She looked down at the writing, trying one last time to read the words, but the meaning still refused to come. This wisdom, whatever it was, would never be for her.

She tore the corner into tiny pieces on the table, feeling like a fiend. Then she reached for the next scroll and tore off its corner as well, and the next, and the next, tearing each one to bits as she went. If somehow this was Simon's secret, he would never find it. He would never go.

The edge of a page sliced into her hand, making her wince in pain. She let the scroll fall to examine the cut, bringing her candle closer. It was tiny but deep in the web of skin between her thumb and palm, and blood dripped on the scraps of paper before her. "Damnation," she muttered, putting the cut to her mouth.

Then she froze. The torn bits of parchment were

moving, shuffling themselves like a deck of gamesman's cards, and the droplets of her blood writhed over them like tiny, living creatures. As she watched, stunned between fascination and fright, three of the bits aligned themselves into a rough triangle, the edges knitting themselves together to form a single piece.

Half-certain she was dreaming, she shredded another corner and dropped it on the pile. The new bits riffled through the others, and two more pieces found each other and knitted themselves into one. But the drops of blood were almost gone, shrinking as if consumed by the parchment. More curious than squeamish, she squeezed another drop from her cut, and the shuffling started anew, the scraps fairly dancing on the table as they writhed and reformed, two of the larger pieces coming together in a rough square nearly the size of one of the original corners.

She picked this up and examined it, her scalp starting to tingle. The words no longer looked like words at all. The characters had stretched and twisted as the parchment re-formed to make what looked like a piece of a maze, tunnels twisting in every direction, doubling back on themselves. "The catacombs," she whispered to the empty air. Her blood had not been consumed at all, she saw; it was still there, a path of red traced through the twisted maze. "Papa . . . this is a map."

Suddenly she heard a sound from outside, hoofbeats on the drawbridge. She ran to the window, the scrap of parchment still clutched in her fist. Simon and Malachi were coming back. Her heart leapt up, and she ran to gather up the parchment, eager to show her love what she had found. Whatever this enchantment was, surely it must be connected to his quest. Then she stopped. What if she were right? What if this were a map to the catacombs that would lead him to his prize? What reason would he have to stay at Charmot?

She kicked open the chest at the foot of her bed with her bare foot and shoved the magical parchment inside, then slammed down the lid. She would show him, she promised her conscience, but not until she knew that he loved her, that he wouldn't leave her once he found his prize. She would tell him everything. Just not yet.

Simon left Malachi in the stables and started across the courtyard. Dawn was only a few hours away, and surely Isabel would be asleep by now, but he had to see her even so. He had to be certain she was all right.

He stopped at the rain barrel and washed what was left of the blood from his skin—what clothes he wore were still black and mostly unstained, he was relieved to see. He plunged his head under the water and washed out his mouth as well. But as he straightened up, he felt a prickling sensation on the back of his neck, as if he were being watched.

A massive black dog was sitting on his haunches just inside the castle gates, staring at the vampire with eyes so blue, they seemed to glow in the moonlight. A crimson tongue lolled from the creature's mouth between curving, ivory fangs, and malice rolled off him in waves, the stench of pure, uncomplicated evil.

For the second time that night, Simon wished he had a sword; for the first time in ten years, he felt real fear. "Begone from here," he ordered, taking a step toward the dog. "Leave this castle in peace." He had grown up on tales of the grim, the devil's black dog who appeared to those about to die, but he had never believed them. Of course, he had never believed in vampires, either. "I said begone!"

The dog stood up, its expression unchanged. With a final look over its shoulder, it trotted through the castle gates, disappearing into the night.

Isabel had begun to think Simon didn't mean to come upstairs at all, it had been so long since she'd seen him ride in. Just as she was deciding if she should go look for him or give him up and go to bed, she heard a knock on the door. Smiling, she opened it barely a crack.

He pushed his way inside and gathered her into his arms. "Surrender or be lost." He kissed her, lifting her completely off her feet, and she laughed as he did it, twining her arms around his neck. His bare skin felt warm against her through the thin linen of the shirt.

"I am lost," she admitted, caressing the wet curls of his hair at the back of his neck. "But I will still surrender." She kissed him, first deeply, then more lightly, a dozen silly little kisses as he spun her around. "So where did you go?"

"To the dance, of course." Holding her this way, he could almost forget the evil he had seen and done that night. He had expected to find her unsettled, perhaps even grieving; he had never expected this. "I told you, I like dances."

"You did not," she corrected. "You said there were dances in Ireland, and you hinted that you went. But you never said you liked it."

"I liked it very much." The wreath of flowers Susannah had left for her was still on the table, and he twirled her across the room to put in on her head. "We used to have a harvest dance in autumn and a May dance every spring."

"And you danced with every maiden there, no doubt," she teased, trying to take it off again.

"Only the prettiest ones." He stopped spinning her around to use both hands to fasten the rosebuds in place. "Though I have to say in God's own truth, there was none there as pretty as you."

"Aye, I'm certain," she said sarcastically, pleased nonetheless. " 'Tis my costume that makes me so fair."

"That's part of it, for certes." He kissed her again, pulling her close until her body molded to his. "Though I think I recognize that shirt."

"Do you, in faith?" she said with a giggle that sounded like someone else, some much more frivolous girl than she had ever allowed herself to be. "Methinks it belonged to me first."

"Aye, you might be right." He turned her in a circle again, a slow, sweet lover's dance. "So you only mean to take back what is yours."

"Just so." He took her hands and turned her in a figure before him with such grace, she could almost hear the music. "Tell me more about those Irish dances."

"As you will, my lady." She couldn't know how beautiful she seemed to him, he thought, a nymph crowned with flowers, dancing in his arms. His frozen heart ached just to see her. "My father was a bard as well as the duke's castellan, so he always sang and played the harp."

"Your father was a musician?" she said with a laugh.

"Aye, he was." He lifted her off of her feet again, making her laugh again as he kissed her. "And a poet as well."

"A poet?" she echoed, touching his cheek. "In faith, I am impressed, sir knight." She rose up on tiptoe to kiss his lightly stubbled jaw. "And is your father's son a poet, too?"

"I was." He stopped dancing to caress her face, thinking of the lays he could sing on the beauty of her eyes if he only had the freedom. "I was a great many things, love, once upon a time." He kissed her now in earnest, and she seemed to understand, enfolding him in her embrace as she opened her mouth to his. He pressed her closer then turned her around in a figure. "You're a good dancer," he teased with a smile as she laughed.

"Am I, in faith?" She ran her hands over his shoulders and down his bare, thick-muscled arms. And to think, the first time she had seen him, she'd thought he might be a monk. "'Tis a wonder, since I've never danced before."

"In faith, I can hardly believe it." His hands encircled her waist, admiring the softness of her curves, and she giggled, flinching away, ticklish.

"I've never done a lot of things." She lay her hands against his chest, the sheer power of him frightening and beautiful at once. "As you could tell, no doubt."

"I had a slight suspicion." He touched her chin as she looked down, turning her face back to his. "I should tell you that I'm sorry." Her eyes widened, and he smiled. "But I am not."

Her frown melted into a smile. "Thank God." He laughed, and she kissed him, her hands sliding over his shoulders. He bent and wrapped his arms around her, lifting her off of her feet. "I am not sorry, either." She brushed back the dark silk of his still-damp hair to press a warm kiss to his cheek.

"Darling . . ." He carried her to the high bed, kissing her mouth as they went, but rather than laying her back on the coverlet, he turned and sat down himself, holding her over him. She framed his beautiful face in her hands, finally able to reach him, to touch him as she'd longed to do for so long. She kissed his forehead, the pale white curve of his high-arched cheek, the dark shadow of his lashes as his hands moved under the shirt she still wore to cradle the curve of her behind. She pulled the shirt off over her head, dragging the flowers from her hair in the process, then kissed him, holding his face to her own as he lifted her onto him, moaning into his mouth as he slid into her.

Their love was softer this time, less desperate, a delicious tension building slowly inside her like scratching an exquisitely torturous itch. She bent her forehead to his shoulder, using the strength of her thighs to rock over him, and he gasped, all but panting as his hands caressed her back.

He kissed her throat, the throb of her pulse no more than a delicate goad to his passion after his orgy of feeding. Her hair fell like a curtain all around them, and he gathered it up in his hand, inhaling her scent as he drew her head back, arching her throat up to his mouth. She moved faster over him, and he wrapped her in his arms, shifting her closer on his lap, driving deeper inside of her with every stroke, and she cried out his name, plaintive and sweet. "It's all right," he promised, a kiss against her ear. "I have you . . . I won't let you fall."

"No . . ." She twined her arms around his back, molding her body to his, waves of pleasure making her feel dizzy as he filled her up, the two of them now one. "I trust you." She clung to him with all the strength her melting limbs could muster as he rolled over her, pressing her into the soft mattress, their bodies still joined. Only when he drove in harder did she let him go, her hands clutching the coverlet, her hips arched up to his. Her climax came slowly this time, rolling through her with such violence, she was blind, the whole world going black. But Simon was there, still holding her, kissing her cheek, and even in the void she felt protected and safe. I love you, she thought, feeling him erupt inside her, his own rolling shudder as he fell into her arms. But even in her innocence, she knew better than to say the words aloud. Nothing had changed; he still thought he was cursed. She could so easily drive him away.

Simon kissed her shoulder, then nuzzled her breast, drunk on the warmth of her flesh even now. He raised up to kiss her mouth, then pulled the heavy bedrug over them. "Come here." He drew her to him, her head on his chest, his arm around her shoulders.

"That was nice," she said, and he smiled as she yawned, as unaffected as a child.

"I'm glad you thought so." He kissed the back of her hand. "As the cad who has ruined you, I feel obliged to please."

"Stop it," she said with an uncharacteristic giggle as she snuggled against his shoulder. "I am not ruined, and you are not a cad."

"Is that so, my lady?" He stroked her hair. "What would you call it?"

"Never you mind." She turned her head to kiss his throat, feeling very drowsy and comfortable. "I should thank you." She laced her fingers with his. "Whatever it's called, I didn't think I'd ever get the chance to do it."

"Dancing," he said, making her laugh. "It's called dancing."

"Ooh, so that's what dancing is like." The moon had begun to set outside her window, a glowing orange ball. The morning would be coming soon. "I didn't realize." She ran a possessive hand along his arm, trying not to think about the moment he would have to leave her. "No wonder everyone gets so excited about it."

"Exactly." He kissed her brow. "What made you think you'd never get to dance, my lady? Didn't you expect to marry?"

"Not really," she admitted. "I could never really imagine it. My father always expected that I would, of course. He used to talk about it all the time, the man who would protect Charmot when he was gone." Her hand closed half-consciously around his wrist. "But I never thought . . . it never seemed to have much to do with me, really. Do you see what I mean?"

"I think so," he answered, watching her face. In truth, he had never thought about what it would be like to be a woman, treated as chattel. The number of his own choices in life had gone from one to a hundred when Francis, the duke of Lyan, had made him a knight, but Isabel, born noble as she was, had never had but one destiny before her at which she could fail or succeed. His fate was at least partly of his own making, cursed or not, but what could she have done to change her path?

"Then when Papa died . . . it just seemed so sudden and so wrong, as if someone had made a mistake. I kept thinking that I must be dreaming, that soon I would wake up, and he would be there to take care of me again." His arm tightened around her, and she smiled. "But I didn't wake up, of course, and the king sent a stranger to be my husband. I should have let him, I suppose . . ." She let her voice trail off for a moment, hoping he would disagree, but he said nothing. "It just seemed so ridiculous that I should marry someone my father had never met, that his castle should go to some stranger," she went on instead. "So Brautus helped me."

He shifted on the pillow, cuddling her close. "Did you miss your mother?"

"I didn't," she admitted with a hollow laugh. "I didn't know her well enough to miss her; I had never known her. Only Papa. She was like a ghost he could see that I could not, this dead peasant girl haunting the castle. Sometimes I miss her now." She turned to face him, pillowing her head on her own arm. "What about your mother and father? Are they still in Ireland?"

"No, love," he said, turning to lie on his back. "Not any more." She brushed the hair back from his forehead, and he smiled. "My da died just before I left home with the duke. He broke his leg breaking a horse, and a fever set in. The whole manor mourned him."

The memory still pained him, she could tell, and she kissed him lightly on the mouth. "I should have liked to have met him."

"Oh, aye," he said with a smile. "He would have loved you." He caressed her cheek with the backs of his fingers. "You would have been embarrassed by the rare verses he would have sung to your beauty."

"You think so?" she said, laughing. "Your mother must have been a lucky woman."

"She was a beauty, too." His expression sobered. "She died when I was three years old, though, murdered by a Saxon raider, so I wouldn't call her lucky."

"Simon, dear God," she said, caressing his hair. "How awful."

He tried to smile, but it was a poor effort. "They used to say I saw it happen, but I don't remember it. I just remember afterward feeling like I ought to die as well, that the world had lost everything in it that was good." He had never spoken of this to anyone, not even his father. But it seemed natural to tell her now. She was looking down at him, her eyes soft and warm with sympathy, so beautiful even in the dark. What would it be like to awaken in sunlight to those beautiful eyes?

He drew her down to him and kissed her, tenderly but deep. "You're wrong, love," she said softly when he let her go. "The world can still be good."

He smiled for her. "I see that." She lay back down with her head on his chest, her arms around him, and she yawned again. "You should go to sleep," he told her, pulling her hair free before she was hopelessly entangled.

"I can't," she protested, still yawning. "The others will be home soon, and I can't let them find us like this." She made herself let him go. "Besides," she went on, "Orlando will be missing you."

Orlando, he thought, remembering. Orlando was still locked up in the catacombs, predicting disaster and cursing the vampire's name, no doubt. The worst part was, he was probably right on both counts. "Oh, I doubt it," he lied with a smile. "Go to sleep. I will stay awake."

"No," she insisted, so drowsy now even this simple word was almost beyond her. "You have to go."

"I will," he promised, kissing her bare shoulder. "I will go before anyone comes back." She smiled but didn't answer, already asleep. He kissed her cheek, and she barely stirred, a tiny snore making him smile. "I love you," he whispered, lying down beside her. "I love you, Isabel."

9

❦ ❦

Isabel slept most of the next day because no one bothered to wake her. By the time she came downstairs, the household was well about the new day's business, almost as if the revelries of the night before had never happened. "Good morrow, my lady," Hannah said, setting food on the table before her. "You must have slept well."

"Aye, too well," Isabel answered, making an effort to sound casual. "Why did no one wake me sooner? It must be past midday." She had dressed herself with particular care, making certain her gown was neat and her hair was tucked away beneath its kerchief so that to all outward appearances she was the same respectable maiden they had all left behind the night before. But she still felt as if she must be putting off some kind of sinful glow, as if everyone must be staring at her behind her back, gaping at one another in shock to see her transformed to a wanton. Everything about her was different; how could she hope to hide it?

"Well past," Hannah said with a smile. "Brautus must

have kept you up half the night telling war stories."

"No, he went to bed early." She took a bite of bread, ravenous in spite of her raw nerves. Indeed, she felt almost shockingly healthy except for being a little sore in spots, but if she thought about that, she really would blush herself scarlet. "We both did." And surely she must sound strange; to her ears, her voice sounded hollow and false, not like her at all. But Hannah didn't seem to notice. "I must have just been tired."

"I shouldn't wonder if you were," the maid said, taking up her spinning, "not after all the worry you've had lately. You're a very brave woman, my lady."

"I'm all right." I'm in love, she wanted to blurt out. I have a lover; can you believe it? "How was the dance?" she asked instead, covering her snicker with a cough.

"Oh, we had a grand time, as always," Hannah answered with a mysterious smile of her own. "So grand, in fact, that our Queen of the May has yet to come back home."

"Susannah isn't here?" Something about this made her shiver, though she couldn't have said just why.

"Not to worry, my lady," Hannah said, twisting her thread with her usual skill, obviously unconcerned. "She took up with some miller's son with a pretty face and no brothers as soon as we arrived; 'tis no great wonder she had no more time for us. I won't be surprised if she turns up with a husband before the day is done." Her spindle full, she pulled off the skein and started on another.

"As easy as that?" Isabel laughed.

"Oh aye, my lady. We common folk don't have nearly the pomp and trouble finding mates as the nobility," she said with a smile that held no small glimmer of pity. "'Sooth, we seem to trip over one another at every turning once the time is right."

"You make it sound so romantic." Was that what she and Simon had done, trip over one another? He was the only man of her class she had ever known well enough to think of marrying, that was true, but was that the only reason why she wanted him? If he had been shorter or blonder or more cheerful, would she still have loved him, just because he was there? For she did love him, of that much she was certain.

"Romance is for those who can afford it," the maid said with a laugh. "Minstrels, mostly, and queens. Most of us are happy enough just being easy together, comfortable like. Your parents were the same, as I remember." She smiled at Isabel again, a wise, motherly smile. "Just you wait, my lady. Someday you will see."

"You think so?" Isabel said, smiling back, but suddenly, she didn't feel like smiling much at all. I don't have to wait and see, she wanted to say; I already know better. But in truth, she did not. If romance was only for those who could afford it, she feared she was deeply in debt. She had no more business throwing herself away on Simon than she did taking a leap over the moon, not when she knew he could never marry her. But I don't care, she thought, stubborn and defiant.

Simon might not care a fig for her; he might be cursed; they might never marry; and she might burn in hell for a harlot after dying an old maid. But today she did not care.

"I do indeed," Hannah said as Isabel stood up to clear away her bowl. "You will have a fine husband, my lady; I don't doubt it for a moment." She didn't mention Simon, Isabel noticed with a bitter, inward smile.

"By God's grace," she answered aloud. "I will pray you're right."

"My lady, you're awake," Kevin said, coming in looking pale. "You should go upstairs." He looked around the hall. "Where is Brautus?"

"I couldn't say," Isabel answered, confused. "What has happened?"

"He's upstairs," Hannah answered at the same time.

"Go and fetch him," Kevin told his wife before turning to Isabel. "Go with her, my lady, and stay."

"I will not," Isabel said, getting up. "Kevin, what's wrong?"

For a moment, she thought he would refuse to answer, but Raymond and some of the other men were coming in behind him. "We went looking for Susannah," he began, obviously unhappy.

"Did you find her?" Hannah said, alarmed.

"No," he said, shaking his head. "But we found three others." He nodded to Raymond, who went back out again. "My lady, they are dead." Raymond came back in leading Mother Bess, leaning heavily on his arm on one side and her gnarled willow cane on the other. "I fear the wolf has returned."

She watched with Hannah standing beside her as the bodies were carried in, her arms crossed tightly over her breasts as if to hold back a scream. "You found them together?" she asked, shocked to hear her voice sound so calm.

"Aye, my lady," Kevin said as the third and last of the dead men was laid before the hearth. The first two were dressed in the leather clothing of soldiers with heavy woolen mantles of a Scottish weave. They looked as if they might have been killed by the same beast as the woman Isabel had seen at the chapel. One's throat was eaten nearly to the bone, and the other had a deep gash in his throat just under his jaw. But the third was no fighter. He was dressed for the festival in a finespun linen shirt and woolen hose and a vest still decorated with a wilted flower. He was younger than the others, too, and handsome, and Isabel could see no mark of violence on him anywhere. But he was dead just the same. "They were arranged in a clearing near the grove," Kevin explained.

"Arranged?" she said.

"Aye," old Wat replied, his leathery face more gray than his beard. "In a triangle, head to foot, with their arms outstretched, like this." He scratched the beginnings of the pattern in the ashes on the hearth, but his wife, Glynnis, struck the stick from his hand with a shriek.

"Old fool," she scolded, rubbing out the scratches with her foot.

"The young one is the miller's son," Tom said, looking even more greensick than Isabel felt as he stared at the dead man's face.

"The one who was with Susannah?" Isabel said, putting a hand on his shoulder.

"Aye, he was with her." He looked back at her, a strange light in his eyes. "But he wasn't the only one."

"What is it?" Brautus said, coming in with a speed to put his injuries to shame. "What has happened?" He saw the corpses and stopped, appalled. "Isabel . . . come away from there."

"Brautus . . ." Without thinking, she ran to him, hiding her face in his shoulder.

"Hush now," he rumbled, holding her with his good arm. "It's all right." She wrapped her arms around him, desperate to believe him. "It will be all right."

Simon awoke from unquiet dreams to find Orlando and Raymond, the peasant from the woods, standing over him. "The sun is down," Orlando said, looking grim. Simon had released him from the catacombs at dawn, but they had barely spoken, the vampire saving his confessions for the night, when he would be wakeful enough to defend himself.

"My lord, you must come," Raymond interrupted. "My lady needs you in the hall."

"Is she all right?" Simon asked him, getting up.

"For the moment," the man answered, pale and obviously frightened. "Please, just come."

He made it to the hall just as Isabel was running to the arms of her Black Knight. "My lord," Kevin said in obvious relief as he came to meet him. "Christ save us, come and see." Brautus scowled at him as he passed, still murmuring comfort to Isabel, but she didn't look up from his shoulder. And once Simon saw the bodies, he was just as glad.

Two were the brigands he had murdered himself, looking no better for their day spent dead in the woods, but the third was worse somehow, a man he had never seen before. "Where did you find them?" he asked, pretending to wince at the wound in the first one's thick throat as if he hadn't been the one to put it there. "Were they together?"

"Aye." Kevin stood just at his elbow. "We were just telling Lady Isabel, they were left in a sort of witch's pattern in the woods."

"Witches my arse," Brautus scoffed. "You there, Sir Crusader—I thought you killed this wolf."

Simon looked back at him, suppressing a smile. In a different world, he would have been quite fond of Brautus, he thought. "So did I," he said. He made a careful examination of his second kill to satisfy his audience, then moved on to the only one he needed to see, the handsome peasant. "No wolf did this."

"No, my lord," Wat said eagerly. "I said as much myself—I said it looks as though he died of fright."

"Nay, Dad, he looks too peaceful," Kevin objected. "Look at his face." Hannah let out a sob, and Isabel made a small sound from behind them as well.

"Hush," Simon warned, giving each man a look that they returned with an understanding nod. "Enough." He turned the dead man's head to one side, silently praying he would not see what he was almost certain he must, but there it was—a pair of tiny puncture marks in his throat.

"Look there," Kevin said, pointing, and Wat made the sign of the cross with a whispered oath.

"I see it." Simon touched the almost dainty wound. The marks were too close together; no man's bite could have made them. But it was almost certainly the kill of a vampire.

"Susannah," Hannah said from behind him. "Someone has to find her."

"Find her?" Simon said, turning around.

"She never came back from the dance," Isabel explained. She looked as pale as the others, but she was no longer huddled in Brautus's arms. "The men had gone to look for her when they found these men lying dead in the woods near Mother Bess's cottage."

"Not even hidden," Wat agreed. "Out in the open for all the world to see."

Simon drew the dagger from his belt and pierced the dead man's breast over his heart.

"Sweet Jesus," Glynnis squeaked, reaching for her husband.

"No blood," Wat said in an awestruck whisper as he held his wife.

"There wouldn't be," Isabel said, reaching Simon's side. "Dead men don't bleed." She touched Simon's arm and nodded, bracing herself not to be sick.

He plunged the dagger into the corpse's heart and twisted, making Hannah scream. But the spurt of blood that should have come did not. A thick red foam formed just around the blade, but that was all. Simon looked at Wat. "No blood."

"Holy Christ," Hannah cried, sinking down on a bench as if her legs would support her no longer. "What is this devilry?" she said as Kevin went to join her. "What has taken Susannah?"

"I don't know, love," Kevin said, holding her close. "Maybe she's still all right."

"Let us hope," Simon agreed, trying to sound like he meant it. Some vampire had killed this man, a vampire with the delicate mouth of a woman or a child. Hannah had the truth of it. Something had taken Susannah. "Double-bar the gates," he said to Brautus, wiping the dagger and returning it to his belt. "Set a guard on the wall over the drawbridge and in back as well. Keep watch over the lake." He met Isabel's eyes with his own. "I'll be back as soon as I can."

Isabel watched him leave the hall, frozen in shock. He couldn't really mean to just charge out into the dark by himself. Orlando was standing just opposite her, staring at the bodies with the strangest look on his face she had ever seen, almost a smile but frightened as well. Feeling her eyes, the wizard looked up, and his face was ashen under his long, gray beard.

"Simon, wait," she called, her paralysis broken as she hurried after him.

She caught him in the archway and drew him back into the shadows of the corridor to the hall. "Where will you go?" She held him by either wrist. "How will you find Susannah?"

"I don't know," he admitted. "I'll start where those men were found . . ." He saw tears in her eyes. "Darling, no." He drew her to him and held her close, feeling her tremble as she clung to him, feeling her tears on his skin as she cried, her face pressed to his chest at the opening of his shirt. "Shhh," he murmured, stroking her hair, desperate love washing over him in a wave. "It's all right."

"It is not." She clung to him with all her strength, her heart pounding with fear and love combined. She couldn't let go of her wits this way; she must be brave for Charmot. But she didn't want to be brave. She wanted to cry and let Simon hold her; she wanted him to keep her safe.

"No," he agreed, kissing her brow. "But it will be." Suddenly the very idea that some other demon might try to come here, might threaten his beloved, filled him with an almost blinding rage. "I will find it." He drew back to frame her face in his hands as he made his promise. "Whatever is in the forest, whatever has taken

Susannah and murdered her lover, I will find it, and I will destroy it."

"And what if you cannot?" she said. "Did you see Orlando's face?"

"What?" He let her go, confused. "No. What does Orlando have to do with—"

"He's frightened, Simon." Raymond passed by them, headed for the wall, no doubt, and she drew him deeper into the shadows. "When the first woman was murdered, Orlando barely batted an eye. When we suggested you might be in danger in the wood by yourself, he acted like it was some kind of a joke, like we were fools to even think it. But now he's afraid."

"I'm sure he is not," Simon promised with a smile.

"Ask him." Watching him smile, so brave and careless, all she could think of was what he would look like if he was wrong, his bloodless body laid on the floor of the hall, his throat torn open, his eyes staring sightless at the beams above. "Does he know what killed those men, Simon?" she asked. Simon is my only hope, the wizard had told her his first morning at Charmot. My warrior and my salvation. But just what did he mean for Simon to fight? "Does Orlando know what is in the woods?" she asked her lover now.

"No." Her question caught him completely off guard; for a moment the lie would hardly come out. "Of course he does not, no more than I do myself."

"Are you certain?" Is he lying? she thought. He sounded unsure, not his usual manner at all. But why would he lie? "Simon, if you know something, I need you to tell me, not protect me. I am not—"

"You are not a child," he finished for her with a smile. He cradled her cheek in his hand. "Trust me, love. I know that." He kissed her sweetly on the lips, and she allowed it, kissing him back. She wanted to be strong, to make him tell her the truth, but she couldn't be certain he hadn't told it already. She didn't want to fight with him, not now.

"Be careful," she said, brusque with feeling, fighting the near-compulsion to throw herself into his arms again as he drew back.

"I will," he promised. Brushing a final kiss across her brow, he left her, following another man into the courtyard.

She went back to the hall where the corpses were being carried away. Glynnis and Hannah were huddled together in a corner, Hannah obviously in tears. Isabel's heart ached as well, remembering Susannah in this room the day before, how happy and pretty she had been. How could she be gone? What sort of monster could have wanted to hurt her?

Mother Bess was sitting by the fire, so close the cinders were in danger of setting her skirts aflame. Kevin had said the bodies had been found barely a stone's throw from her door. "Mother Bess," Isabel said, going to join her. "Are you well? Is there anything you need?"

The old woman looked up, startled, then she smiled. "Come and sit with me, my lady." She took Isabel's hand between her own. "To think that I should live so long," she said softly, a tremor in her voice.

"You will live a great deal longer, Mother," Isabel said with a smile.

"Brave little girl." She gave her hand a squeeze before she let it go.

"I'm not a little girl anymore," Isabel answered. "And I don't feel very brave."

"Not to worry, child," the old woman said with a nod. "Your mother had the sight; her vision was true." She touched Isabel's cheek. "But you are such a pretty thing."

"Thank you." In truth, she had no idea what the dear old creature was talking about, but she supposed it really didn't matter. After all that had happened, she felt like she might babble a little herself.

"Your mother knew you would be pretty," Mother Bess said, searching her face with eyes grown cloudy with age. "She said you would charm the wolf."

"The wolf?" Isabel repeated. "Mother, the wolf is dead. Simon killed him, remember?"

"The wolf cannot die, my darling. You know that. Even your fool of a father must have told you that." The last of the bodies was carried past them, the soldier with his throat torn out, and they both made the sign of the cross. "Much that is dead can still rise."

"My father would have called that superstition, Mother," Isabel said with a smile. "Is that why you call him a fool?"

"The Norman would not see fire burning in his bed," the old woman scoffed. "But your mother loved him; she would have no other." A tear slid down her withered cheek. "She knew he would give her our champion."

A cold tremor passed through her, though why she couldn't have said. "I think you must be upset, Mother Bess," she said. "You're not talking sense. Let me get you some broth or some wine—"

"You need not be afraid, child," the old woman said, catching her by the wrist with surprising strength. "You will beat him in the end." With her free hand, she caressed Isabel's cheek. "But you will mourn your man, I think. I grieve for that young man."

"Simon?" Any other time, she would have humored the woman without paying her any real mind. But tonight her words were so near to Isabel's own fears, they seemed to reach her very heart. "Do you mean Simon?"

"He has a mark on him as well," Mother Bess nodded. "But I cannot read it."

"Why do you say I will mourn him?" Isabel demanded. "What do you think will hurt him?"

"The wolf, my child," the old woman said, sounding surprised by the question. "The wolf will bear no rivals."

"'Tis a dark, ill night, old mother," Brautus said. Isabel had been so engrossed in what Mother Bess was saying, she hadn't noticed him behind her. "A cottage alone might make a poor shelter, don't you think?"

The old woman drew back from Isabel, glaring at him. "Tell me what you mean," Isabel insisted, more confused than ever. "What wolf?"

"You should burn in hell, old man," Mother Bess said. "You and your fool of a master."

"You should have some soup and give your bones a rest," Brautus answered her. "And your tongue as well."

"She knows nothing?" the old woman demanded, gesturing at Isabel. "You have told her nothing?"

"And what should I have told her?" he scoffed. "My lady is too old for fairy tales."

"Maybe I'm not," Isabel interrupted. In truth, whatever the ancient crone thought she should know, it didn't sound like any fairy tale she had ever heard. "Tell me."

"Things are bad enough already," Brautus said. "We don't need this old witch making matters worse with a lot of pagan foolishness."

"Tell me, Mother Bess," Isabel repeated. "Pay him no mind; this is my castle, not his." She took the old woman's hand. "Who is this wolf who cannot die?"

The old woman touched her cheek and smiled. "You are so like your mother." Then her expression clouded, her gaze stealing over Isabel's shoulder to Brautus. "But yes, I am hungry," she said, letting her go. "I will have some soup."

"You are needed in the kitchen, my lady," Brautus said. She turned to glare at him, and he smiled, looking tired. "I swear to you, poppet, it's nothing." He touched her cheek as well. "Haven't we got enough to frighten us already?"

Isabel wanted to argue, but what would be the use? "I will bring your soup, Mother," she said, getting up. "We can talk later." Giving Brautus a final baleful glance, she headed for the kitchen.

When Simon returned to the castle, he found Orlando waiting in the stable. "Did you see the girl?"

"Not a sign." He climbed down from Malachi's back. "How are the others?"

"Frightened but quiet." Isabel was right, Simon thought; the wizard looked frightened himself.

"Orlando, it's all right," he said, unfastening the horse's saddle. "I killed two of those men myself, and the third . . ." He let his voice trail off, loath to even say it.

"The third was killed by the girl," Orlando finished for him. "Did you turn her?"

"No, I never saw Susannah last night either." As he unsaddled and rubbed down his mount, he explained how he had spent the night before, starting with a slightly censored version of his time with Isabel and ending with the vampire he had made, the knight, Tristan. "He bit me back," he said with an incredulous smile, still shocked to think of it. "And you were right, by the way. I could never have done that and not known it. I've never felt anything like it." He stroked Malachi's neck. "I suppose Tristan must have turned Susannah."

"A new-made vampire with no one to show him how?" Orlando said. "Not likely." He sat down heavily on a bale of hay, wiping his face with a cloth.

"Then who?" Simon had never seen his small friend so worried, even the night they had met. "Orlando, what are you thinking?"

"Kivar." He looked up, pale and grim. "It is Lucan Kivar."

"You can't be serious." Simon almost laughed, the thought was so ridiculous. "Kivar is dead—"

"No," Orlando cut him off, shaking his head. "Not dead, just driven from his solid form, from his vampire body."

"Which amounts to the same thing," Simon said.

"No, it does not." He took his seer's stones from his pocket and rattled them in his fist. "If somehow he has found another host, another way to possess a human form; if he has found you—"

"He would have attacked me long ago," Simon pointed out. "I agree that something strange is happening here, strange even for us, but why should we think it has aught to do with Kivar?"

"The way the bodies were arranged," Orlando said. "Two killed by you, his vampire son, and one by a vampire daughter." He shuddered. "It is an old device." He dropped the stones on the straw-covered floor and bent over them for a moment. "I see nothing," he finished with a sigh.

"Because there is nothing to see." Simon hated the notion that he was somehow connected forever to the monster who had made him, that he was Kivar's vampire son. He hated it so much that Orlando had learned long ago not to say it for fear of sending him into a rage. That he was doing so now only proved how worried he was. "That kind of pattern is known here, too, you know," he said. "These people come from druid stock, remember? A native vampire might think he was a warlock, might try to use the old magic to cure himself or to gain more power." But Tristan wasn't from this plain, he thought in spite of himself. "In any case, we should keep a close watch on those bodies tonight."

"Yes." Orlando gathered up the stones. "Come then."

"You go; I'll be along." He scratched Malachi between the ears before he left the stall. "I want to make certain Isabel is all right."

Isabel paced her tower room, a dozen different terrors spinning in her head. As soon as she heard Simon's footsteps coming up the stairs, she flung open the door and rushed into the corridor to meet him. As soon as she saw him, she threw herself into his arms.

"I was so scared." She clung to him with all her might, her cheek pressed to his chest. You will mourn him, the old woman's voice spoke in her head.

"It's all right, love," he promised. "It's all right." He kissed her, and she rose up on tiptoe to reach him, her arms entwined around his neck.

She kissed his cheek, his jaw, his throat, fear becoming passion in a single moment, a kind of lover's madness. He lifted her off her feet, carrying her back into her room, and she wrapped her legs around him as well.

"Did you find Susannah?" she asked as he kicked the door shut behind them.

"No, love." He kissed her deeply. "I'm sorry—"

"No, don't be sorry." She kissed him, crushing his mouth under hers. "You're safe." She held him to her, caressing his hair, weak with longing as he kissed her throat. "I need you to be safe." He pressed her to the cold stone wall, his hips pushed hard against her, and she slid down his body, her legs still twined around his. "I need you." She dragged up her own skirt, melting as his mouth found hers.

"I need you." He sounded just as desperate as she felt, and his hands moved over her feverishly, brutal and tender at once as he reached under her skirt. He crushed her hard against his wall, his sex against her stomach, then grinding lower as he lifted her up again, and a hot wave of desire tore through her like lightning, making her gasp as they kissed. His hands slid under her behind, holding her easily, and she laughed, caressing his neck, kissing under his hair. He was strong; he could hold her forever. He could keep her safe.

She kissed his eyelids, his brow, nuzzled his cheek as his mouth found her throat and moved lower still, bathing her skin with his tongue. His hand stroked her flesh, her inner thigh, then higher, and she writhed against his touch, her breath coming faster. "I want you," she said, bending her head to his shoulder, sweet waves of bliss radiating through her as his touch pressed deeper. Her breasts felt swollen and deliciously tender as he kissed them through her gown, suckling her nipples through the cloth, first one and then the other. "I want you inside me."

His hand opened her sex, rough with desire, and she moaned against his shoulder, stifling a scream. Then suddenly his hand was on her cheek and it was his sex filling her up, a single, breathless stroke that seemed to touch her very soul. She laughed, dizzy with pure, sweet joy, and he moved, a steady, brutal rhythm like the beating of her heart. "Angel," he murmured, hoarse with desire. "Isabel . . ." Her hips rose to meet him, matching her rhythm to his, and he shifted her closer, thrusting in deeper, making her cry out.

"Yes . . ." She was crying, and he cradled her close, kissing her cheek, their bodies still moving as one. "Simon, please don't stop."

"Never." His kiss moved to her throat, turning cruel, a bite, and she cried out again in pleasure, not pain. A different kind of ecstasy rushed through her, making her swoon in his arms as her climax rose and fell and rose again. She was dying, surely, but she didn't care, not if he was with her, not if he would never let her go.

Simon had not meant to bite her, but he couldn't stop. His demon's fangs were tearing her flesh; her blood was on his tongue, and the pleasure was like nothing he had ever felt before. Her body embraced him as he fed, pliant and burning with life, her soul in his mouth, liquid fire like he had drunk so many times before. But this was no stranger, no meaningless prey; this was Isabel, his love. Tearing his mouth from her throat, he passed his tongue over the wound, a final thrill of taste as his demon's magic hid the mark. She sighed in his arms as if she felt the loss as deeply as he did himself, the loss of this demon's kiss. He kissed her mouth instead, adoring and breathless, and his body shuddered, spilling into hers.

"Simon," she murmured, caressing his face with her hands as she brushed her mouth across his cheek and lips. He wrapped his arms around her, molding her body to his as he carried her to the bed, crushing her beneath him as they fell. But he couldn't stay; the dawn was coming. He could not let himself sleep in her arms. He felt tears rising in his eyes, tears of her blood he could not let her see.

"Simon?" He was getting up, she realized in shock; he was leaving her again. "Simon, no." She sat up, reaching for him. "Stay here. Stay with me."

"I can't." He sounded tearful, but his face was turned away. "The dawn will be here soon—"

"So let it come." She turned his face to hers. "My

love, I swear it isn't real." She kissed his cheek, her heart aching with love. "This curse isn't real."

He gathered her close for a moment, hiding his face over her shoulder. "I wish it were not." He kissed her hair, fighting back tears. "I so very much wish it were not."

He was holding her so hard he hurt her, but she could still feel him pulling away, retreating into the pain that shut her out. "Tell me, Simon," she ordered as he kissed her cheek. "Tell me what Orlando has told you; why has he said you are cursed?"

"Orlando?" He drew back. "No, darling, it isn't Orlando—"

"Then what?" He turned away. "Simon, stop. What do you want me to do?" If he said to stay away from him, she would murder him on the spot, she thought. "Do you mean for me to keep you as a plaything forever, my lover I keep in the cellar?" she joked, touching his shoulder.

"No," he promised, turning back to her with a bitter smile.

"Do you mean to leave me then?" Her face flushed hot, her pride long ignored but not forgotten. "Am I the plaything instead?"

"No." He knelt on the floor before her and took her hands in his. "I would marry you, beloved, if I could."

"Then do it." She thought she must be going mad; joy and grief were so entwined inside her heart they seemed to be the same. "Ask me to be your wife."

"I can't." He kissed each of her palms. "I know you think . . . but you're wrong." He looked up at her. "When this curse is broken, I am yours."

"When this curse is broken." She looked away, her hands limp and still in his grip. "Will that ever be?"

How could he answer her? he thought. For ten years he had searched for salvation and not found it; how could he promise her that he would find it now? "I don't know." He rose to his feet. "I—"

"Don't." She looked up at him. "Please, don't tell me you're sorry."

He smiled, but it was not with joy. "I will not." He bent and kissed her forehead. "Sleep well, love."

"You, too." She watched him go, needing all the will she had to stop herself from running after him. When this curse is broken, I am yours, he had promised. Then broken it would be.

10

❧ ❧

Simon found Orlando snoring on the ground near the bodies, his lantern long burned out. He examined the corpses himself, but apparently none of them had so much as twitched all night. These three were well and truly dead, their souls dispatched for heaven or hell as suited God, not evil. Simon rather envied them. He thought again of Isabel's face when she asked him if his curse would ever be broken and the coward's answer that was all he had to give. All his fine promises to the contrary, he had broken her heart.

The sky was growing lighter. A line of dawning purple traced the castle wall and glowed on the surface of the lake. The sun would kill him; this was one of the great, unchanging truths of his vampire life. To kill in darkness was to live; to stand in the light was to die. But how did it happen? Orlando had described undead bodies bursting into flames, consumed into ashes in a moment, but how would that feel? Would his consciousness pass into hell in an instant, becoming a demon indeed, or would his soul move on to judgment as if he were a man? Orlando had no answer for such a question; he did not think of hell or paradise as Simon did, did not believe in the same God. And Simon's own theology was not equal to the task. The priest in his home village had never heard tell of a vampire.

The first pale rays of sunlight pierced the trees along the lake shore, reaching for the shadow of the castle where he stood. He felt a prickle on his skin similar to the sensation he would feel walking into a church, only stronger, reaching deeper through his flesh to the bone. In a moment, he would explode into hellfire, every cursed particle that made him transformed at the same instant into flame. He waited, entranced, as still as the corpses lying dead before him, watching as the sunlight crawled across the ground, moving ever closer to his feet.

"Simon!" Orlando rushed at him, flinging all his weight against him to push him to the open cellar door. They plunged together through the opening and fell backward down the stairs as sunlight swept over the wall. Smoke rose from Simon's clothes and boots as the wizard scrambled back up the steps to the door, climbing like a beetle on his hands and knees as Simon felt the burning rising up inside him, pain like nothing he could have imagined. A scream formed deep inside his mind that his throat was too far lost to voice, drowning out every thought of guilt or truth or salvation. Then Orlando slammed the door, and the burning stopped.

"Are you mad?" the wizard demanded, limping as he

came back down the stairs. "Ten years of fighting, of searching, and now, with the prize all but within your reach, you think to surrender?" Simon made no effort to answer him; he had no answer to give, no explanation the dwarf could ever understand. He sat up on the cold, earthen floor, bowing his head to his hands.

"Never mind, warrior," Orlando said, patting the vampire's shoulder as if he might have been a grieving child as he passed. "Come, you must rest. You will have much work to do tonight."

Isabel walked out into the courtyard, yawning in the early morning light. Kevin and Tom were coming down from the castle wall as she emerged, and Raymond's cousin and Wat were headed up. Another group of men were coming from the stables, carrying shovels and picks, and Kevin and Tom went to join them.

"What are you doing?" she asked, going to meet them.

Kevin looked at her, surprised. "We're going to bury those bodies, my lady. I thought we'd put them in the orchard, near the back where those trees have died out—"

"No." Suddenly all she could think of was what Mother Bess had said. *Much that is dead can still rise.* She had tried again the night before to speak to the old woman, but she wouldn't say any more, and in her mind, she thought Brautus must surely be right, that the tales she told were nonsense. But in her heart, she

ll right," she said with a nod. "I will wait for you
ere."

"Good." He grinned. "See if you can make up with
rautus; that should keep you busy."

"Oh, Brautus will come around," she promised. "It's
eally you he dislikes, not me. He thinks I've given you
far too much consideration here, that I've treated you
far better than you deserve."

"And so you have." He sounded almost cheerful, the
Irish rogue again.

"Yes, but Brautus doesn't know it," she retorted,
blushing as she smiled. "Once he sees you're not some
scoundrel after my castle, he should take to you well
enough. Everyone else seems to like you."

He took her into his arms. "It isn't your castle I
want," he said softly, almost a growl, as he bent to kiss
her. For half a moment, she thought about the others
watching and what they might think. She was the lady
of Charmot, after all; she should think about her dignity. But as soon as she felt his lips touch hers, every
such thought was forgotten.

"So what is it?" she said, speaking just as softly as he
roke the kiss. "What is it you want?"

His answer was to press her closer and kiss her more
eply, the only answer he could make. "Keep the gate
rred and the drawbridge up," he ordered, letting her
"We should not be long."

Not to worry, sweeting," she promised with an imp-
mile. "Brautus may be furious with me, but he and

couldn't be sure. "We must take them to the church,"
she said to Kevin. "They must be buried in sacred
ground."

"The church is an hour's ride away from here, my
lady, and that on horseback," Kevin said. "No one here
will care to venture so far from the castle, not with a
killer in the woods." Several of the other men mumbled
their agreement. "Not in daylight, anyway."

"Not in daylight?" she echoed. "Kevin, that's ridiculous. Daylight is safer—"

"Not without Sir Simon, I should have said," he corrected. "If he thinks we should take these men to the
church tonight, I think there are some who would go.
But not now."

"Not on my order, you mean," she retorted. Once
again, they all seemed to accept Simon's right to rule
here completely without question, stranger that he
was and strange as his habits might be. Never mind
that she had been their lady all her life, that she had
spent the last ten years shut up behind these walls to
keep them safe.

"It isn't that, my lady," one of the other men
protested. "We want to oblige you, truly. But . . ." He
looked around at the others for support.

"Sir Simon is a knight," Kevin finished for him. "He
can protect us. You cannot."

"No," she said coldly. "I suppose I cannot." They all
looked miserable, at least. "Then we will wait for
Simon."

* * *

Simon awoke at sunset to find the entire household in the castle courtyard. "What is this?" he asked Orlando, coming down the steps.

"Lady Isabel insists the dead men must be given proper Christian burial at the Chapel of Saint Joseph," the wizard explained. "They expect you to lead them there."

"You jest," Simon answered. But in truth, that was exactly what it looked like. The wagon was hitched to its team, and the three bodies had been laid inside, covered over with blankets. A whole procession's worth of men were waiting beside it, armed and obviously anxious. "I will talk to her."

"I would wait a moment, if I were you," Orlando advised. "She's busy arguing with her captain."

"Brautus, can't you see I'm frightened?" Isabel was saying in the meantime. Brautus had come down, prepared to go with the others, but the very thought was more than she could bear. "If I had my absolute choice, we would drop those bodies in the lake, and no one would leave the castle. But that would be wrong. Someone has to take them to the church. But not everyone, and not you. I don't mean to protect you by keeping you here; I mean for you to protect the household." He made a disgusted little snort that made her want to hit him, but she took his hand instead. "I am the lady of Charmot, and I need you. Will you abandon me?"

If she had struck him, he couldn't have lo[ ] shocked. "Never," he said, his jaw clenc[ ] Shooting a final glower in Simon's direction as toward them, he turned and went into the cast[ ]

"Brautus!" she called after him, but he was g[ ]

Simon reached her side. "Shall I try to s[ ] him?"

"God's faith, no," she said with a bitter little "He'd probably try to kill you."

"I wouldn't blame him." Her eyes widened, an[ ] smiled. "I would in his place. He has been the Bl[ ] Knight for quite some time, I hear."

"Yes," she said, smiling back. "He has."

"So what is this about going to the church?" he asked.

"Simon, we have to," she said. "We have no i[ ] how those men were killed or who two of them w[ ] we owe them a Christian burial." There was some[ ] more, he could tell. Something had convinced he[ ] to bury these men at the church would protec[ ] somehow, keep her castle safe from the evil th[ ] killed them in the first place. Who was he to[ ] otherwise?

"Very well," he nodded. "But you are stayi[ ]

"Simon—"

"Lady Isabel." He touched her chin, turn[ ] up to his. "I will comply with your wishes [ ] will carried out. But I will not risk your sa[ ]

If he meant to be mocking her, he h[ ]

I have been holding this fortress together for quite some time now. I think we can manage one more night."

Something about her words made him shiver, demon that he was. "Just be safe." Kissing her softly one last time, he turned to the men who were waiting, pretending not to notice what he and their lady were doing and making a poor job of it. "Come, Kevin," he said. "Let's see this done and come home."

Isabel watched him mount Malachi as if he had been born to ride him, watched the men of her father's castle follow him without a moment's question. You can help him, Orlando had promised. You can save him from this curse. The little wizard, riding his new pony, stopped at the gate and turned to wave to her, and she smiled and waved back. She would help Simon. She even knew how.

This time the gates of the chapel swung open as soon as Simon knocked. "My lord," Father Colin said, coming out to greet him. "Kevin sent word what had happened." He stared for a moment at Simon's face, his eyes clouding with confusion, but after a moment they cleared with no further sign he recognized him at all. "Please, all of you, come inside."

Three fresh graves had already been dug in the churchyard's consecrated ground. "We cannot know what manner of Christians these strangers might have been," the priest explained to Simon as the bodies were laid to rest. "But all in the village know the miller's son,

Jack, was a godly man." An older man and woman who must have been Jack's parents stood beside his grave, the woman sobbing in her husband's arms. "Their only son," Father Colin finished with a sigh.

Simon felt sick just watching, the guilt he felt writhing inside him. These good people had done nothing to deserve their pain, yet he had brought it to them even so. Could even the Chalice be worth such a price? Even if it existed, even if he could find it, why should he think himself worthy of the salvation it was supposed to offer? He turned away as the priest began the funeral mass, picking up a fallen shovel, the sacred ground suddenly burning under his feet like the sands of the desert as he walked away with Orlando following close behind him, carrying a lantern he had brought from the wagon.

It seemed a century since he had stood here in this garden, but in fact it was only a matter of weeks. This was where he had made his first kill at Charmot; this was where the curse he had brought on this plain had begun. The corner where he had buried Michel and his men was just as Isabel had described it to him the night she had made him promise to protect her castle; the ground in one grave-sized plot had obviously been disturbed. Moving closer, he could see it had sunk in even deeper, until it looked only half-filled with earth.

"So there it is, wizard," he said. "Do you still think Isabel imagined it?"

"No," Orlando admitted. "But I still don't know how

it happened or what manner of creature is inside."

Simon glanced back at the others, still engrossed in the funeral. "There's only one way to find out."

All the time he was digging, he expected Michel to rise up, but the ground under his feet didn't stir. After a few minutes, his shovel struck what was unmistakably a corpse, making a nasty, squelching thud. "Stand back," Simon ordered as a terrible stench rolled up from the grave. Orlando nodded, but he stayed where he was, holding the light.

Simon laid the shovel aside and bent down in the grave, bracing himself for a pitiable sight as he brushed the last of the dirt away with his hand. But what he saw still made him cry out in shock. Staring up at him in the dim light of the lantern was his long-lost patron, Francis, the duke of Lyan.

"Holy Christ," the vampire rasped in his own native Gaelic, a language he had not spoken in years, the words burning his tongue as he stumbled backward, almost falling on the corpse. "Sweet Mary of God . . . this cannot be." The duke had been buried in the cursed mountains where he died; Simon had dug the grave himself. And even if he had not, his body had been without life for ten years; it should have rotted and crumbled to dust long before now. Yet here was the face Simon had loved so well he had followed it across the world, lifeless and pale but intact. He brushed more of the earth away and found that the head had been cleaved from the shoulders, and a wound gaped in the chest over the heart. He stepped back and looked up at Orlando, who still stood at the edge of the grave. "How can this be?"

"Kivar," Orlando said. "It must have been Kivar."

"Why are you so shocked, my love?" a woman's voice spoke from the shadows. "You put him there yourself." Susannah emerged from the trees, even more beautiful in cursed death than she had been in life, her Maying gown translucent in the moonlight. "You told me," she finished with a beatific smile.

"I told you?" Simon said, climbing from the grave.

"Two nights past, in the grove," she answered. "Do you not remember?" She came closer, madness gleaming in her eyes. She had not just been taken by a vampire; her innocent mind had been broken. "Don't you remember your promise, my lord?" She laid a hand on his chest, an obscene parody of her old flirtatious smile on her lips. "You told me that you loved me."

"Susannah, I did not," Simon said, taking her hand.

She frowned. "You promised I would be lady of Charmot." She bent her cheek to his hand like a kitten begging a caress. "I didn't want to kill Lady Isabel, but you said you must."

"Susannah, listen to me," he said, putting a hand on his sword. "I never saw you that night. I never made you any promise—"

"You made me what I am!" She smiled, holding her pale arms up to the moonlight as if to admire their beauty. "I am perfect now, you said." She looked at him in hunger that could almost seem like love. "You said I will never die."

"Susannah, I did not do this," Simon said, his heart aching with pity for her even as his stomach crawled with revulsion.

"Kivar," Orlando repeated. "He must have changed his shape to look like you."

"Is she dead?" Susannah said. "I must weep for her."

"Susannah!" Tom came running toward them, his boyish face alight with relief. "You're alive." Before Simon could stop him, he had run to the vampire and taken her into his arms.

"You see?" she said, smiling over his shoulder, her fangs pure white in the moonlight. "Tom still loves me, at least." She tilted the boy's head to one side, baring her fangs for the bite.

"No!" Simon roared, his horrorstruck paralysis broken. He raised the sword and struck Susannah's head from her shoulders, the mouth still screaming as it fell. Tom stumbled backward as Simon drove his sword point into the vampire's breast, the body lurching and writhing as he pinned it to the ground, then exploding over all three of them in a shower of foul, blackish blood.

The boy stared at him, aghast. "You killed her."

"No, Tom." He took a step toward him, using his vampire's power to entrance him. "She was already dead." A trickle of blood flowed down the boy's neck from the vampire's bite, but he didn't seem badly hurt. "Susannah was not here."

"Not here," Tom answered, his eyes locked to Simon's. "Susannah is dead."

"Tom!" Kevin came toward them, freezing when he saw his son. "Holy Christ, my lord . . ." Simon, Tom, and Orlando were all three covered with the vampire's blood. "What happened?"

"A demon," Simon answered. I didn't want to kill Lady Isabel, Susannah had said. But you said you must. "Take care of him, and of Orlando." Kivar or whoever had murdered Susannah meant to kill Isabel as well. "I have to go back to Charmot."

11

❧ ❧

Isabel lit the candles in her bedroom, moving quickly, barely wincing as a drop of melting tallow burned her finger. Compared to what she meant to do, that tiny hurt was nothing. She fished her father's torn and crumpled parchments from the chest at the foot of the bed and threw them on the table along with the purse of coins Mary had given her and the silver cross she had found in the churchyard, then dug through another, smaller cask on the table beside her bed until she found the tiny dagger that had once belonged to her mother, a simple peasant's knife with a handle of bone and a blade so thin and sharp it could cut through leather and barely leave a mark.

She sat down at the table and arranged the shredded corners of her father's code she had already torn from the parchments before her, then used the knife to carefully cut away the ones remaining and added them to the pile, tearing them to pieces as she went. Setting the rest of the scrolls aside on the floor, she spread the bits in a single layer, making sure they touched. Then she picked up the knife.

"Forgive me, Papa," she whispered. This magic was not for her; she had no business attempting it. But she had no other choice. Gritting her teeth against the pain, she sliced open her palm, spilling her blood on the parchment. Spinning and tumbling in a chaotic frenzy, the pieces writhed and shifted on the table, some tearing themselves into even smaller bits as others joined together until at last she saw a single page before her. Tunnels twisted over most of it like water snakes, but she could make out a larger, rounded gap in the center where three of the tunnels converged—her father's study. A single character sketched in her blood marked this spot, and a scarlet trail led out from it into the labyrinth, marking a pathway just as she had guessed. Somehow, she had made a druid's map.

"This is it," she whispered, tracing the path with her fingertip, thinking of Simon's curse, his belief that the key lay somewhere in the catacombs. "This has to be it."

A gust of icy wind rushed through the open window, much too cold for May, and the candles on the table sputtered and went out. Still holding the map, she got up to take the candle from her bedside to relight them and almost screamed aloud. Simon was standing behind her.

"God's faith," she said, pressing a hand to her chest. "You scared me."

He smiled. "I'm sorry."

"Aren't you always?" she retorted, but she couldn't really be angry. "What are you doing back here so soon?"

He touched her, picking up a lock of her hair and examining it with a bemused smile as if he had never seen its color before. "Where else should I be?" He looked just the same as always, his angel's face just the same, and his voice with its hint of Irish brogue was just as deep and soft as ever. But something was different; a different sort of light was shining in his deep brown eyes.

"You went to the churchyard." She backed away from him a step, her skin prickling with unreasonable fear, the map still clutched in her fist behind her back.

"Oh, yes," he nodded. "That." He touched her cheek, and an icy shiver raced down her spine. His hands were always cool to the touch, but never like this. "That didn't take long." He traced the shape of her mouth with his fingertips. "Didn't I say I would be back as soon as I could?"

"Yes." She turned her face away from his touch, the tip of her tongue barely tasting his skin as she flinched. He tastes wrong, she thought, her heart beating faster. But surely that was madness. "But I didn't hear your horse or the wagon."

"You must not have been listening." He moved closer, putting a restraining hand on her upper arm when she started to move away. "What are you hiding, love?"

"Nothing," she insisted, ducking to escape, but he kissed her, a rough, brusque kiss that was like nothing he had ever done before, his tongue stabbing into her mouth as his hand tightened almost painfully on her arm. She made a small sound of protest, and his arms closed around her, crushing her to him even as she put her wounded hand against his chest to hold him off.

"Stop it," she ordered, tearing her mouth from his. "Simon, let me go." He did taste wrong; it wasn't madness or her imagination. "What is the matter with you?" She tried to break free, but he wouldn't allow it, pushing her back against the table. "I said stop!" She raised her hand to slap him, and he caught her wrist.

"What's this?" He brought her palm to his mouth, tasting her blood, and for a moment, she thought she must be losing consciousness; the outline of his body seemed to melt and waver before her eyes. Then his tongue swept down the cut, cold as a snake, and he was solid again, a jolt of fury passing through her. "Why have you hurt yourself?" he said with an exaggerated tenderness that she didn't believe for a moment. This man was not Simon. He let go of her wounded hand, now healed, she saw with horrified surprise, and took hold of the one that still held the druid's map. "Oh, my," he said, catching sight of it. An evil smile that was nothing like her lover's spread over his face, making her blood run cold. In the distance she heard hoofbeats, Malachi crossing the drawbridge, the shouts of the men standing guard.

"Who are you?" she demanded, trying to break his grip.

"Aren't you the clever girl?" he said, still smiling, paying her struggles no mind as he lifted her wrist to examine the map more closely. "Did you work this out all by yourself, or did the little wizard help you?"

"You are not Simon." She reached behind her with her free hand, hoping to reach the dagger to stab him or even the purse so she could bash him in the face. But her fingers found the cross instead.

"No," he admitted, his voice changing, growing thicker. "But I will be."

He moved to kiss her again, and without thinking, she punched him, the chain of the cross tangled in her fist. He howled in pain out of proportion to the blow she had managed, flinching backward. She saw the shape of the cross burned into his jaw, still smoking. "Bitch," he snarled, slapping her hard across the cheek, sending her sprawling as the real Simon burst through the door.

"Get away from her!" he roared, the sight of his own image striking his beloved making him livid and dizzy at once. The other vampire turned on him, baring his fangs, and he saw the cross-shaped wound. "You will not touch her again." He bared his own fangs as he advanced, his sword held out before him.

"Think you not?" the other vampire rasped as his shape melted and changed to the shape of Michel, the brand still livid on his thick-lipped face. "I will touch her in ways you have not yet imagined."

Isabel huddled against the side of the bed, the cross still clasped in one hand, the map crumpled in the other. The demon who had struck her had changed his shape to a shorter, stockier bull of a man with a thick French accent—Michel, she realized with horror. Simon advanced on him, protecting her, but he was a demon as well, she saw, a monster with the same cruel fangs.

"I killed you once already," Simon snarled, advancing on this creature, whatever it was. Isabel was safe; that was all that mattered. "I see no reason why I cannot do it again."

"You didn't kill me, precious son," Michel said with a thin, bitter smile that looked completely out of place on his coarse, drunkard's face. "You released me." His features shifted again, his body convulsing as he grew taller to become the duke of Lyan. "Were you glad to see my face again?" he said in the duke's own kindly tone, but his smile was unmistakable, the leer Simon saw in his dreams. "I know how sorely you have missed me."

"Kivar," Simon said raggedly, the word catching in his throat.

"You have done so well, my Simon," he said, for all the world Francis, the duke of Lyan, returned from the grave. "For centuries, I waited for you, knowing you would come." He smiled, retreating slowly in a circle as Simon advanced. "But I never dreamed you would be such a success as this." He turned his gaze on Isabel, his smile becoming the devil's leer again, obscene on the face of the good man Simon had loved. "Look at the treasure you have found."

Isabel scrambled to her feet, tripping on her skirt but determined to stand even so. "Who are you?" she demanded. "What are you?"

"Don't you recognize me, pet?" The demon's face was changing again, his body reforming. Suddenly her father stood before her, looking just the way he had the morning before he died. "You know me in your blood."

"No," she said, shaking her head, trembling all over. She wanted to run to Simon, to hide behind him from this horror, but how could she? He was a horror himself. Every detail she had ever perceived in his arms and forgotten came back to her in a rush. His skin was cool, not warm. He had no heartbeat. But he was her beloved—even now he meant to protect her. You will mourn him, Mother Bess had said. He carries a mark himself.

"What did you think I was doing all those years in the catacombs, sweet daughter?" the demon said. "Writing my memoirs?"

"He lies, Isabel," Simon said. "You know he lies; you have seen what he is."

"You have the evidence there in your hand," the demon insisted. His voice was so familiar and suddenly so kind. She wanted to hear him, to stand there and listen to him speak to her forever, to give him whatever he asked if it would keep him from leaving her again.

"Why did you leave me?" she asked him, taking a step toward him. "Why did you never tell me the truth?"

"Darling, he's entrancing you; it's a trick," Simon insisted, taking a step toward her. "Any vampire can do it."

"Vampire," she repeated, but the word meant nothing. "Papa . . ."

"Come to me, 'Bella," the demon in her father's shape entreated. "Bring me the map."

"Yes." Suddenly everything made sense, every doubt she had ever felt was gone, her confusion clearing like soft clouds before the wind. "You made it." She took a step toward him. "It belongs to you."

"No!" Simon roared, human voice becoming wolvish howl as he transformed. Isabel screamed as he lunged for Kivar, the ancient vampire melting back into the shape of Michel as the fangs of the wolf tore at his throat.

Isabel watched as the two creatures rolled as one across the tower room, Michel shifting again into the great black dog she had mistaken for the peasant's grim, and she grabbed for Simon's fallen sword. But where could she attack? Simon rose up, fangs bared and hackles raised, and suddenly he was a man again, her lover transformed to a monster. The dog lunged at his throat, and he grabbed it by the scruff of the neck, shaking the great beast like a rat even as it tore at his arms and chest with its curving, ivory fangs. The dog changed back into a man, another stranger, tall and thin with hair the same shade of red as her own.

"You cannot kill me, Simon," Kivar said, laughing, and Simon punched him in the face. He laughed harder as he fell back against the table, licking the trickle of borrowed blood from his lips.

"Watch me," Simon answered, charging him with all his strength and lifting him from the floor. He flung him backward toward the open window, and Kivar's eyes widened as he felt himself falling, but still he laughed, changing back into the dog as he fell, twisting in midair. Simon rushed forward, flinging himself toward the window as well, but something stopped him—Isabel, grabbing him from behind.

"No," she said, falling back from him again. "Don't."

He turned back to the window just as the dog hit the ground at the foot of the tower, crumpled and broken, but in a moment, he was up again. Still a dog, he turned and looked back at the castle before plunging into the lake, disappearing in the dark.

"Isabel!" Brautus shouted, running in, sword drawn. "What is it?"

Simon turned again. His love was watching him in horror, tears streaming down her face. "Isabel," he said, starting toward her.

"Stay back!" she ordered, holding up the cross, and he recoiled, blinded with pain. "Don't touch me!"

"Darling, please," he said, weeping blood tears of his own. "Let me make you understand."

"Would you entrance me, too?" she demanded.

"No, I swear." He reached for her, the cross holding him at bay. She had no evil in her heart, no malice, and he had betrayed her, brought hell itself into her sanctuary. "That creature was never your father—"

"And what are you, beloved?" Even now, she could not help but love him; even stained with blood, his face was beautiful, the face of her angel. But how could she believe him? "What is it you want?"

"Just you," he promised, moving closer in spite of the pain, desperate to reach her. "I love you, Isabel."

"No," she said softly, barely louder than a whisper.

"Yes," he promised, coming closer still. "I love you." He reached out to touch her.

"No!" she screamed, backing away, and Brautus attacked, plunging his sword into Simon's stomach. Isabel's screams dried up into a gasp as the vampire stared down at the blade, then back up into Brautus's eyes. "No," she said more softly, almost a whisper. "Brautus, no . . ." She took a step toward him, a sob rising in her throat.

But her lover didn't fall. Suddenly he started laughing, so much like the demon, the vampire who had fallen from the window, she thought she must be dreaming. "Simon?"

Simon fell to his knees, still laughing, and Brautus let go of the sword. "The Black Knight," the vampire rasped, drawing the blade from his stomach, his frozen flesh hissing as it healed.

"Sweet Christ," Isabel said softly, clutching the cross. "Save us, please, dear God . . ."

"He will," Simon answered, letting the sword fall from his hand. "You are innocent."

"And why are you not?" She moved closer, her hand outstretched. She wanted to touch him, to comfort him, but she was afraid, not just for herself, but for Charmot. He looked up at her, the anguish in his eyes like a knife in her heart. But could a demon feel grief? "Tell me, Simon." She held the cross out before her, and he flinched as if it hurt him as it had hurt the other creature. "What are you?" She wept for him, but she feared him, too.

"Vampire." He crouched on the floor, his face turned away, and she thought of the wolf he had become. The wolf . . . Mother Bess had said that the wolf cannot die. Brautus made a noise beside her, and Simon looked up at him, a strange, scary smile on his face. "I am a vampire."

"Begone!" Brautus said, taking the cross from Isabel and thrusting it forward, making Simon recoil. "In the holy name of Christ, begone!"

"No," Isabel said, but Brautus held her back in a grip of iron. "Simon, please, just tell me how to help you." Surely now he would tell her the truth; surely now he could have no more reason to lie. She was the lady of Charmot; she had a duty to protect her people. Her angel was a monster, a vampire. But she loved him even so; even now she wanted nothing more than to comfort him. Surely somehow she could do both. "I want to believe you, Simon. I want to—"

"No." If Simon could have willed his death, he would have at that moment. But he could not die any more than he could live. "There is nothing to believe." Lucan Kivar was returned. The monster had come to his love's very tower, he had touched her. Simon had brought him to her. He staggered to his feet, and Brautus held the cross out again, holding Isabel back. But he didn't need the talisman. Simon wouldn't touch her. "I am sorry, my love." He would protect her even if she hated him; he would save her from Lucan Kivar. He loved her, and he could not stop. But he could leave her. He could keep her safe.

"No!" Isabel lunged for him again, but Brautus held her in a grip of iron. "Simon, stop!" But he was gone.

He fled out the door, moving faster as he reached the stairs. "My lord, what has happened?" Hannah asked as he passed her in the hall, and he broke into a run. He was not her lord and never could be. Malachi was still waiting in the courtyard where he had left him, and he swung into the saddle just as Kevin and the others came charging through the gates.

"My lord!" Kevin shouted. "My lord, wait!" Simon spurred Malachi into a gallop, scattering dogs and gravel in every direction. In a single, mighty leap, they cleared the wagon and thundered through the gates, jumping again as the drawbridge was raised to land with a scramble on the opposite bank. Rearing once as he brought the horse around, the vampire fled into the night.

Isabel heard the horse on the drawbridge and stopped fighting Brautus. It was too late. She would never catch him now. "Damn you," she murmured as he let her go, crumpling to the floor, great gasping sobs threatening to choke her as she fell. Simon had said that he loved her. Simon was a vampire. She touched the sword he had pulled from his own stomach, the blade that should have been thick with his blood. It was as clean as if it had just been lifted from the grindstone and hot enough to burn her fingertips. Her lover was a demon. "No," she said softly through her tears, sinking even deeper until she lay face down on the rug. "It can't be true."

"Oh, no, you don't," Brautus said. He bent down and took hold of her arms, hauling her upright again with no great show of tenderness. "We have no time for that." She stared at him, aghast, as he wiped her eyes with the tail of her apron as he had done when she had fallen down and skinned her knee as a child. "You are the lady of Charmot, remember?" he said more gently as Kevin came running in behind him.

"Lady Isabel, are you all right?" the groom demanded, pale and agitated.

"She's fine," Brautus answered. "Tell us what happened at the churchyard."

"Sir Simon . . . something tried to attack Tom," Kevin said.

"Sir Simon attacked him?" Brautus said.

"No," Kevin said with a frown. "Sir Simon saved him. He is downstairs now. But Sir Simon left us at a gallop. He said he had to come and save Lady Isabel." Isabel gasped, swaying on her feet, and Brautus took hold of her arm.

"He saved me," Isabel said. "If he is evil, Brautus, why did he save me?"

"Hush now," Brautus said, tightening his grip. "Kevin, where is that granddam of yours?"

"Sleeping in our rooms, I think," Kevin answered, looking more confused by the moment. "Lady Isabel, what has happened? Why did Sir Simon flee the castle? Does he need help?"

"Tell Mother Bess to come to the solar," Brautus answered for her. "Tell her Caitlin's daughter needs her help."

"What are you talking about?" Isabel demanded. Caitlin had been her mother's name, but she could not remember Brautus ever mentioning it before. "She wanted to tell me before," she said, remembering. "But you wouldn't let her." The wolf cannot die, the old woman had said. But you will beat him in the end. Simon had transformed to a wolf. Simon was something called a vampire, something Brautus seemed to know but she did not. "You knew!" she said, looking at him in horror.

"Forgive me, my lady, but hush," Brautus ordered, giving her a shake.

Kevin looked back and forth between them with a frown. "Aye, Brautus," he said. "I will bring her." Nodding once to Isabel, he left.

"You knew," she said again, tearing her arm from Brautus's grip.

"No, love, I did not," he answered. "If I had, he never would have crossed the drawbridge, I can promise you." He looked pale, suddenly, and shaken. "But come. It is time to let the old witch say her piece."

Malachi thundered down the forest path with Simon crouched low over his neck. Suddenly the stallion stumbled, sending the vampire sailing over his head without a moment's warning like a stone launched from a flail. He slammed full force against a tree before crashing to the rocky ground, his spine giving way with a horrifying snap. Malachi reared over him, still fighting for his footing, the rope that had tripped him still tangled around his legs.

"Easy," Simon said, trying to stand, but his limbs were shattered, beyond his control. "Easy, boy." He managed to roll out of the pathway, but one of the horse's hooves still came down hard on his leg, crushing it to pulp beneath the animal's weight. "It's all right," he said soothingly, the pain making him feel faint. "It will be all right." He was a vampire; he would heal in an hour or so, but if Malachi should fall trying to avoid him, he would not.

"That's it," he said softly as the horse stopped

prancing to nuzzle him with his nose. "We're fine."
But he couldn't seem to make his arms work to reach
up to him, and he was still restive, obviously still
upset. Suddenly he reared up again, kicking Simon in
the side, stoving in his ribs. The vampire cried out,
unable to stop himself this time, and the stallion galloped away.

"Shit," Simon muttered, borrowing Isabel's worst
oath as he rolled himself onto his back.

"Stop your crying." Kivar had taken back the shape
of the brigand, Michel, along with his manner and
voice. "It's not as if you can die." He hauled Simon up
by one arm, making him scream as his broken bones
scraped and twisted inside his flesh, then threw him
over his shoulder like a freshly dressed stag at the hunt.
"Come, my son," he grunted, shifting him to a more se-
cure position, making him swear again in pain. "You
and I must talk."

Isabel waited in the solar, the cup of warm wine meant
to revive her after her ordeal untouched. Brautus said
nothing, sitting by the fire, and she didn't ask him to
speak. She wanted to hear Mother Bess first. She went
to the loom, to the tapestry her mother had been
weaving up until the day she died and Isabel was born.
All her life, she had studied it, trying to conjure up
some sense of the woman who had made it, the
mother she had never known. What would her mother
tell her now? I love him, Isabel would say to her. I want

to save him. Would the pretty peasant girl call her a fool?

The door opened, and Mother Bess came in, leaning on Kevin's arm. "Welcome, old gran," Brautus said, rising to meet her. "Come and sit by the fire."

"Never you mind where I sit," the old woman snapped. "You and your lord nearly made quite a mess, don't you think?" She smiled at Isabel, patting her cheek. "But we'll soon put it right."

"I don't know what you mean, Mother Bess," Isabel said. "I don't understand any of this."

"You will, poppet," Brautus promised as the old woman snorted at him again in disgust before she sat down. "It's all right, Kevin. You can go." The groom looked at Isabel, obviously uncertain, and she nodded.

"It's all right." He nodded back and left them, closing the door behind him.

Brautus took out a scroll of parchment very much like the ones Isabel had taken from her father's study. "All right," he said gruffly, looking first at Mother Bess, then at Isabel. "Shall I begin?"

"You know naught of the beginning," Mother Bess said scornfully. "But aye, you may as well."

"Thanks," he muttered, turning to Isabel. "I was with your father when he came here to Charmot. We had fought together many years already, and I knew that he meant to make this place his final home. But he never once mentioned any need to take a wife. He had loved a demoiselle once in his youth in France, but she betrayed him, and he swore he would never love another."

"Foolish Norman," Mother Bess muttered, earning herself an impatient glance from the knight.

"But one day just after we had finished clearing the land for this fortress and the architect was drawing out the walls, we looked up to see a maiden coming across our brand-new bridge," he went on. "The most beautiful creature your father, or indeed any of us, had ever seen." He smiled at her fondly, and she made herself smile back. She could not doubt he loved her, that everything he had done had been for love. But all she could think of was Simon's face as he left her. I could have stopped him, she thought. I could have made him explain; I could have saved him.

"You had not been born yet, you'll recall," Brautus was going on. "So this baggage walked straight up to Sir Gabriel like she knew him and said, 'I will marry you.' And he looked back at her for barely a moment before he said, 'Yes, you will.' And that was Lady Caitlin."

"She was a pretty thing," Mother Bess agreed.

Any other time Isabel would have found this story fascinating. She had certainly never heard it before. But she didn't see what bearing it had on her present situation. Charmot was apparently besieged by demons from every side, one of whom had told her that he loved her. And she, poor fool, still loved him back. What did she care how her parents had come to be married?

"I don't understand," she repeated. "What does my mother have to do with Simon?"

"Caitlin's father was a protector of the druid's grove," Mother Bess explained, as if this should mean something to her. "Your grandfather, my very dear Lady Charmot." Isabel looked at her blankly. "Sweet God, did that Norman tell her nothing?" she demanded of Brautus.

"Don't speak that way about my father," Isabel said, her temper starting to rise. "He was your lord, if you'll recall, of noble blood—"

"Your mother's blood was far more noble than his," the old woman cut her off with a dismissive little scoff. "Her line reached back to ancient days before the druids came to the southern lands of Britain, when the Normans were still nothing but savage pawns of Rome." She leaned forward to take Isabel's chin in her gnarled and wizened hand. "You come from druid stock, sweet girl. You are a child of the grove."

"Yes, but what does that mean?" she demanded. "What good is that to me, or anyone else?"

Mother Bess let her go with a sigh. "Ruined . . . go on then, Brautus."

"No one expected your mother to conceive a child, druid blood or not," Brautus said. "But when she did, she had a dream, a vision, she called it. She said her child would be the champion of her ancient line, that the child in her womb would avenge her race and overcome the wolf."

"That sounds horrifying," Isabel said dryly, though in truth her show of not caring was losing strength by the moment. Simon had changed himself into a wolf. "What does it mean?"

"The stories say that in ancient days in the first lands of the druids, one of their women was taken by the gods and gave birth to a demon," Brautus explained, handing her the scroll. She unrolled it, but the crumbling page was covered in the same strange text as everything else in the catacombs; she couldn't read a word.

"It is no story, old man," Mother Bess said with a bitter laugh. "This demon grew to manhood hating the druids and his mother's people. He cursed them, using his immortal power to murder all of those who opposed him and make slaves of the rest. And his favorite form was that of the wolf."

"So he changed," Isabel said, looking up from the scroll. "He could change."

"Oh, yes," the old woman nodded. "But he was not all-powerful, as he believed. Some of the priests managed to escape him and come south, and they brought their wisdom with them, and their sacred blood. They wrote what they remembered of the wolf as a warning to their progeny, for they knew that someday he would find them and use all of his cunning to destroy them."

"And you think Simon is this person—this demon wolf?" Isabel said, hardly crediting her ears.

"Simon?" the old woman said, looking at Brautus. "That young man . . ." She looked back at Isabel. "Dear Christ, can it be so?"

"He is a vampire," Brautus nodded. "He said it himself."

"But what is that?" Isabel demanded. "You act as if you know—"

"I do know, love," he cut her off. "A vampire is a cursed creature that can only live in darkness, feeding on the blood of the living." He looked more pale than ever. "Your father and I had heard such tales at war, and I saw enough to know that they were true."

"The demon drank the blood of his victims, and his children did the same, mortals that he poisoned with his own immortal blood," Mother Bess said. "No weapon could harm him; he could not die." Her eyes glittered in the firelight. "But neither could he live."

"I stabbed him, poppet, remember?" Brautus said, taking Isabel's hand. "He did not die. He did not even bleed."

"The druids wrote that their gods could not destroy the wolf because he was one of their own," Mother Bess explained. "But they drove him from their forests and across the sea, and they cursed him for all time, condemning him to live in darkness, to never see the sun."

Isabel stared at them, aghast. "There is but one God in heaven," she said, standing up as if she'd heard enough.

"He could not live as mortal men," Mother Bess went on, relentless. "He could taste no meat nor drink anything but living blood. He was the vampire."

"Your father believed as we do, poppet," Brautus said, putting a hand on her arm, pressing her back into her chair. "He loved your mother very much, but he would not believe these pagan tales of demons and druids and gods."

"No more do I," she answered. "I will not believe it." *God Himself has banished me from the light*, Simon had told her at their first meeting. He had never eaten so much as a crust of bread or drunk so much as a sip of water in her presence; he spent the daylight hours buried underground. He said himself that he was a vampire; she had seen him transform himself into a wolf. But he loved her; he had said that, too. He was barely older than she was herself; he could not be some ancient pagan evil. He had been at Charmot for weeks; he could not mean them harm. "I believe in Christ, in the grace of God Almighty." But what in Christ's teachings explained how Simon had transformed himself into a wolf before her very eyes?

"And so do we, my lady, and so did your lady mother, I do swear it on my life," Mother Bess said, taking her hand. "But she believed in the old ways as well, that there was good and evil in the world that God knew well but perhaps his priests did not."

"She did not argue with your father, but she trusted in her vision," Brautus said. "She was certain that this wolf or vampire or whatever he was would be coming to Charmot and that the child she carried in her womb would be the one to vanquish him. She made your father promise to protect the wisdom of the druids in their catacombs, and she began this tapestry. It became a kind of joke between them." He unrolled the weaving and held it out to her. "We always assumed the maiden was meant to be Lady Caitlin herself, that the wolf was bowing down to the son in her womb. Then when you were born a girl, and Lady Caitlin died . . ." He looked at Mother Bess. "Some people thought they knew better."

"Knew the truth, you mean, and so we did," the old woman answered. "Caitlin knew it herself. She just feared to frighten her pigheaded husband with the knowledge that his daughter would be faced with such a task. She never expected to die; she thought she would have time to teach her daughter who she was, to prepare her for what she would become."

"After she died, your father refused to hear any more talk of a prophecy that would endanger his child," Brautus said. "And I agreed with him; I thought it was all a lot of peasant nonsense, more than he thought it, in fact." He glared at Mother Bess. "Despite what some would tell you, he had great respect for the wisdom of the druids, Christian that he was. He just did not wish to give them his daughter. He refused to believe that you, his precious child, were meant to battle some demon—you were a girl, for pity's sake. He searched the catacombs all of your life for some evidence of some female warrior who had attempted such a thing in the past, but he never found a word to support it." He stopped, taking a deep breath. "What else he might have found, I cannot say."

Isabel's blood had run so cold, she felt numb. "Do you mean to tell me I'm supposed to murder Simon?" she said, her voice sounding hollow in her ears.

"Slaughtering a monster isn't murder," Mother Bess said grimly.

"Your father thought your husband would fulfill the prophecy, if somehow it really was true," Brautus said. "That was why he was always so concerned that you should marry a man who could protect Charmot. That, he believed, was your true destiny." He smiled with sadness in his eyes. "I believe it as well. That is why I became the Black Knight."

Isabel looked down at the tapestry, the tiny red-haired maiden and the wolf with his head laid in her lap, gazing up at her in love. I love you, Simon had said, on his knees before her, weeping tears of blood. "No . . ." She looked back at them, the knight and the peasant crone, both of them waiting for her to say she would do what they wanted, that she would kill her love to save Charmot. But how could she? Even if she had the strength, even if she knew how to kill a demon who could not be killed, how could she kill Simon? You cannot kill me, the demon in her father's shape had told him. The second demon . . .

"There were two of them," she said suddenly, standing up.

"Two what, poppet?" Brautus said with a frown.

"Two vampires." She laid the tapestry aside to pace the tiny open space before the hearth, the room suddenly feeling too small. "The first one came and tried to hurt me, to take—" She reached into her pocket and took out the crumpled parchment she had made somehow with magic and her blood—her mother's druid blood. "To take the map," she finished. "He looked like Simon at first, but it wasn't him. I could tell it wasn't him. He wanted this map."

"What map?" Brautus said.

"This map of the catacombs," she said, handing it to him. "Don't even ask me how it came to me."

"Where is this other vampire now?" Mother Bess said, not disbelieving, just confused.

"He went out the window," she answered. "Simon came in, and they fought. They both changed, not just Simon. The other vampire's face kept changing." She trembled at the memory, but she wouldn't let herself stop. "He changed into someone Simon knew, then a man I believe was Michel, then . . ." She looked at Brautus. "He changed into my father."

"Holy Christ," he murmured.

"He asked me again for the map, and I almost gave it to him—I would have if Simon hadn't stopped me. It was like I couldn't help myself." She looked down at the map again, remembering the monster's voice, the tender voice of her father. But her father would never have kissed her that way; he would never have hurt her. "Simon attacked him. He protected me. He changed into a wolf, and the other one changed into a dog—a big black dog I had seen before, Mother Bess, and taken for the grim. They fought, and Simon pushed him out the window." She looked at Brautus. "Then you came in."

"Yes," Mother Bess said, staring into the flames. "The wolf could make a son."

"So how do I help him?" Isabel demanded. "If this other vampire is this wolf I'm supposed to kill, how do I help Simon?"

"Help him do what?" Brautus asked with bitter humor.

"Save him," she answered. "You both seem to know so much about demons and vampires; tell me how to save my love."

"He cannot be saved, little girl," Mother Bess said, patting her hand. "If he is a child of the wolf, he is damned."

"No," Isabel said, pulling away. "I will not believe that." She turned back to the tapestry. "He came here for a reason." She looked up. "Where is Orlando?"

"Locked up in the cellar," Brautus answered. "I didn't want him running off to help his master."

"Good," she answered, taking the map back from Brautus and putting it into her pocket. "I want to talk to him."

"Wait, my lady." Mother Bess caught her by the wrist in a grip so tight, it hurt her. "You are the champion," she said. "If you do not destroy the wolf, Charmot and all who live in this forest will be lost."

"I believe you," Isabel answered. "But I have to know which demon to destroy."

12

❖ ❖

Simon woke up in the dark. The pain was gone, so he knew he must be healed, but he still couldn't stand. He was sitting against a rough stone wall with his hands over his head, shackled at the wrists, and his legs straight out before him. Heavy chains were shackled to his ankles as well.

A spark flashed in the dark. "Awake at last." A vampire who looked like the thick-witted brigand Michel stood beside a table at the other end of the damp, low-ceilinged cave. But in truth, Simon knew he was Lucan Kivar.

"I killed you," Simon insisted, struggling to pull his arms free. He had broken chains before in his demon state; he could break these.

"You know quite well you did not." He lit a second candle. "Even if you had been too stupid to realize it yourself, that insect you keep with you would have told you." Simon gave the chains another rattling pull, and Kivar smiled. "You're wasting your strength." He carried the candle to another corner of the cave, illuminating a huddled mass that sat up as he squatted beside her and became a girl, bound and gagged. "Those chains will hold even a vampire for quite some time." He touched the girl's cheek, and she flinched, her gag muffling a scream.

"Who is she?" Simon asked, struggling to keep the horror he felt from his tone.

"No one," Kivar answered. "Would you ask the cook the name of the sheep when she served you mutton?" He stood up and smiled. "Of course, being an Irishman, you might."

"What do you know of Irishmen?" Simon scoffed with a deadly smile of his own. "The only one you ever met cut off your head and stabbed you through the heart before you could get acquainted."

"Is that the way it went?" He frowned. "I thought Roxanna stabbed me through the heart." He shrugged. "Not that it matters." He came back to Simon, leaving the candle beside the weeping girl. "Did you kill her, by the way? I know she would have asked you to do it." A shadow of fury passed over his thick-featured face, pasty white in the flickering light. "Stupid girl."

"Would you care?" He held his wrist chains stretched taut, pulling them with all his strength but silently now, and he thought he felt them begin to give way just a bit.

"Of course I would," Kivar answered, his careless smile returning. "I care for all my children." He touched Simon's cheek, and Simon snapped at his hand like a dog, unable to stop himself. This monster had kissed Isabel, pretending to be him, stealing his very shape. "But I must say, Simon, that you are my favorite so far."

"What about Susannah?" Simon said, refusing to rise to the bait. "She was your newborn, was she not?"

"A momentary diversion." His mouth twisted in a bitter leer that made him look more like the living man whose corpse he had stolen. "You killed her, too, I suppose?" He went back to the table and opened a leather pouch very much like the ones Orlando carried, only larger. "Did you at least fuck her first? She wanted you to so badly."

"You killed her," Simon answered. "Not me."

Kivar looked back at him over his shoulder, considering. "Yes," he decided. "You could say that, I suppose. But if so, then I also killed you." He went back to taking objects Simon couldn't see out of his pack and setting them on the table. "Are you dead?"

The iron shackles cut into Simon's wrists. "You tell me."

Kivar looked up at the ceiling with a wry half-smile. "Not yet." He lifted a curving, golden dagger to the light, and the girl on the floor began to struggle, trying again to scream. Simon couldn't be certain in the dim light from across the cave, but he was sadly afraid he recognized her, the child of a woodcutter who had taken refuge with her family at Castle Charmot the first night Isabel had seen him as the wolf. If it were she, she was barely more than twelve or thirteen years old.

"It's all right, sweeting," he called out, making every effort to sound braver and more certain than he felt. "He isn't nearly so scary as he thinks."

Kivar set the dagger aside. "No, perhaps not." He palmed another, much smaller object from the table. "But you are." He turned back to Simon. "I should thank you for this body, by the way." He looked down at his scarred but powerful hand. "Not so elegant or intelligent as our mutual friend, the duke, of course." He clenched his fist and smiled. "But it should serve my present purpose well enough." He held the object in his hand up to Simon's eyes—the signet ring Francis had always worn, the proof of his noble title, given to him by the king. "But I do miss being Francis."

"You were never Francis," Simon said, trembling with rage. "His soul escaped to heaven long before your demon spirit touched him."

"Not so," his tormentor said with a smile. "His mind was still all but intact when I took possession of it; I could hear his thoughts quite well. As for his soul . . ." He shook his head like a man who has heard a child prattle a fairy tale. "Of course, the mind does deteriorate over time, even under my command. Still, I owe him a great debt. I could never have kept up with you so well without his help. Orlando is a clever little maggot." He suddenly grabbed Simon's right hand in a grip more powerful than any shackle and slipped the ring on his finger. "His one regret in all his stupid life was that he had not made you his heir when he could have so easily," he said softly as Simon made his face like stone, refusing to react. "So see how I repay him for his service?"

"And I will repay you," Simon answered, his lips drawing back in a smile that was more like a grimace. "Next time I will finish you."

"I bid you do your worst, my son," Kivar said mildly, unimpressed. He took a step back as Simon lunged to the length of his chains, and this time Simon felt a definite slip; the bolts that held him to the wall were definitely bending. "But spare me your ignorant prattle of heaven and souls, if you please." He walked away again. "I was immortal when your God was still being invented under some sheepherder's tent."

"Then why are you so keen to have His chalice?" Simon retorted. If he could get himself free of these shackles, he was almost certain he could reach that golden knife before Kivar could stop him. He might not destroy the devil completely, but he could destroy the body he possessed, cut off the head and cut out the heart as Kivar himself had apparently done to Francis. At least the girl could escape.

"His chalice?" Kivar said with a mocking laugh. "Simon, do not be a fool if you can help it. The Chalice is mine, my birthright. It has nothing to do with your God." He returned to face him, holding the knife. "Has that little worm, Orlando, not told you yet what the Chalice holds?"

"Salvation," Simon answered.

"No such thing!" he cried. "Salvation is another pretty story, another myth your priests made up to keep you savages from eating each other alive." He smiled wryly. "But you should not feel badly; in my time, it was the same."

"So what good is the Chalice?" In truth, the devil's words meant nothing to him; if Kivar had said he was on fire, he wouldn't have believed him even if he smelled the smoke. Simon had been burned by too many crosses and repelled by too many innocent souls to doubt his God was real or that He took a hard but definite interest in the affairs of the damned. Isabel, he thought before he could stop himself. Isabel had driven him from her with a cross, invoking the name of the Christ. What must she be thinking now? How must she feel? He didn't dare to dwell on it, or he would never escape this trap. "Why search for it?"

"The Chalice is healing," Kivar answered, a strange, triumphant madness burning in his eyes. "The Chalice makes you whole." He clasped Simon's face between his hands, studying it. "You are afflicted with death, my son, a disease of the blood, not a curse. The Chalice could cure you." He let him go slowly, backing away. "But perhaps I do not need you any more." He turned quickly and snatched up the girl from the floor, baring his fangs, and she let out a despairing, mewling kitten's moan. "You look at this and see a soul," the ancient evil said softly as he removed her gag, sounding genuinely puzzled. "You fear for her more than you do for yourself, even now, this empty-minded little beast whose name you do not even know." He let her fall again, her head striking the stone floor with a tiny crack. She shuddered and went limp.

"I am a knight, Kivar," Simon answered, watching the other vampire's face, his expression impossible to read. The laws and life of chivalry were not something he had found much cause to think of since he had become a vampire. They just were, a part of him like the arm that wielded his sword, the code of his life. His father and the duke had both been men of honor, protectors of the innocent, and he had loved them, had lived and breathed only to make them proud. So he had become the same. Even as a damned soul, a vampire loosed upon the world, he had never found a way to give up the habit.

"Yes," Kivar said, turning on him. "A knight— exactly." He picked up the dagger. "I had heard tell of this new creation in the world, this knight, and it amused me to think of taking one as my son. But after watching you for all these years, I begin to understand your weakness." He came closer. "And I have seen your Isabel." He traced the dagger's point down Simon's throat, and with an effort, Simon allowed it without flinching. Kivar could not easily kill him with a knife, and if he had truly wanted to do so, he could have done it already. Besides, in another few moments, Simon might have worked himself free. "She is not a knight, but she is strong, stronger than you, I begin to fear. Perhaps I have chosen badly."

"Leave her alone," Simon ordered, the words catching in his throat in spite of his resolve. The very idea of this monster touching his beloved was more than he could bear; the killing rage rose up inside him, turning his vision to red.

"I cannot," Kivar answered. "But I will not abandon all my hopes for you just yet." He held the blade to Simon's throat, curved like a scythe. "This knife could behead you like a blade of grass with a single flick of the wrist," the ancient vampire said, the voice Simon had first heard from him in his true form returning, calm and cold. "Do not move." He sank his fangs deep into Simon's throat, sucking stolen blood from his vampire's veins as his body went rigid with fury. The terrible hunger that ruled him, knight or not, rose up like a fever, gnawing at him like a serpent, driving him to madness, and still the devil fed, drawing deeper, pulling at his very heart. Only when Simon was empty and aching, burning to be filled again, did Kivar lift his head.

"The sun will come to claim you soon," he said, stepping back, wiping his mouth on Michel's dirty sleeve. "There is an opening in the earth above us, and now you are too weak to free yourself and escape." His voice seemed to waver and echo inside Simon's head. All he could think of was feeding, gorging himself on blood and taking his revenge. "But you can be strong again."

Kivar lifted the girl from the floor again, her head now lolling on her shoulders, but she was still alive. Simon could hear her heartbeat roaring in his ears, feel it throbbing through his weak and starving flesh as if it were his own. "Take the beast and feed from her as you were created to do," Kivar said, slashing the dagger across the girl's wrist, filling the cave with the scent of her blood. "Then you will be my son."

He laid the girl across Simon's lap, passing her wrist across his face to smear his mouth with her blood. Simon lurched up in his chains like a man possessed, a howl of agony erupting from his throat, but he did not take the bait; he did not bite her. "If you are still a knight, then let the dawn consume you. Do so that your innocent might live," Kivar finished, backing away. "But if you have the strength to take what is yours by all that is right, I will come to you again."

"Kivar!" Simon shouted as the ancient left him in the dark.

Isabel waited in her father's chair in the catacombs as Brautus led Orlando in. "My lady!" the wizard said, rushing forward as soon as he saw her face. Expecting nothing but hostility after keeping him locked up in Simon's room all night, she was surprised; he looked and sounded genuinely relieved. "Are you all right?"

"Yes," she nodded as Brautus helped the little wizard into a chair. That wasn't quite the perfect truth, as she was confused, terrified, and rather nauseated, but it seemed the wisest response. "But there are questions I would have you answer, if you will." She set the purse Mary had given her and the silver cross she had found at the church on the desk between them. The druid's map she kept in her pocket. "Questions about Simon."

"I have one as well," Orlando answered. "Where is he?"

"I don't know." He barely glanced at the items before them, showing no sign that he recognized either one. "After he turned into a wolf and threw the second vampire out my bedroom window, I asked him to tell me what he was and how he came to be here, and he left the castle rather than give me an answer."

"The second vampire?" Now he looked alarmed. "What was his name? What did he look like?"

"We were not properly introduced," she answered. "As for what he looked like, I fear it would be easier to tell you what he didn't. First he looked like Simon. Then when Simon himself appeared, he turned into another older, kindly-looking man who was a stranger to me but whom Simon seemed to know well. Then he changed into another man I believe was a brigand knight named Michel." She glanced at Brautus. "Then for a moment, he was my father. At the end, he turned into a dog. So I truly couldn't tell you who he was."

"Kivar," Orlando murmured, going pale.

"Simon said that word as well," she said, remembering. "Is that this creature's name?" She waited, but the wizard did not answer. "Orlando?"

"You should ask Simon," he said grimly. "You should never have sent him away."

"I didn't send him away," she answered.

"I did," Brautus said. "Why should I not have done it? Is he not a vampire?"

"You say that word as if you know its meaning," Orlando answered Brautus. He turned to Isabel. "Do you know, my lady?"

"I did not before last night." She picked up the cross, remembering how happy she had been even in her fear when Simon left her for the chapel with the others, remembering the tears of blood that he had wept in her room. "I wish I did not now." She saw pity in the wizard's eyes, but he said nothing. "Orlando, is Simon my kinsman?"

He looked at her blandly, his face a perfect mask. "He said he was, my lady," he answered. "I can only choose to believe him."

"Aye," Brautus said as a knock came on the door. "And we can choose not to." He opened it, and Glynnis came in, carrying a tray of food.

"You should eat, my lady," she said, watching the wizard as she set it on the desk between them. "And we thought Master Orlando might be hungry, too."

"Thank you, Glynnis." She filled a trencher for the wizard and set it before him, but he didn't touch it, watching for her to start instead. "Orlando, good heavens," she said, taking a bite of bread that tasted like sawdust in her mouth, so little did she want it. "What have I ever done to make you believe I could poison you?"

"Nothing, my lady," he said after a moment. "Forgive me." He began to eat as Glynnis left.

"This purse was found on the dead woman we thought was killed by the wolf," she said, pushing her own food away. "I saw Simon change into a wolf last night. I can't help but notice how much this resembles your other purses and bags." He kept eating, never even glancing up. "Is it yours?" she persisted. "Did Simon . . . ?" The question stuck in her throat, but somehow she made it come out. "Did Simon murder that woman?"

"You know him, Lady Isabel," he answered, his brown eyes meeting her green ones. "What do you think?"

"I want to think he did not, that he could not do such a thing," she answered. "But I can't forget what I saw." He looked away. "Orlando, I understand your wanting to protect Simon," she began again. "But you must understand that I must protect Charmot. I am sworn to it."

He smiled his bland little smile. "And I am sworn to my master." Brautus snorted in obvious disgust, but she remembered the words Orlando had spoken to her in this room on his first morning at Charmot. Simon is my only hope, my warrior and my salvation, he had told her. My soul is in his hands. How could she expect him to betray him? "What do you wish me to tell you?"

"Ah, now that's an easy one," Brautus answered for her. "Tell her how to kill him."

"I don't think he has to tell me that," Isabel said. "I think I already know." Orlando looked at him, surprised. "Sunlight," she said. "Is that true, Orlando?" Simon had three vows that she knew of—to avoid human contact, to never eat food, and to never see the sun. The first he had broken with her fairly regularly from the first day he had arrived. The second had already been explained—as a vampire he fed on the blood of the living. But why avoid the sun? Mother Bess had said the druid gods had cursed the wolf, banishing him to darkness. "Is this why Simon can never go out in daylight?" But Orlando only smiled at her as if he hadn't heard. She thought perhaps he looked a little paler, and he had stopped eating his breakfast. But she couldn't be certain, and she couldn't afford not to be. "I don't want to hurt Simon," she said, standing up. "But I can't let this other demon hurt Charmot. Orlando, I want to save him, but . . ." Tears rose in her eyes, and she turned away, staring hard at her father's books to keep from breaking down. That was when she saw it.

"You have to help me, Orlando." She took the bottle from the shelf, the ruby red bottle that felt so cold to the touch. He had told her it was deadly poison, all but snatching it out of her reach. "If you don't, I will open this and empty out whatever is inside." She turned to find him still smiling, if anything more broadly than before. "Outside in the courtyard," she continued. This time she was sure he had gone pale, and his smile disappeared. "In the noonday sun."

"No!" He leapt to his feet. "Give it to me!" He tried to rush forward, but Brautus held him back. "Please, my lady, you must not."

"Then you must help me." He seemed so desperate, she felt horrible. It was not in her nature to threaten or torture anyone, even at such need. But he'd given her no better choice. "Will sunlight kill Simon?"

"Yes," he admitted, near tears. "But as my god or yours may judge me if I lie, you need not fear him, my lady."

"And why should she not?" Brautus demanded. "Because he is her kinsman?"

"No," the wizard answered. "Because he is truly not a demon, for all he is a vampire." He looked up at Isabel with pleading in his eyes, so powerful she felt near to weeping herself. "He would say I am a fool, but I swear on the treasure you hold that is more dear to me than life, he is just what he has always told you, a good man under a curse."

"Orlando, I saw him," she answered, wanting desperately to believe him. "I saw his fangs. I saw him turn into a wolf."

"Only to protect you," he insisted. "It is Kivar that you should fear, not Simon. It is Kivar who will take down this castle stone by stone to find the prize he seeks. Only Simon can protect you. Only he can destroy Kivar forever."

"Why should I believe you?" Simon had tried to protect her from this Kivar; he had done everything she had ever asked to try to protect Charmot. But what of her mother's prophecy?

"Let me go to him," the wizard begged. "Let me bring him back to you." He struggled free, and Brautus allowed it. "He loves you, Isabel," Orlando said. "Even if he has not said as much, I promise you he does. Let him save Charmot."

"He has said it," she answered, the memory threatening to make her cry again. "I want to help him, Orlando."

"Then believe him," the wizard persisted. "Allow him to return."

Behind him, Brautus nodded. She could read his mind; he wanted to trap Simon somehow here at the castle, somewhere open to the sun. But she would not. "All right," she said, taking a deep breath. "I will let him return." She looked down at the bottle she still held, so cold it seemed to burn inside her palm. "But if you lie, if you betray me, your treasure is forfeit."

"I do not lie," he promised. "Let me go, and I swear I will return to you your protector." He smiled slightly, a very different smile from the one he'd hidden behind like a mask. "I will bring you your Black Knight."

"No," she said, meeting his eyes with her own. "I am going with you."

"No!" Brautus protested. "Let him bring the vampire back here where we can deal with him together."

"We cannot deal with him at all," she answered. "Simon is not coming back through the gates of this castle until I am certain he is what Orlando says he is, a good man under a curse who will protect us, not harm us." She wouldn't let Brautus send him away again, wouldn't give Mother Bess the chance to turn the household against him. If Simon truly was a monster who could not be saved, she would deal with it herself. And if he could be, she would find a way to do that, too.

"And how will you know that?" Brautus said. "If someone must go with the little one, fine, I will go; I will take Kevin and the other men with me—"

"Brautus." She put a hand on his arm. "If my mother was right, if Simon is the creature we believe him to be, then this quest is mine alone."

"No one ever said that," he said, his jaw set hard.

"No one had to say it." Ten years of confusion and resentment over what her father might have wanted and what she was meant to do with the legacy he had left her was melting away. For better or worse, this was her destiny. "I'm sorry I was born a woman, Brautus. I'm sorry my father is dead. But he is, and I was, and this is my destiny."

"Isabel, you must trust in me," Orlando said. "Whatever destiny you think you must serve, you must trust in Simon's love."

"I want to trust him," she answered, meeting Brautus's eyes. Trust me, she tried to say to him without speaking, and he nodded as if he understood. "But I must also trust myself."

"So you mean to go alone?" Brautus said. "You think I can allow that?"

"Orlando will be with me," she answered.

"A wizard roughly the size of an acorn," the old knight scoffed. "A fine, strong guard indeed."

"I don't need a guard." She thought again of her mother's tapestry, the maiden charming the wolf. To her knowledge, she had never charmed anyone; how was she meant to be that maiden? But if not her, who else? "What good is a sword against a demon, if he really means me harm?" she said. "If I fail, Charmot is left to you."

"Don't say it." He cradled her cheek in his palm. "Your father would never ask so much of you, my lady. You are a better warrior than he could ever have guessed."

"No such thing," she scoffed. "Come, Orlando. We will find my Black Knight together."

Simon watched the sun crawl in a ragged beam across the cavern floor, his useless breath now coming in panting gasps of fear. For an hour he had watched it, pale at first, then brighter, moving ever closer. In his mind, he could already see himself burning, his flesh exploding into flame, his clothes consumed like parchment in the fire. The girl still lay across his lap, her head against his shoulder; her blood oozed from her wrist onto his stomach, soaking hot and sticky through his shirt; he felt every pulse of her heart. She was dying; even if he did not touch her, she would die. But he would not touch her. One long draught of her innocent blood down his throat, and he would have the strength to break the chains that bound him and escape into the dark. But one draught would never be enough for the hunger that consumed him; he would devour her, an innocent; her death would be his crime, no longer Kivar's. He would not do it. His maker had set him a test meant to prove he was a monster, not a knight. But Kivar was wrong.

He clenched his fist, and Francis's ring pressed into his skin, a warning and a comfort. The need for vengeance shuddered through him like another physical pain, but it was wrong as well. Francis was in heaven with God; he had no need for vengeance. If Simon was consumed in grace, he would join him.

"Forgive me, Christ," he murmured, his voice coming out as an animal's growl, the name of the Almighty burning his tongue. "Forgive me all my sins." Paradise would be Ireland, a green land by the sea. "Forgive me all the death I have caused, the pain that has delighted me in the blackness of my sin." He would be with Francis and his father; he would see his mother's face again. His eyes burned with tears that would not come; he had no blood left inside him to weep. "Save me by Your grace, and take me home." The sun was moving closer; he began to feel its warmth on his skin, a shadow of the burning that would come. "Abandon me not to the dark." Abandon . . . he was abandoning Isabel. She is strong, Kivar had said. Perhaps I have chosen badly. He would go to her, destroy her, and Simon could not stop him. Simon would be dead, consumed at last by the light. Orlando could not protect her; Brautus could not. The devil would take her.

"No!" He screamed so loudly, the ground shivered around him, dirt raining down on his face, but still he could not pull free of the chains. Still he had no strength.

"My lord?" The girl stirred against him, lifting her head. "My lord, I am frightened." She clung to him, her heart beating faster, and the hunger twisted inside him, the fangs growing deadly in his mouth.

"It's all right." Her throat was now within his easy reach, even with him chained to the wall; all he had to do was bend his head to be free, and still the sun was creeping closer, the fire rising hot inside him. "You have to run away."

"No," she said, crying, her face pressed to his shoulder, burning his skin with her tears. "He will find me."

"No," Simon promised, trying to soothe her, to keep his voice natural and calm. A child, he kept telling himself, repeating the words in his head to try to drown out the roar of her blood and the beating of her heart. A beast, Kivar had called her, no better than a sheep. But she was not a beast; she was an innocent child. "He will not find you, not in the sunlight. He cannot harm you in the light."

"He can," she insisted, clinging even more tightly to him, so tightly he could feel her pounding heart against his chest. "I know he can. I want to stay with you."

"I said go!" She screamed and fell back as he lunged forward, eyes glowing green and fangs extended, the bolts that held him creaking, ready to give way. "Run," he ordered even as his body fought to reach her, out of his control "Run, and don't look back."

"Yes . . ." His demonic power to entrance was still intact; she could not disobey him. She backed away, unable to defy him even in her terror. "My lord . . ." Still bleeding, her heartbeat still like thunder, she turned and fled the cave, scrambling into the light.

Simon fell back against the wall, great sobs of pain and anguish wracking through him, howls of grief that echoed through this cave that was his torture and would be his tomb. Soon it would be over; soon he would be free. Isabel was lost. But he didn't know what else to do.

Malachi had returned to the castle alone with a scrape on his leg but otherwise unharmed, and they followed the clear trail he had left through the forest—it looked as if he had galloped straight through the brush all the way. "What scared you, sweeting?" Isabel murmured, bending close over his neck to avoid a low-hanging branch. "Was it Simon?"

"Listen," Orlando said, stopping beside her. "Did you hear that?"

"I think so." She thought she had heard a terrible sound like the howl of some wounded animal, but it had come and gone so quickly, she could have thought she had imagined it if Orlando hadn't heard it, too.

"This way," Orlando said grimly, taking the lead.

A mile or so deeper into the forest, they heard another strange sound, softer but continuing this time. "Lisette!" Isabel cried, leaping down from Malachi to run to a girl huddled by the pathway, hidden in the brush so well, Isabel had almost missed her altogether. "Poor darling, you're hurt," she said. "Orlando, she's bleeding."

The girl was hysterical, barely coherent. "Sir Simon," she was sobbing. "He's sick." She seemed to be covered in blood, but the only wound Isabel could see was a deep cut on her wrist. "Something terrible . . ."

"Did he do this?" Isabel asked gently as she bound up the cut. Orlando came closer to hand her his cloak, and she wrapped it around the girl. "Did Sir Simon hurt you?"

"No," Lisette insisted. "He didn't . . . another man, like a demon he was . . . he took me from my father's house to a cave and tied me up and left me, and then he came back with Sir Simon. Only he was hurt; Sir Simon was hurt, knocked out, like, and the other man chained him to the wall."

"What other man, Lisette?" Isabel said, stroking the

frightened child's hair, trying to calm her. "What did he look like?"

"Michel," she answered. "That Frenchman—I saw him when he first said he was coming to Charmot; I was hiding in the barn when he questioned my father, trying to find his way to the castle. But he didn't sound like himself."

"Lucan Kivar," Orlando said, turning pale.

"Sir Simon woke up, and he and Michel talked to one another, but none of it made any sense." She looked up at Isabel. "I was so scared, I couldn't think, but Sir Simon told me it would be all right. But there was something wrong with him. The villain threw me on the ground, and I hit my head, and when I woke up, he was gone. Michel was gone, and my wrist was bleeding, and I felt so weak."

"Where was Simon?" Orlando said, obviously fighting to keep an even tone.

"Still in chains," the girl answered. "I was lying in his lap . . . I was just so scared. I didn't want to leave him; I was afraid Michel would find me. But there was something wrong with Sir Simon; he . . . I don't know." Her face was pale as milk, and her eyes were wild with fear.

"Did he bite you?" Isabel said, laying a hand on her cheek.

"No," she promised. "But . . . he had teeth like a wolf, and his eyes were on fire, green fire. He made me run away." She huddled against Isabel, who held her closer, cradling her in her arms.

"You see?" Orlando said. "You see he did not harm this child—"

"Where is this cave?" Isabel said, cutting him off.

"Not far," Lisette said, pointing. "I couldn't run any farther."

"It's all right." She smiled at the girl. "Master Orlando is going to take you back to the castle. You're safe now."

"I am going with you," the wizard insisted. "You won't know what to do."

"I know enough." She knew that cave, had played there often as a child. Part of the ceiling was open; it had let out the smoke when she built a fire. It would let in the sunlight. "Lisette is badly hurt; she needs looking after." He started to protest, and she caught his arm. She still had the bottle in her pocket; she could threaten him again. But she didn't. "You will have to trust me."

His eyes searched her face. "Yes," he said at last, laying a hand over hers. "I will trust you."

13

❧ ❧

Isabel pulled the cross from her pocket and held it out before her, the chain entangled in her fingers as she ducked into the cool dark of the cave. Groans and howls of pain echoed back to her like the death throes of some great beast, and she shivered, tears rising in her eyes.

She found Simon chained against the wall, just as Lisette had described, the sunlight streaming through the roof less than the length of her arms from his feet. He looked up as she emerged from the tunnel, his nostrils flaring as if he smelled her more than saw her. "Isabel . . ." She could no longer doubt he was a vampire; cruel fangs curved long and white from his mouth as he suddenly screamed in agony, and his eyes glowed yellow-green with demon fire. But he was still Simon, too.

"Did you murder Susannah?" Her throat felt thick with unshed tears, choking her to death. She could still see her, the beautiful Queen of the May. How could she love the monster who had killed her? "Did you murder that girl at the church?"

"No," he answered, fighting for his voice. The hunger that was killing every shred of humanity left inside him leapt up in delight at the sound of her heartbeat and the smell of her skin, torturing him more sorely than any trap Kivar could have devised. He lunged against the chains again, the shackles slicing deep into his flesh. "Innocent . . . never the innocent." He had to warn her, to make her understand, but his mind was gone; he couldn't form the words. "Not Susannah . . . Kivar."

"And why should I believe you?" Smoke was beginning to rise from his clothes; she could smell the leather of his boots beginning to burn. But how could she save him? If she released him, would he kill her?

"Get out." His demon eyes were pleading, and his voice was tender, even as it twisted in a wolvish growl, the voice of her beloved. "Get out, Isabel."

"I will not." She was coming closer, moving through the light, and he roared in frustration, the chains that held him squealing in protest, ready to give way as the demon inside him fought to be free. "I cannot."

"Isabel, no!" He thrashed in his bonds as she came closer, screamed as she reached out to touch his cheek as if her hand might have been made of molten iron, his lips drawn back from the terrible fangs in a snarl, the final warning of the wolf. But she was not afraid.

"Yes." She touched his mouth, touched the fangs and looked into his glowing demon's eyes. "I love you."

"No," he tried to answer, tried to warn her, but it was

too late. With a final roar, he snapped the chains and crushed her in his arms, rolling to the blessed cool of the darkness as the sunlight finally reached the empty cavern wall. Pinning her beneath him, he arched over her, sinking his fangs into her throat. Lacing his fingers with hers, he felt the cross she held pressed like a brand against his arm, but he didn't care; the pain was nothing. All that mattered was the blood, the sweet, precious life of his beloved. The demon held him completely as he fed, adoring her and killing her at once, satisfied at last.

"Simon . . ." She stroked his hair, twining her leg around his as she had when he made love to her, and a delicious weariness crept over her, a will to surrender. His fangs hurt her, tearing her flesh, but it was an exquisite pain, as natural as breathing. The part of her that ached for him so dearly had been born for just this pain, or so it seemed as he held her. His hands caressed her as he fed, and she had never felt so loved, so needed. But it had to stop.

"Simon . . ." He heard her voice and cherished it, the sound as vital as the blood that fed him, and he felt her hand entangled in his hair, pulling hard enough to hurt him. "Simon, stop." She sounded calm, utterly fearless, the voice of the maiden on the battlements who had prayed for his immortal soul. The hunger inside him was waning, the demon slowly being sated, but her blood was still delicious, too sweet to leave a single drop untasted. He raised his head and kissed her, exploring her mouth with his tongue before he sank his fangs into her lip, drawing gently at the wound, still drunk with feeding, with the ecstasy of being filled at last.

"Simon." She gently drew her mouth from his. She should have been frightened; she should have been confused, but she was not. Somehow she knew what to do. "Stop," she said, caressing his cheek as he gazed down at her, his eyes deep brown again and rapt with wonder. "I love you," she whispered, raising up to kiss his brow. "Love me, Simon. Let me live."

"Yes." He wrapped his arms around her, pressing her close, and the demon fell away. She was his love, his Isabel. "I love you." He kissed her cheek, cradling her head in his hand, and she turned her face to his and kissed his mouth.

"Ouch . . ." She winced, touching her sore lip and pulling a wry face.

"Darling . . ." He touched her cheek, heartbroken with remorse. "I hurt you."

"No," she started to say, then stopped with a laugh. "Well, yes." He took her into his arms again, and she held him, weak but happy. "But I'm all right." He kissed her again more gently, tracing his tongue over her lip, and the soreness seemed to dissolve, the deep puncture healed. "Saints," she swore softly as he drew back. "That is quite a trick."

He smiled. "I'm glad you like it." He bent and kissed the wound he had left on her throat, the tender flesh so cruelly torn it made him want to cry. "I could have killed you." He kissed it again, but the punctures were too deep for his demonic magic to heal. "I wanted to kill you."

"Brautus and Mother Bess wanted me to kill you." He raised his head and looked at her, shocked. She smiled, touching his mouth. "They said it was my destiny to kill the wolf that would destroy my people," she explained. "And we thought the wolf was you."

"No," he promised. "I swear it is not." The cross's chain was still entangled in her hand, and he bent and kissed it, kissed the cross and let it burn his mouth.

"Simon, no," she protested, alarmed, as she pulled it away.

"I did not kill Susannah. I released her from the same curse that has fallen on me. I would have tried to save her, to give her some hope of salvation, but she meant to kill Tom." The burn was already healing; he was strong again; her blood was strong. "I did not kill the woman you saw at the church. I saw her, and I fed from her, but I did not kill her."

"Like you fed from me," she said, trying to sound casual, not jealous. The woman had been slaughtered; how could she be jealous of her? But she was. She was jealous of every other woman he had ever touched, vampire or not, jealous even of the pain they had felt in his arms.

"No." He brushed the hair back from her brow, her face so beautiful it hurt to look at her, but he would look forever if he could. "Not like I fed from you. Nothing has ever been like that." He thought again of how close he had come to destroying her forever, and the memory made him tremble. "Why did you come looking for me? Didn't you know I could hurt you?"

"I told you; I wanted to kill you." The very idea made her feel faint. In truth, she was already faint, she realized, light-headed and weak from the loss of so much blood. But she couldn't bear to let him go. "But I couldn't do it." Tears welled in her eyes. "I couldn't watch you die. Even if you were a demon, even if you meant to murder me and everyone I loved, I couldn't watch you die."

"No, my love." He kissed her eyelids, weeping with her. "Angel, please don't cry." She touched his cheek in wonder, her fingertips wet with his tears of blood. "I'm sorry. I'm so sorry."

"No," she protested. "Please, don't . . ."

He kissed her, stealing her breath, desperate with love, and she held him, aching but content. "I love you," he promised, kissing the corner of her mouth as his hand moved between them, raising her skirt. "I love all that you love." He moved inside her, and she sighed, her body enfolding him, warm and wet. "I am yours, your demon."

"Mine," she murmured, rising to meet him as her eyes fell shut.

"I will protect Charmot." He kissed her as he moved in deeper, his hands moving over her hips, up her sides.

She was his, more precious to him than any holy relic or even salvation itself. She was his salvation. "I will protect my love."

"My knight." She ran her hands over his shoulders, swooning in his arms. She felt so weak, so fragile, but he held her; he loved her. She didn't have to be afraid. "My demon." He moved faster, and she laughed, the ecstasy beginning, every muscle in her body tingling with life. She reached to kiss him, clumsy with want, and he brought his mouth to hers, his tongue sliding over her own. She was the maiden, and he was the wolf; somehow she had won him to her thrall, not to kill but to love. She called out his name as her climax erupted, and she felt him breaking free as well, the waves that shuddered through her passing from her flesh to his. On and on it rose and fell until she thought her heart must burst, and still he held her, still he was with her, her vampire love, until at last the waves subsided.

"Isabel . . ." His voice seemed very far away, calling from a dream, but his body was close, his arms wrapped around her as he rolled onto his back, drawing her close to his chest. "Sleep, my love," he murmured, kissing her cheek, and she let herself obey him, giving herself over to the dark. "Sleep until the night."

Simon felt her arms go slack around him, her breath fall deep and even. Her heartbeat was still weak but steady; she would be all right. He held her closer, crushing her to him, fierce with love, but still she barely stirred. Kivar would never touch her. He would protect his love.

An hour after sunset, Simon rode back through the gates of the Castle Charmot with Isabel cradled, still dozing, in his arms. "Wake up, darling," he murmured as Brautus came to meet them. "We're home."

Isabel blinked, still so tired she could barely hold her eyes open. "Oh, dear." Brautus looked like a thundercloud, standing on the steps with his fists on his hips.

"So at least you're alive," he said as Simon climbed down.

"Of course I am alive." Simon lifted her down and started to let her go, but she swayed on her feet. "I'm fine," she insisted as he scooped her up again.

"Of course you are," he muttered, kissing her cheek as he carried her inside. Brautus followed.

Orlando was waiting in the hall with Mother Bess beside him. The wizard bent his head to his folded hands on the table as soon as they appeared, mumbling a prayer of thanks, but the old woman didn't look relieved at all. "What have you done to her?" she demanded of Simon, as Brautus drew his sword.

"Brautus, stop," Isabel insisted through a yawn. "It's all right." Simon looked rather stormy himself, she noticed, facing the captain with a challenge in his eyes. "Put me down." He didn't respond, so she gave his hair a tug. "Simon, put me down."

He set her on her feet but kept a firm hand on her elbow in case she should wobble again. Brautus, old dragon that he was, looked ready to eat him alive, and he couldn't blame him; in his place, Simon knew he would feel just the same. But he couldn't afford to back down and beg forgiveness, not with Kivar so close and so ready to attack. All the way home, he had felt the ancient evil's gaze upon them, watching from the woods, and whether this feeling was real or his fretful imagination mattered very little. Kivar would come. "Sorry, love," he said, squeezing Isabel's hand, his eyes still focused on Brautus.

"What's that on your neck, then?" Brautus asked Isabel, looking at her no more than Simon was. They looked like a pair of angry he-wolves, squaring off to fight, and she, she supposed, was the bone they were disputing. "What did he do to you?"

"He bit me," she answered, her tone matter-of-fact. "But I lived." Still holding Simon's hand, she turned and faced the hall, the others who were gathered there as always for the evening meal. "Sir Simon is my love and my choice," she said. "He will be my husband." She looked back at Brautus. "He will be lord of Charmot." A murmur of wonder rippled through the room, and she held Simon's hand more tightly. "Anyone who cannot bear his rule is free to go; I will do all I can to help you find a new home." She looked back at Brautus and Mother Bess, standing together, an odd alliance indeed. "But this man will be my lord."

"Congratulations, my lady," Hannah said, coming forward to embrace her. "This is happy news indeed."

"Aye, it is," Kevin agreed. He glanced back at his grandmother, and from his expression, Isabel thought she must have told him much while they were gone. But still he offered his hand to Simon. "We will be glad to have Sir Simon for our lord."

Simon smiled, a dozen conflicting emotions pulling at his heart. "Thanks, Kevin," he said, taking the groom's hand. He could see Orlando watching him in despair. This was just what the wizard had warned him might happen, just the distraction he had feared. Brautus was watching as well and looking no happier, watching Isabel. "And what about you, captain?" Simon said, letting her go to face him. "I have wronged you, I know, whether I meant to do it or not." He looked at the old woman standing just behind him. "Those who call me a wolf are not completely mistaken," he admitted. "But I do love your lady with all my cursed heart, and I will not give her up." He offered his hand. "Can you let me have her?"

"Do I have a choice?" he grumbled. Isabel frowned, crossing her arms to resist the urge to reach out to him herself and beg him for her heart's desire as she would have done as a child. Simon was not a treat or a toy; he was her love, and Brautus must accept him or decide that he could not. "Aye," he said at last, clasping Simon's hand. "I know I do not." He pulled the vampire into an embrace. "But keep her safe, or I will be the one to vanquish the wolf."

"I will," Simon promised, more moved by this cold surrender than by the warmth of all the rest save Isabel herself.

"Excellent," Isabel said with a laugh, and most of the hall laughed with her. They didn't realize what had just happened; they only knew their spinster lady would be wed. "Simon, come," she said, taking his hand and drawing him away from the crowd. "I have to show you something."

"You should rest," he answered. He touched the wound on her throat, now bruised to a black and purple welt. "Every time I think about it—"

"So don't," she cut him off, softening her sharpness with a smile. "That is what I want to show you." She caught Orlando's eye and waved him over, glancing at the crowd as it continued to disperse. "I think I may have found the way to help you more than you know." She reached into her pocket as Orlando joined them. "You said when you first came here that my father came to you in a vision to send you to Charmot." She looked at the wizard and smiled. "I'm assuming now that you were lying."

"Yes," Simon admitted. "I'm sorry, love—"

"As well you ought to be," she interrupted, a glint of real temper in her eyes. "I mean to punish you for the rest of our lives for telling me such a lie. But in the meantime . . ." She handed him the druid's map.

"What is this?" He had a vague recollection of Kivar's trying to take something from her the night before in her room, but he had been too engrossed in trying to save her life to worry about what it was.

"A map to the catacombs," she answered. "You said there was something at Charmot that could save you from your curse, and I took you to the catacombs because I thought whatever you were seeking must be there." He was studying the map, a look of wonder on his face. "You and Orlando seemed to agree."

"Where did you get this?" It was indeed a map to the catacombs, marked with the sign of the Protectors of the Chalice over the chamber where Sir Gabriel had made his study and a trail made in what his demon senses told him without question was his love's own blood. "How did you know—"

"I didn't," she admitted. He handed the map to Orlando almost absently, looking now at her instead. "My father . . . he had made scrolls of his own, chronicles of the castle and notes on his study of the druids, and he marked each scroll in one corner with a code, symbols I could never read." She explained how she had taken the scrolls from the study and how she had by accident discovered their secret. "I knew it must lead to whatever you and Orlando were trying to find," she finished, suppressing a smile at the stunned look on his face. "Last night when you went to the churchyard, I finished it so I could give it to you when you returned." She shrugged. "But we got a bit distracted."

"Just a bit," Simon agreed, smiling in spite of himself. In truth, he felt a little dizzy. All this time spent searching for the Chalice, he had barely believed it existed, believed he was doomed to be alone forever, a monster despised by all who knew him for what he really was. Now in a single day and night, Isabel had looked into the demon's eyes and sworn her love, had fed him from her very heart and lived to love him still, had declared to all he was her choice, her beloved, vampire or not. And now, it seemed, she had given him the Chalice.

"So what is it?" she asked him now. "What are you trying to find?"

"It's called the Chalice," he answered. "According to Orlando, it can save me from my sins, make me a man again, not a vampire." You are afflicted with death, my son, Kivar had said, not a curse. The Chalice is healing, not salvation. But Kivar was a liar.

"And you think it's here?" she said, weak again with relief. "Orlando?"

"All this time." The wizard was purple and seething with fury. "All these weeks spent searching, and all the time the key was hidden in your tower. Stupid, silly girl—"

"The hell I am," she retorted, making Simon turn his head to hide his smile. He had been about to leap to her defense, but she didn't seem to need him. "If you two had told me who you were and what you wanted instead of lying to me and treating me like a leper in my own castle, I would have shown you my father's scrolls from the very beginning." She included Simon in her general glare. "Though I doubt very much you would have known how to use them, even if I had."

"She's right, Orlando," Simon said. "Would you have known we needed Isabel's blood to make her father's code do its work?"

Before the wizard could answer, the sound of a bell from outside broke through the general hum of the hall. Someone was ringing the bell on the other side of the moat as if the imps of hell were hanging from the clapper. They looked at each other, Isabel going pale. Someone meant to summon the Black Knight.

"Forgive me, Isabel," Orlando said, bending over her hand. "But now, I fear we will see just what this wasted time will cost."

Kivar had not just stolen Michel's corpse but his horse and his armor as well. "Will no one answer my challenge?" he called out in the French knight's slurred and lazy voice. He made the destrier rear and turn about like a seasoned veteran of the lists. "Where is this Black Knight?"

"I'm dreaming," Isabel said, standing between Simon and Brautus on the battlements with Orlando and Kevin close by. "I've had this dream before." In truth it had been her constant nightmare since the moment she had heard the name Michel. Only now he was a vampire.

"It will be all right," Simon promised, drawing her close to his side.

"Can you kill him, then?" Brautus asked.

"Where is the beauteous maiden of Charmot?" the brigand shouted, brandishing his sword. "Fight me or bring me my bride!"

"Yes," Simon answered.

"No," Orlando said at the same moment.

"I killed him before," the vampire said stubbornly.

"Apparently not," the wizard replied, his tone more gentle than his words. "Simon, without the Chalice . . ." He caught sight of Isabel's face and let the sentence die.

"This is probably a foolish question," she said. "But what happens if we refuse to let down the drawbridge and open the gate?"

"Kivar comes over the wall," Simon answered. "Or under the lake or out of the sky. He's a vampire, love— worse than a vampire. For ten years his spirit has been living inside the bodies of dead men—I killed the man you see myself, I promise you. He can turn into a dog or a vapor." His hand had tightened on hers so much he knew he must be hurting her, and he made himself loosen his grip. "He doesn't need the drawbridge to get in."

"So why bother with this challenge?" Brautus asked.

"It amuses him," Orlando said. "He knows Michel intended to kill the Black Knight, and he enjoys the joke of allowing him to do it." He looked pointedly at the ring Simon now wore, the ring that the duke had regretted not giving him before his death. "It is one of his favorite tricks."

"He may not know I'm here," Simon pointed out. "He may still think I died in his trap."

"Not likely," Orlando answered. "He will have made certain one way or the other."

"But he doesn't know whether or not you have the Chalice," Isabel said, making them all turn to look at her in shock. "He knew I had the map, and he knew what it was. And apparently he wants it."

"Oh, yes," the wizard nodded. "Very much."

"So let me fight him," Brautus said. "You and the acorn go down and find this Chalice, whatever it is—"

"No," Simon said, cutting him off. "He'd know at once he was fighting a mortal man, and he would abandon the game. The only one with any hope of keeping him busy is me."

"And what good will keeping him busy do?" Isabel asked. "If Orlando is right, and you can't kill him—"

"Kivar is immortal, but Michel's body is not," Simon answered. "He never should have left Francis for me to find; I know now how to drive him out. If I can cut off his head and cut out his heart, his spirit will have to abandon its host. We don't have any other corpses lying around the castle that I don't know about, do we?"

"You mean other than you?" Orlando said. "It's too risky—if Kivar took possession of you—"

"If he could possess me, he would have done it when I killed him the first time," Simon cut him off, putting an arm around Isabel when he saw her horrified face. "He has other plans for me, I'm afraid."

"So what about this beheading and heart ripping," Brautus interrupted. "Can you do it?"

Simon smiled. "Oh, yes."

"Simon." Isabel put a hand on his arm and pointed. "Look."

Kivar had stopped circling and shouting to hold his mount perfectly still, facing the castle. He raised the visor on his helmet and smiled, showing his fangs, his eyes glowing green in the dark. "He heard," Kevin said, panic in his voice. "He heard every word you said."

"Very likely," Simon agreed, staring back. He pressed a kiss to Isabel's brow. "But I am not afraid."

14

❧ ❦

Isabel watched Brautus help Simon into the painted armor of the Black Knight in his tiny cellar room. "I am afraid," she said, leaning against his bed. "I don't want you to fight him."

"You and Brautus will take the others across the lake in boats," he answered, strapping on the spiked plates that covered his arms. "Even if I fail, Kivar won't be interested enough in the people of Charmot to make the effort to hunt you down. All he really cares about is the Chalice."

"You're not listening." Brautus's chain mail hauberk was a bit long for him, hanging almost to his knees, but through the shoulders and arms, it was a good fit. "I said don't fight him."

He laid his gauntlets aside. "You know I have to fight him." He cradled her cheek in his palm, making her look at him. "You made me promise I would, remember?"

"That was Michel, a man." She pushed his hand away. "Not this demon in a dead man's body, this thing that can't be killed."

"He can be killed, and I will do it." He made her meet his eyes again. "I am sworn to it."

"Oh, shut up." She batted him away again, moving out of his reach. "Ever since I met you, you've been telling me what you are sworn to do and not to do, and it's always exactly the opposite of whatever it is I want." He looked at Brautus, hoping for guidance, but the knight just shrugged, barely trying to hide his smile. "I know you have to fight him," she admitted, turning back to him. "But I still don't want you to do it."

"I know." He looked almost exactly the way she had pictured him in her desperate dreams before she had ever seen him, her true Black Knight, a deadly angel loosed from hell to protect Charmot. But he wasn't that; he was Simon, her beloved, and she'd only just found him. How was she supposed to let him go? "I don't want to fight him," he said now.

"Yes, you do," she cut him off. "You're fairly itching to go out there and hack him to pieces and take your revenge—"

"And why shouldn't I be?" he demanded, cutting her off in turn. "I want him gone, destroyed forever. I want to be free of him for good." He framed her face in his hands, refusing to let her pull free this time. "I want to be what you told your people I was," he said more gently, gazing into her eyes. "I want to be a man again, your husband. I want to grow old with you, to see our sons grow up in sunlight."

She didn't answer for a moment, the willful girl inside her battling the woman. "Or daughters," she finally retorted. "We could have daughters."

"Aye," he admitted with a smile. "We could." He kissed her, and she wrapped her arms around him, pressing herself against him with all her strength for a moment, memorizing every tiny portion of the way he felt before she let him go, and she could feel him doing the same, running his hands through her hair just before she pulled away. "Go with Brautus," he said, still holding her hands in his. "I will find you when it's done."

"No," she said, shaking her head. "I'm staying here with Orlando."

"Poppet, enough," Brautus said. "You can't—"

"I can," she interrupted. "Orlando and I will wait down here outside the catacombs while Brautus leads the people safety. As soon as you dispatch this Kivar, we're going to find your Chalice."

"As simple as that," Simon said, smiling in spite of himself.

"Why not?" she retorted, smiling back. "I have a map."

"We've no more time to argue," Brautus said with an air of surrender. "Whatever this Kivar might be, I doubt he'll wait forever."

Simon took the devil's mask helmet and put it on his head. "How do I look?"

"Terrifying," Isabel answered, trying to sound careless and ironic in spite of the tears in her eyes. She touched the helmet's leering grin. "So go and frighten him to death."

Simon hadn't worn armor in so long, he had almost forgotten how uncomfortable it was. He stopped halfway across the courtyard to fidget, resettling the chain mail shirt on his shoulders, the devil's-head helmet cocked at an odd angle as he tilted his head from one side to the other, loosening his neck. "You make quite a picture, my lord," Kevin said, holding Malachi's reins in one hand and a lethal-looking black lance in the other. "Brautus's kit fits you well."

"Well enough." He swung into the saddle, Malachi planting his feet to hold himself steady, an old hand at such business, and Kevin handed him the lance. "You should hurry," Simon advised him. "The others have already gone."

"Tom will watch out for his mother." He adjusted Simon's stirrups. "Besides, someone will have to open the gate."

"That's true enough." His voice sounded hollow and hoarse behind the helmet, but at least whoever had designed it had been clever enough to make the "eyes" wider than they looked, the actual openings set behind hooded lids of steel and tilted up at the corners to give him a clear view on either side. "Just keep an eye out and be ready to flee if you have to."

"Godspeed, my lord." The groom stepped back and

touched his forehead in salute before running to open
the gate.

Kivar was ringing the bell again as Simon rode out
on the drawbridge at a trot. "Finally," he laughed, turning his horse to face him. He rode Michel's horse, the
same armored destrier Simon had frightened so badly
in the chapel yard after he had slain its master, and its
eyes were wild with fear, its muzzle flecked with foam.
What dark act of will had Kivar practiced on this creature to make him bear his weight? "I like your costume," the ancient vampire said. "As depressingly
moral as you knights can be, you have a great flair for
occasion." He seated his lance with graceful ease, as if
he were born to it. Michel had been a professional
fighter; how much of his skill could the demon have
stolen? "But then, you are no longer a knight."

Simon seated his lance as well. "Why would you say
I am not?" Malachi was pawing the ground, eager to be
under way, and he smiled. "Did you not call for the
Black Knight of Charmot?"

Kivar's smile turned darker. "So I did." Without further warning, he urged his mount into a gallop, star-
tling the animal—an amateur's mistake. Malachi
charged back almost before Simon's own spurs
touched his flanks, by far the superior beast. They
came together at the center of the drawbridge, Kivar's
lance shattering on Simon's breastplate as he leaned
in to take the full force of the blow, trusting his vampire strength to hold him in the saddle. His own lance

point found a ridge in Kivar's armor just below the shoulder and levered him neatly off his horse. He quickly brought Malachi around, his lance still whole, as Kivar climbed back to his feet, clumsy and apparently stunned.

"Well done, my son," he said, drawing his sword. "I didn't realize how little this barbarian knew his own craft." His horse was trapped behind him against the gates, and it screamed, pawing at the drawbridge, desperate to escape. "But then the body only remembers so much."

Simon bore down on him again with the lance, the rules of engagement be damned, catching him solidly in the throat with the point before he was close enough for Kivar to reach Malachi with his sword. He jumped down from the horse's back to shove the lance's blade all the way through the ancient vampire's throat, nearly beheading him with this single hit. Kivar struck at him with Kivar's heavy broadsword, but Simon barely felt it, the blade glancing off the thick chain mail armor, his vampire body impervious to the bruises and scrapes of a mortal man.

"I will kill you," he said, ripping the helmet from Kivar's head, watching his face contort with rage, unable to speak with Simon's lance through his throat. "I will scourge your filth from this world for all time." He drew Sir Gabriel's sword and struck the vampire lord's borrowed head from his shoulders, his blade passing smoothly through the Frenchman's thick, dead neck.

But just as he was raising the sword to cut out the dead heart, the head began to laugh, Kivar's high-pitched, lunatic giggle ringing out all around him. The headless corpse reached up and grasped Simon's sword, severing three of its own fingers as it did so but snapping the blade like a twig.

"Fool!" the head cried out, the eyes coming alive again with demon fire. "My precious, beautiful fool!" Simon grasped it by the ears, crouched over the headless trunk, and a rush of cold wind, stinking of the grave, swept up and over him, knocking him backward, the head still clutched between his hands.

"Kivar!" he shouted, struggling to rise, both horses now screaming and stamping in fright. The foul head he held went soft in his grasp, rotting away in a moment, and the body dissolved into a gray-black, slimy fluid that oozed from its armor into the cracks of the drawbridge. "Kivar!" Kevin opened the gates again, rushing out as the horses rushed in, but Simon barely saw him. Flinging the filth he held away, he grabbed the broken fragment of his sword and sprinted for the castle, tearing off his helmet as he went.

Isabel gazed at the carving of Saint Joseph, absently clearing the cobwebs from his face. "I am surprised that you're here, Isabel," Orlando said from behind her. "Why aren't you watching Simon fight?"

"I didn't want to distract him," she answered. "I used to do it on purpose, back when Brautus was the Black

Knight. I would stand on the battlements and watch, and if things were going badly, I would scream, or I'd cry out 'God-a-mercy, sir knight, you are killed!' if Brautus made a hit. Sometimes I would pretend to faint; that always seemed to work." She hugged herself, the underground passage even colder than usual, and imagined the battle above them now, her heart's love fighting a demon he knew he couldn't kill. "May God forgive me."

"I would think he has already." Orlando smiled as he patted her arm. "Brautus never actually killed any of these poor knights, did he?"

"No," she admitted. "But some of them were very, very embarrassed."

A door slammed above them as if it had been caught by the wind in a storm, and suddenly a terrible stench filled the passage, as if someone had opened a tomb. "Kivar," Orlando cried as they turned toward the stairs. "Run, Isabel—"

"Run where?" A freezing wind swept past her, the stench so strong, she thought she would be sick. She turned back toward the door to the catacombs as the stone carving on its face began to tremble and the shape of the monk began to crack, screaming as a skeletal hand broke through the stone, dried ribbons of sinew still hanging from the bone.

"The cross," Orlando called out over the sound of breaking stone and rushing wind. "Where is the cross?"

She fumbled in her pocket, her eyes locked to the stone as it crumbled away. The desiccated corpse of the monk stepped down from the door where it had been entombed, the skeleton still draped in the rotting tatters of the cleric's robe, his flesh dissolving further into dust with every step. Only the eyes looked alive, the glowing green eyes of Kivar.

"Isabel," he said, his voice echoing in the air around her rather than from his lipless grin. He held up one hand and saw the weapon of Saint Joseph he still held, a rough wooden stake, and he laughed, saying something more in a language she couldn't understand before he flung it away.

"Stay back," she ordered, trying to sound brave as she held up the cross.

"Not this time, little one." He struck it from her hand so hard she felt her wrist give way with a snap, her flesh crawling at his touch as the talisman skittered away. "Now come." He grabbed her broken wrist, and she cried out in pain. "Where is the map?"

"I don't have it." How could she have ever mistaken this monster for Simon? This was his true form, this ancient, rotting corpse.

"What a sweet little liar." He yanked her closer, the smell making bile rise in her throat. "Shall I kiss you for it?" She screamed as he bent closer, but he didn't do as he had threatened, snatching the map from her pocket with his other hand instead.

"Release her!" Orlando shouted, holding up a fistful of something from one of his pouches. He flung the powder at Kivar, shouting some sort of incantation, and the skeletal vampire burst into flames, the rotting robe consumed in an instant. But the flesh and bone would not burn; with another icy blast of wind, the fire went out.

"My turn," Kivar said with a snarl, raising his free hand toward Orlando. The wizard rose up and sailed back into the wall as if he'd been flung by a giant, then slid to the floor, apparently lifeless.

"I won't open it," Isabel insisted as Kivar turned her toward the door again, tearing at the bony hand that held her fast.

"Won't you?" Kivar slammed her palm against the door, slicing a gash in her flesh with the sharp-edged, broken stone, and it swung open with a crash, the rusted hinges screaming. Holding the map out before him, he dragged her through her father's study and into the pitch-black tunnel beyond.

Simon ran through the castle and down the stairs, armed with nothing but fury and a broken sword. "Kivar!" He found the stone door to the catacombs shattered and Orlando slumped against the wall. "Orlando!" He fell to his knees beside the wizard and shook him. "Orlando, where is Isabel?"

"Gone." He looked up, blood running into his eyes from a scrape on his forehead. "Taken by Kivar." He pointed at the broken door. "There was a dead saint buried in the stone . . . Joseph." He was holding Simon's sleeve, but his grip fell away. "We are lost."

"No." The vampire shook him again, refusing to be patient. "Tell me how to use it—the Chalice. If I find it, how do I use it to destroy him?"

"Kivar has the map," the wizard pointed out. "He has the girl, the protector's blood—"

"Just tell me!"

"I don't know!" He struggled to his feet. "I always assumed that when we found it, somehow you would know, that some book or ancient carving would have told us by then or it would be an instinct . . . I don't know."

"Lovely." Looking around the passage for some better weapon, Simon found a rough wooden stake encrusted with cobwebs and dirt—the weapon of Saint Joseph. "Maybe this will work."

"Simon, how will you find them?" The wizard chased him into the study. "If Kivar finds the Chalice first, he will become more powerful than any demon in creation, a god in his own right. How will you find him first?"

"Isabel's blood." He smiled a madman's smile. "I can smell it."

"Of course . . ." The wizard smiled. "Come, warrior. Lead on."

Isabel stumbled in the dark, struggling to stay on her feet. She had no doubt that if she fell and broke both legs, Kivar would drag her the rest of the way. The glow from the creature's eyes cast the faintest of glows on the damp cave walls, glittering occasionally on a trail of some phosphorescent powder on the floor.

"Your friend, Orlando." They crossed over the gleaming track and plunged into another dark tunnel. "As he ever was, so clever and so wrong."

She wanted to answer, but she wasn't sure she had the strength. She had been exhausted and weak from the loss of the blood Simon had taken from her when she came back to Charmot; now she was bleeding again, and the pain from her wrist was making her feel faint. Not to mention she was being dragged through a labyrinth by a rapidly disintegrating corpse. Given her absolute preference, she would have screamed until she passed out dead. But screaming wouldn't save her—or Charmot. "Simon is going to catch you," she made herself say as they rounded another sharp corner. "He is going to destroy you."

"Is he?" He turned sharply again, so quickly she had to put up her free hand to stop herself from crashing into the wall before he yanked her on. "How do you know he's not destroyed himself?"

A picture of Simon lying beheaded on the drawbridge of the castle with Malachi standing over him rose up in her mind, but she pushed it away. "He isn't." She made herself think of her mother instead and her tapestry, her vision of the great deed her child would do to save her people. This creature, this Kivar . . . this was the wolf. "I would know."

The vampire laughed. "Perhaps you would."

They rounded another, softer curve, and the ground fell off steeply before them, leading them down in a spiral that seemed to go on forever. Kivar muttered something in his ancient tongue and moved faster.

Simon could smell the scent of his beloved growing stronger and sweeter in the chill. In his eagerness to reach them, he didn't notice the way the ground sloped sharply downward until it was almost too late. He staggered, the stake held out before him, and Orlando lunged past him and grabbed it, pushing it aside just before Simon was impaled. "Thanks," the vampire muttered, shaking, clapping his friend on the shoulder before he climbed back to his feet.

Isabel heard a scuffle from somewhere far behind and above them, no louder than a rat in a wall, and she smiled. Simon was coming; he would find her. Then Kivar laughed, a bitter little chuckle, and her hope turned cold. "Not so graceful, is he?" he said, his smile plain in his voice. "Come along, little one."

"Simon, be careful!" she cried out, planting her feet to hold him back one more moment. "He knows!"

Kivar caught her hard by the hair, making her gasp with pain, but she would not scream, not with Simon close enough to hear her. "Aren't you the brave little beastie?" the creature said coldly, turning to continue down the slope.

Alive, Simon thought, the meaning of her words barely registering as they echoed back through the dark. Alive and still conscious. Exchanging a look with Orlando, he quickened his pace.

The passage opened up as it leveled off, and Isabel stumbled as Kivar suddenly stopped. "Of course," he said, laughing. "What else would they do?" He raised his hand as he had done to attack Orlando, and a torch blazed up before them, then another, then another, forming a half-ring of fire. Behind the torches were columns of stone carved to look like the trunks of great trees, so intricate Isabel blinked, thinking for a moment they were real, great oaks growing under the earth. Even the ceiling was carved to mimic a canopy of summer leaves frozen forever in time. The ring seemed to end against the opposite wall of the cavern, melting into a smooth, flat slab of rock.

"Behold the labors of your fathers, little one," Kivar said, drawing her into the ring. "See what their folly has wrought."

"Were they so foolish?" Just inside the ring were two smooth obelisks of stone, shoulder high and set a man's arm span apart. "Did they not escape you?"

"For a time." He gazed up at the rock face, his demon's eyes triumphant. "But that time is over." He turned back to her, letting go of her wrist to reach for her shoulders, and she knew her moment had come. Before he could catch her, she attacked, falling on him in a fury, gouging at his eyes, the only part of him that seemed alive. He screamed, clawing at her hands, kicking her legs from beneath her and driving her to the ground. "Little bitch," he snarled, crouched in front of her with both her wrists in his grip. One eye was torn completely from its dry and skinless socket, hanging useless on the flap of parchment that should have been his cheek. The other was whole but oozing, obviously blind. "Do you think I need to see you?"

"I will kill you," she promised, trembling with horror but furious, the daughter of a druid and a knight. "The time that is ending is yours."

He yanked her back to her feet and shoved her between the obelisks, the loss of his sight apparently no great hardship in his quest. He slammed her bleeding hand against the top of one, pulling her arm nearly out of the socket to do it, and a sickening shudder passed through her, the cavern turning dark to her eyes in spite of the light of the torches. He tore open the flesh of her other wrist with his ruined teeth and fangs, gnawing at her like a dog, and this time she did scream, unable to hold it back. He pressed her bleeding wrist to the other obelisk, and her body felt like it was being split in two by lightning, the whole cavern shuddering around them.

"Here it is, little one," Kivar said, tearing her gown down the back and ripping the fabric to shreds to bind her hands to the stone. "Here is your great destiny."

Simon stepped into the light behind them, the stake held out before him. "Be careful, my son," Kivar warned him as he moved to strike. "I would hate to snap her neck." Isabel was bound to some sort of stone pillory with her blood flowing freely down either side, and the ancient vampire stood behind her, a wasted skeleton cradling her head between his bony hands. "Look what she can do."

The wall of stone before them was suddenly glowing with light, a cold, blue glow that spread outward from the center. Isabel writhed in her bonds, the power that coursed through her tearing her apart, and the light grew brighter, the stone turning to what looked like ice, white then translucent, a frosted window to another world. At first Simon thought he saw the torches he could touch reflected in the shining surface, then he realized that no, the ring continued on the other side. The icy wall turned clearer still, and he could see an altar just opposite the position where Isabel was bound, a high stone table draped down the center with a cloth of gold. The other side was not a cavern but a grove, a shining forest in daylight, and his heart leapt up in spite of all to see it, a sun that would accept him, a light that did not burn his eyes. At the center of the altar stood a single cup.

"The Chalice," Orlando murmured, awestruck beside him. "It is the Chalice."

"This is the birthright I would offer you, my son," Kivar said. "This is the realm I would give you to rule." Isabel's heart was growing weaker; Simon could hear it. She was dying. He didn't have time for trances and dreams.

"Let her go!" he shouted, turning away from the vision before him.

"Let her live," Kivar answered. "Not as this animal that time will decay, this food for worms and the carrion crow, but as a goddess." His eyes were destroyed, but he turned to face Simon as if he could still see him, one skeletal hand entangled tenderly in Isabel's red hair. "Go forth and take the Chalice, use it as I will instruct you, and we shall be as one. Together we will save her; we will make her a queen."

"No," Orlando warned. "He lies."

"Silence!" Kivar turned his body toward the wizard's voice, but when Orlando took a silent step to one side, he didn't react. He didn't see him.

"Why should I share the Chalice with you?" Simon answered, taking a silent step closer. "Why should I not use it for myself, become a mortal man again as I have always wanted? Even if you kill me afterward, I will die in grace."

Kivar smiled, showing his vampire's fangs inside the dead monk's rotted mouth. "Because your little lamb will die as well."

"She's dying already." He moved closer still. "You've made certain of that." He raised the stake, and Orlando's eyes went wide, but Kivar did not react. "Why should we not die together?"

"Because you are no martyr, Simon," Kivar said. "You are no knight, or you would not be here now." He smiled again, his one remaining eye glowing like fire, blood red, but blind. Looking back, Simon could see the Chalice through the veil of ice, so thin now it was transparent. One more moment, and it would be gone; the Chalice could be his.

But before him, he saw Isabel, the mortal innocent who had shed her blood to save him, the woman that he loved. She slumped between the obelisks, hanging now from her bonds, soaked in her own blood, too weak to stand. But her eyes were alive; she could see him, and her mouth silently breathed, "No."

"You will be a god," Kivar was saying. "You will be my son."

"God is in heaven," Simon answered, driving the stake into the demon's heart. "And my father is with him."

Kivar let out a single scream, and the skeleton he possessed lurched upward, exploding in a moment into dust. Falling back, Simon saw him not as he had known him in the caliph's palace but as he must have been before, a young man with green eyes and shining red hair so much like Isabel's he could have been her brother. The ghost-like form looked down in horror and turned toward the Chalice, the veil of ice turning thicker and whiter again. "No!" he roared, the sound reverberating through the cavern as he rushed forward, his form dissolving as he went. He reached the veil just before he disappeared completely, diving for the forest beyond it, and the wall exploded in a hundred thousand shards of ice, falling to the ground as stone, the cavern wall collapsing into the rubble, the window to the Chalice lost.

"Isabel!" Simon ran to her and tore away her bonds,

catching her in his arms as she fell. Her head fell back over his arm, the welt he had left on her throat livid purple against the deathlike pallor of her skin. He gathered her closer, listening with vampire perception, desperate with fear, and finally he heard it, the delicate throb of her heart.

Isabel felt her angel's arms around her, and she smiled. For once he felt warm. She tried to speak to him, to hold on to him and tell him all would be well, but she couldn't seem to move or speak at all. Letting her eyes fall closed at last, she surrendered in contentment to the dark.

15

❧　❧

The king's agent had been waiting in the solar of the castle Charmot for most of the long, late summer afternoon, so long that he began to wonder if the castle's lord and lady were even there at all. But just as the sun was beginning to set, the door opened, and his mind was put to rest.

"Well met, my lord," the lady said, making him a curtsey as he rose from his seat. "I do apologize for keeping you waiting. I am Isabel of Charmot."

"My lady," he answered, rather dazzled as she took a chair. The legendary beauty of this cursed manor was even more exquisite than her myth proclaimed—he had never seen a woman so fashionably pale. "Your presence is most . . . charming. But to be honest, it is your husband I must see."

"My husband is occupied elsewhere." She motioned him to a chair with a smile. "But he will be joining us presently." She took up a bit of sewing, the perfect picture of domestic tranquility. "Was the king displeased with our tribute?"

"Oh, no, the money was lovely," the agent answered. A former clerk, he had only acquired his title by virtue of his brains; the customs and niceties of these born nobles still made him rather nervous. "But His Majesty is a bit concerned for your safety."

"How very kind." In truth, she didn't sound impressed. "You may assure him I am perfectly safe."

"Yes, but . . . what of the Black Knight?" He expected she might scream or faint or at least burst into tears at the mention of the demon who had kept her prisoner so long, but she didn't seem to miss a stitch in her sewing.

"My husband vanquished him," she answered with another placid smile. "Obviously."

"Yes, of course." He fumbled with his papers. "Wonderful . . . we're all quite pleased." He hesitated to bring up such an indelicate matter to such a delicate creature, but it was the main purpose of his mission, so he supposed he'd better have it out. "But there's still the matter of your husband's identity, my lady. Or I should say, Your Grace."

"You should indeed." The man now standing in the doorway was a perfect match for his lady, in beauty at least, and the agent thought he looked more than a match for any demon loosed from hell. "She is the duchess of Lyan."

"Don't be cross, darling," his lady scolded gently with another secret smile. "You must admit, it's all rather confusing."

"Confusing, yes," the king's man said eagerly. The so-called duke was giving him such a look, his guts felt like pudding all of a sudden. "That is just the word." Simon took the chair beside his wife. "His Majesty remembers the duke of Lyan with great fondness from his youth." He spread the scroll with the listing of nobles in front of them on the table and pointed, avoiding the other man's eyes. "But it seems he left England—or Ireland, rather—some fifteen years ago on Holy Crusade. There is no record of his having any progeny before he left or that . . ." He looked up into the new duke's eyes and gulped. "Or that he ever returned."

"He did not." Simon smiled, and the agent's heart leapt up in wild relief. "Nor did he have any child." He took the parchment to his side of the table and pointed himself. "My father was this man, Seamus of Lyan, a native Irishman and the duke's castellan. When he died, the duke took me with him on Crusade."

"As his squire!" Everything was suddenly quite clear and quite wonderful, the agent thought, and the king was a madman to have ever doubted this most excellent young man's claim. "And he made you his heir."

"Yes." Simon turned to Isabel, and she shook her head over her sewing, suppressing a smile. "I have his signet ring to prove it."

"Of course, of course," the king's man said, rolling up his scrolls. "Your seal was quite in order on your oath of fealty to England." The suggestion that the ring might have been stolen now seemed utterly absurd, and he was quite ashamed to think he had been the one to make it. "But I fear your estates in Ireland have fallen into disarray, Your Grace—the troubles with Wales and with France, you know."

"I expected as much," Simon nodded. He would return to Ireland someday, but he still had much to do before he could. "My first concern is Charmot. I was quite sincere in my request to garrison a royal force within these walls. I have business that will force me to be away from home for some small time, and I wish my wife and my retainers to be safe in my absence."

"And your children," the agent agreed with a jovial wink. "No doubt you'll have an heir to think of before the year is out."

"Pray pardon me, my lords," Isabel said, standing up. "I will leave you to your business."

"Of course." Simon took her hand and kissed it. "I will be with you soon."

"Oh dear," the king's man said when she had gone. "I hope I did not give offense."

Simon smiled. "Not at all."

He found her later in the tiny cellar bedroom they now shared. The elegant gown she'd worn for England's toady had been cast off in favor of one of his own linen shirts; her hair was loose on her shoulders; and a chaos of Orlando's books and parchment scrolls was scattered before her on the bed. "The king's agent was very helpful," he said, stretching out beside her. "He seemed to think we could have a full garrison in place within the month."

"Brautus will be pleased." She smiled at him before taking up another scroll. "He needs people he can order about as he likes; otherwise he gets cranky."

"He's a good captain." He took her hand and pressed it to his cheek, savoring the good, strong rhythm of her pulse. After seven weeks, she still was not completely mended, but she was better. "So what are you reading?"

"The same old matter as always." She showed him the original parchment Orlando had found in Kivar's mountain palace, the sketch of the Chalice that had first set him on his quest. "This is rather obviously Joseph's stake," she said, pointing to the cross of objects underneath the cup. "So this is probably some particular sword."

"Probably." He sat up, leaning with her on the pillows. "Orlando thinks there must be other portals to the Chalice grove besides Charmot."

"Let us hope so." She studied the drawing for another moment before she set it aside. "You will find it."

He put an arm around her shoulders and smiled, kissing the top of her head. He sometimes thought he had never been so certain of anything in his life as Isabel was about everything at every moment. "I will." He touched her chin and turned her face up to his. "Then we can be married indeed."

"Oh, we are quite married already." She laid a hand

against his cheek. "Don't you forget it, your grace."

"Oh, I will not." He pressed her close and kissed her, and she put an arm around his neck, resisting the urge to cling to him with all her might and cry. He had to find the Chalice and the other vampire he had made; she knew these things and understood. But she could not like it.

"I don't want you to leave me," she allowed herself to say as he drew back from the kiss.

"I don't want to leave you ever, and I'm not going yet." He kissed her more deeply, shifting her closer in his arms. "And in the meantime, I'll have back my shirt."

Epilogue

Isabel stood in the churchyard beside Father Colin, tears streaming down her face. Before her was a large, impressive crypt inscribed in beautiful letters with the name of Francis, duke of Lyan, and just beside it was a smaller stone, marked simply Susannah, covered with the last rosebuds of fall.

"She was a kind and lovely girl," Father Colin said, patting her hand. "She dwells in golden castles now."

"Yes." She laid the last wreath on the stone. "I know she does."

"Forgive me, my lady," said Phillip, coming toward her. One of the new royal garrison, he was barely twenty, with ears the size of oak leaves that turned bright pink whenever he spoke to her. "But we should be going. The sun will be going down soon."

"Will it?" She looked up at the darkening sky and smiled. "Then yes, we should go."

Simon and Orlando rode into a tiny village halfway between Charmot and the Scottish border, Simon on

Malachi and Orlando on his little pony, and found a raucous festival raging in the street. "You, sirrah," Simon called to a young man with a tankard in each hand. "It's too soon for All Hallow's. What's the occasion?"

"The sheriff, my lord," he answered with a grin.

"Married?" Orlando asked.

"Nay, lad—dead as a doornail." The fellow was so merry with ale, he seemed to have taken the wizard for a child, gray beard and all. "Ten years of abusing our women and stealing our crops, and now the bastard's dead."

"Did someone murder him?" Simon asked.

"Nay, my lord, you mustn't think that," the drunkard promised. "He went to bed last night wicked as ever and hale as a bull in April and woke up this morning stone dead. Or didn't wake up, I should say. As near as we can tell, an adder got him in the night—there's two nasty marks on his neck, but that's all."

"Bad luck for him," Simon answered.

"Aye, but good for us." Raising one of his tankards in salute, he staggered back into the throng.

"So," Orlando said with a sigh when he had gone.

"So," Simon agreed. "I'd say we were on the right track."

POCKET BOOKS
PROUDLY PRESENTS

The second book in the
Bound in Darkness series

THE DEVIL'S KNIGHT

LUCY BLUE

Coming soon in paperback
from Pocket Books

Turn the page for a preview of
The Devil's Knight. . . .

Siobhan climbed the winding staircase, desperate to escape the prying eyes and questions of her brother's men. She had thought they were her men as well, that she and Sean were partners in a single quest for freedom, not only for themselves but for their people. But now she knew better. Sean was the knight with a quest. She was nothing better than a pawn.

The room at the top of the druid's tower was dark but for the glow of a full moon outside the window. Someone had leaned a spotted mirror against the wall opposite the door, and she gazed at her shadowy reflection. This was the prize Sean thought could win a manor? She could almost laugh. Her handed-down tunic was worn as a rag, frayed at the neck and split up one sleeve, and her leather breeches were worn soft as linen, she had kept them so long. Even for a boy, she was a disgrace. Her face was clean, but one cheek was smudged with a familiar fading bruise from her bowstring's recoil.

And she bore other bruises as well. On her neck were five distinct round marks, made by the grip of her dead Norman husband. Four had faded to a dull yellow-green, but the one over her pulse was still almost black. He could have killed me, she thought as she touched it, remembering the fury in his green-gold eyes. "Tristan Dumaine," she whispered, barely making a sound as her lips formed the shape of his name. The devil's knight, her enemy; the

Norman they had murdered. He had called her beautiful.

She untied her braid and loosened the waves of her hair on her shoulders, blue-black in the tender light. Like silk, he had said when she had let him touch it. She drew her own hands through it just as he had done, letting it fall through her fingers. He had been desperate to escape. He had known they meant to kill him; she had never let him think anything else. She had only touched him to humiliate him, to prove she was a brigand like the rest. He would have told her any lie to gain the upper hand; she had known he was lying when he said it. But how might it have felt to think he told the truth?

She caught her own gaze in the mirror and scoffed, disgusted at her foolishness. She was a warrior, not a woman, whatever Sean might think.

A sudden movement in the mirror made her start, her hand going by instinct to her sword, though she knew it must be Sean or one of his men, come to fetch her back to the fire. "Go away," she ordered, turning toward the door. "Leave me in peace."

"In peace?" The voice came from the shadows by the window, and it made her blood run cold. "Why should you have peace?" A shape emerged in the darkness, a man built like a mountain, and the voice went on, mocking and familiar. "Murderers belong in hell."

"Tristan?" Her tongue felt dry in her mouth. She could barely form the word. He moved into the light at last, and she felt her knees go weak. "No . . . you are not here."

"Where else should I be?" His face, so bruised and bloodied when she'd seen it last, was whole again, the skin pale but perfect. His dark blond hair gleamed like burnished gold in the moonlight, and his green eyes glittered with malice. "Is this not my castle?" His mouth curled in the smile that haunted her memory, cruel and sweet at once. "Are you not my wife?"

"You are dead." He held no weapon she could see, but she trembled even so. He towered over her, his shoulders twice as broad as hers—he could cover her fist with his palm. Even now, in terror and shock, she could remember the strange sensation she had felt when his hand closed over hers, a fearful thrill. "They took you away, Bruce and Calum. You were dying."

"Are you certain?" Tristan mocked her, moving closer. This was the moment he had dreamed of in a fever for weeks, ever since he had become a vampire. The moment he would finally kill Siobhan. He had meant to let her see his face, to frighten and torment her for a moment before he wrung her neck or bled her dry. But now that he was here at last, a moment just wasn't enough. "Did your friends ever return?" Her huge blue eyes were wide with fear, but she did not look away. Any other woman faced with the husband she had helped to murder would have had the decency to scream or faint, but not his beautiful monster, Siobhan. She might turn pale and tremble, but her hand was on her sword. "These creatures charged with cleaning up your mess, where are they now?" She drew the sword, her eyes defiant, and he smiled. "Shall I tell you, sweeting?" He took another slow step closer. "Would you care to guess?"

"You could not kill them," she insisted.

"You might be amazed." She was inching backward toward the door. "I can kill whomever I like." In a moment, she would make a run for it, he knew. His little warrior could sense she was outmatched.

"You were dead!" she shouted, her voice rising to a

woman's shrieking pitch to give away her fear. "I saw you."

"You saw I was dying." He should kill her now and let himself be done. But somehow he could not. "You should have made certain, my love." He raised the dagger he had stolen from her brother's belt. "Your brother, Sean, should have made certain."

"No, I just saw him an hour ago," she said, shaking her head. "You can't have killed him—"

"Can I not?" He wanted her to say what she had done, to hear her say again how she despised him. Then he could let it be over between them. Then he could take his revenge. "I have not killed him yet, Siobhan," he said, moving closer. "But I swear to you I will."

"No!" She struck him with the sword, a blow that should have cleaved his arm in two. But he barely flinched. He grabbed her wrist, wrenching the sword from her grip, and she heard a small sound, like steam on an ember. Looking down, she saw the sleeve of his shirt was ripped open, its edges stained with blood. But the flesh beneath the rip was whole. "Holy Christ," she whispered, feeling faint.

"Be careful, love," he teased her as the tension in her arm went slack in his grip. "You might not want to call Him." He held the dagger to her throat, tracing its tip down her skin. "Blasphemy is mortal sin. But then, why should you care?" Her heart was beating faster; he could hear it. At last she was truly afraid. "What is an oath to you?" He let the dagger scratch her flesh, teasing himself with her blood, and she gasped, a sweetly feminine sound. But in her eyes he saw as much fury as fear. Even now, if he allowed it, she would murder him. "You swore before God's altar to love me, to obey me, remember?" he taunted. "You laughed as you said it, knowing it was a lie." He took a step closer, and she struggled again in his grip, tearing at his fist around her wrist. "Or have you forgotten, sweet wife?"

"No," she answered, struggling to make herself be still. She knew now what he wanted; he wanted her to be terrified, to hear her beg for mercy. But she would not. "I have not forgotten." She made her free arm fall to her side, taking a deep breath. Then she looked up into his eyes.

"You wanted me dead, but you are a coward, just like your brother," he said, glaring down at her with such rage, she thought she might die just from his eyes.

"I wanted this land to be free," she made herself answer, her voice barely shaking with fear. "I wanted you to leave our people be—"

"Your people?" he scoffed with a laugh.

"Aye, my lord," she retorted, new fury making her feel less afraid. "My father's people, born to this land as Sean and I were born to it, born to freedom—"

"Freedom to starve, you mean," he said, laughing again. Even now, looking death straight in the eyes, the little fool would not give up her cause. "If I should let you live, if I should leave you be, as you say, what then? What will your people say to you this winter, now that their crops are destroyed?"

"You know nothing of this land." He sounds like Sean, she thought, almost laughing herself in pure madness. A slave can be contented if his belly is full, her brother had said not an hour before, and she had slapped him for it. "You know nothing—"

"And what do you know, little monster?" he retorted. "How to fight and to fuck like a man." His smile cut through her like a knife. "What good will you be to your people?"

"Bastard!" she screamed, all sense and reason shattered in rage. She lunged for him, grabbing for the hand that held Sean's dagger, and she felt the blade swipe across her cheek. But he hadn't been expecting her attack; she had momentum. She forced the dagger back into his shoulder just above his heart.

His eyes widened for a moment, then he smiled. "Well done." Still holding her fast by the wrist, he yanked the dagger from his flesh. As she watched in horror, the gash she had made closed over, sealing itself with a hiss. "At least this time, you tried to kill me yourself." He pressed the dagger's hilt into her free hand. "Would you care to try again?"

She slashed him this time, across his throat and down the muscles of his chest, ripping through his shirt. Again the wound opened, but no blood came out. A few scant drops welled at the edges of the wound, then the flesh was healed.

"What ails you, love?" he teased her. "You look as if you see a ghost."

"Demon," she whispered, looking up into his eyes. "You truly are a demon." She let the dagger fall.

"Yes." She tried to back away a step, and he caught her by the shoulders, his smile melting into a scowl. Now was the moment for revenge, he thought. She was terrified; her heartbeat thundered in his ears. He let his palms slide up her arms, and she shivered, now too frightened to resist his touch. His hands encircled her delicate throat, and she gasped, biting her lip. No brigand mob could save her now. No one would even hear her scream. "I am the devil, come to scourge you for your sins." She closed her eyes against him, her lashes black against her death-pale cheek. She was his now for the taking, just as he had dreamed. One last, swift movement of his wrist, and her life would be snuffed out forever. "I am your husband." One tear slid down her delicate cheek, glistening in the moonlight. "Is that not so?" he demanded roughly, hungry for her voice, to hear her speak once more.

"Yes." His touch was almost tender, more a caress than a threat. She had dreamed of this moment night after night, the terrible sweetness of his touch if somehow he should return. Lovers she had taken, but no man had ever touched her the way Tristan did; no man had ever dared. But now he did not mean to touch her but to kill her. His hands and voice were cold. "You are my husband," she said.

"Then kiss me." Her eyes flew open, and he smiled, his bitter, devil's smile. "Kiss me good-bye."

He was mocking her, tormenting her before her death as she had tormented him. But she didn't care. She slid her hands over his shoulders, rising to her toes to reach him. He seemed surprised; his green eyes widened, then she closed her eyes and touched her mouth to his. A thrill raced through her stomach as his arms enfolded her, desire more potent than fear. Holding him with all her might, she gave herself up to his kiss.

"Siobhan . . ." He could not murder her, not yet. He could not give her up. He crushed her closer, capturing her in his arms.

His mouth on hers was brutal, demanding surrender, his tongue pushing inside, darting against her own. Alive, she thought. Her husband was alive.

couldn't be sure. "We must take them to the church," she said to Kevin. "They must be buried in sacred ground."

"The church is an hour's ride away from here, my lady, and that on horseback," Kevin said. "No one here will care to venture so far from the castle, not with a killer in the woods." Several of the other men mumbled their agreement. "Not in daylight, anyway."

"Not in daylight?" she echoed. "Kevin, that's ridiculous. Daylight is safer—"

"Not without Sir Simon, I should have said," he corrected. "If he thinks we should take these men to the church tonight, I think there are some who would go. But not now."

"Not on my order, you mean," she retorted. Once again, they all seemed to accept Simon's right to rule here completely without question, stranger that he was and strange as his habits might be. Never mind that she had been their lady all her life, that she had spent the last ten years shut up behind these walls to keep them safe.

"It isn't that, my lady," one of the other men protested. "We want to oblige you, truly. But . . ." He looked around at the others for support.

"Sir Simon is a knight," Kevin finished for him. "He can protect us. You cannot."

"No," she said coldly. "I suppose I cannot." They all looked miserable, at least. "Then we will wait for Simon."

* * *

Simon awoke at sunset to find the entire household in the castle courtyard. "What is this?" he asked Orlando, coming down the steps.

"Lady Isabel insists the dead men must be given proper Christian burial at the Chapel of Saint Joseph," the wizard explained. "They expect you to lead them there."

"You jest," Simon answered. But in truth, that was exactly what it looked like. The wagon was hitched to its team, and the three bodies had been laid inside, covered over with blankets. A whole procession's worth of men were waiting beside it, armed and obviously anxious. "I will talk to her."

"I would wait a moment, if I were you," Orlando advised. "She's busy arguing with her captain."

"Brautus, can't you see I'm frightened?" Isabel was saying in the meantime. Brautus had come down, prepared to go with the others, but the very thought was more than she could bear. "If I had my absolute choice, we would drop those bodies in the lake, and no one would leave the castle. But that would be wrong. Someone has to take them to the church. But not everyone, and not you. I don't mean to protect you by keeping you here; I mean for you to protect the household." He made a disgusted little snort that made her want to hit him, but she took his hand instead. "I am the lady of Charmot, and I need you. Will you abandon me?"

If she had struck him, he couldn't have looked more shocked. "Never," he said, his jaw clenched tight. Shooting a final glower in Simon's direction as he came toward them, he turned and went into the castle.

"Brautus!" she called after him, but he was gone.

Simon reached her side. "Shall I try to speak to him?"

"God's faith, no," she said with a bitter little smile. "He'd probably try to kill you."

"I wouldn't blame him." Her eyes widened, and he smiled. "I would in his place. He has been the Black Knight for quite some time, I hear."

"Yes," she said, smiling back. "He has."

"So what is this about going to the church?" he asked.

"Simon, we have to," she said. "We have no idea how those men were killed or who two of them were; we owe them a Christian burial." There was something more, he could tell. Something had convinced her that to bury these men at the church would protect them somehow, keep her castle safe from the evil that had killed them in the first place. Who was he to tell her otherwise?

"Very well," he nodded. "But you are staying here."

"Simon—"

"Lady Isabel." He touched her chin, turning her face up to his. "I will comply with your wishes and see your will carried out. But I will not risk your safety to do it."

If he meant to be mocking her, he hid it very well.

"All right," she said with a nod. "I will wait for you here."

"Good." He grinned. "See if you can make up with Brautus; that should keep you busy."

"Oh, Brautus will come around," she promised. "It's really you he dislikes, not me. He thinks I've given you far too much consideration here, that I've treated you far better than you deserve."

"And so you have." He sounded almost cheerful, the Irish rogue again.

"Yes, but Brautus doesn't know it," she retorted, blushing as she smiled. "Once he sees you're not some scoundrel after my castle, he should take to you well enough. Everyone else seems to like you."

He took her into his arms. "It isn't your castle I want," he said softly, almost a growl, as he bent to kiss her. For half a moment, she thought about the others watching and what they might think. She was the lady of Charmot, after all; she should think about her dignity. But as soon as she felt his lips touch hers, every such thought was forgotten.

"So what is it?" she said, speaking just as softly as he broke the kiss. "What is it you want?"

His answer was to press her closer and kiss her more deeply, the only answer he could make. "Keep the gate barred and the drawbridge up," he ordered, letting her go. "We should not be long."

"Not to worry, sweeting," she promised with an impish smile. "Brautus may be furious with me, but he and